IMPERFECTIONS

Edited by
Rain Stickland

ISBN-10: 0994950055
ISBN-13: 978-0994950055

DEDICATION

This book goes out to all struggling authors, in the hope that they take their courage firmly in hand and take the plunge to publish their work.

Any true writer will tell you that there is plenty of room for all of us, and that readers are always looking for their next favourite author.

Never give up your dream!

CONTENTS

ACKNOWLEDGEMENTS

This book took the concerted efforts of a number of very talented individuals. Every one of the authors you will read in these pages has put their heart into their work. Thank you to each of you for bringing this book to life.

Thanks also go out, once again, to the very talented Amanda K. Woods, for her vision when it comes to the creation of beautiful covers.

FOREWORD

The seeds for this project began when I decided in the summer of 2015 it was high time I put my money where my mouth was…and start publishing my fiction! Little did I know that I would end up publishing two novels before getting around to putting together this anthology.

I really wanted other authors to come forward, too, and get the amazing stories in their brains onto the printed page. There are so many tales to be told, and readers should have access to all of them.

So I begged and pleaded for my fellow writers to contribute to *Imperfections*, knowing I was asking them to have faith in me that I wouldn't embarrass them (or maybe steal from them—I'm sure the thought crossed *someone's* mind at some point).

However, the writers I know seemed to be only

too happy to have an outlet for their creativity, and this book is the result of that willingness to take a chance.

Dystopian fiction isn't really a genre, though it might seem like it. The thing is, almost any genre can have dystopian elements to it. Science Fiction, Fantasy, Horror, Suspense, you name it.

This particular book's aim was to have a variety of genres, depending on the authors' preferences, but with one common theme: Imperfections. So without further rambling on my part, I'll let you get on with the serious business of reading! I hope you enjoy what we've created for you.

Much love,
Rain

WITHOUT LEAVE
by Rain Stickland

He'd been walking for days. There were no cars in sight, of course. The collapse of the power grid meant no one could fuel up their vehicles anymore. Blake wasn't sure what idiocy had led to that little problem, especially since the Northeastern Blackout of 2003 nearly seventeen years ago had highlighted how problematic electric pumps were, but there wasn't anything to be done about it now. Not only had the grid collapsed, but every portion of society had as well.

The crappy duty-boots he wore were falling apart, and he wasn't surprised by that either. The Canadian Armed Forces had yet to be properly outfitted by Justin Trudeau's Liberal Party, to make up for Stephen Harper's Conservative Party stripping funding from everything they could. There just hadn't been enough time to deal with the backlog of issues, apparently. That meant they didn't have proper boots, their sidearms were still the old Browning pistols, and even their protective gear was crap. And now it didn't even matter.

Blake didn't know if he was AWOL or not. He still had a direct superior who was probably pretty pissed off that he'd lit out, but there was no one else up the chain of command that he was aware of, so he wasn't worried about it. What difference did it make now? A majority of the world's population was gone. No fuel meant no grocery store deliveries, which meant most city-dwellers had starved to death, or were killed in the riots.

When the various military organizations throughout the world had finally gotten their shit together and started dropping shipping containers full of food, there had been very few people left to eat it. Even then they had fought each other to the death over it. By his estimation maybe one percent of the urban populations had survived. Probably not even that, though the community gardens had certainly helped a few.

For the first few months he hadn't worried about his own family, because he knew they were fairly well prepared for anything. The only real concern would be people trying to steal what they had. His dad believed in preparedness. They had a stockpile of supplies in addition to growing their own food, and there were weapons, too. His father hadn't gone crazy on all that stuff, but there was enough that they should be able to survive from one planting season to the next.

Eventually, though, Blake started to feel an urgent need to get himself home. It wasn't just that he was worried about his parents and sister. In truth, he really missed them. He'd been gone a long time, and with the world falling apart he longed to see them again and spend what time he had left with them.

Mactier hadn't changed a bit since he'd left. The tiny Ontario town either didn't want to change, or no one was interested in coming in and doing anything with it. That was fine with him. It was nice to come home and have everything remain the same. It felt welcoming. Never mind the fact that there were probably a lot fewer people in it than there had been when he left.

His folks' place was outside of town, so he kept moving past the hardware store and library to cross over the railway tracks. He reached Kitty Bay Road and headed south toward the bottom point of Stewart Lake. It was just about noon when his right boot-heel hit the crushed stone driveway of home. When Blake saw the shattered glass sidelight at the front door, however, he instinctively stepped off the noisy path and moved forward through the grass instead.

The nine-millimetre he hadn't bothered to turn in when he left his post was in his hand, without him consciously being aware of drawing it, before his boot touched the first step of the front porch. When he got to the door he stopped to listen. Strange sounds carried through the broken window. He couldn't identify them at first, but after a few moments he was horror-struck.

His fingers closed around the sun-warmed metal of the knob, and dread clutched at his heart as he slowly turned it. He really didn't want to see what was in the house, but if there was a chance his family was still alive he needed to help them.

In one swift move, Blake was through the door with his gun raised. In a split second he'd aimed at the first intruder and blown a hole through his head. He shifted his aim to the next, and then the next, followed by a fourth. There was no need to worry about hitting anyone important. Everyone he loved was dead on the floor.

It wasn't until the fifth bullet entered another intruder's head that the rest of them were able to react to the threat. The three remaining men bolted for the window behind them. Blake shot the one closest to him. Six down and two to go, and he still had seven bullets left to do the job. The man in the lead crashed through the closed window, and the other attempted to follow. He was bent over the sill when Blake's next bullet penetrated his back at an upward angle.

Blake stalked over, grabbed the wounded man's ankle, and yanked him back into the room. He wasn't going anywhere anytime soon, so it was safe to pursue the one who was getting away. Blake planted his boot on the sill and launched himself over the garden bed beneath. The only problem was, the escapee was already at the tree line. Blake pushed his body to the limit, trying to reach the man before he disappeared into the dense brush. His tracking skills were limited, and he knew there was a very good chance he would lose him.

An hour later he was forced to accept temporary defeat, but at least he would have someone to interrogate—assuming he was still alive. In the meantime, he had something more important to do.

Jogging back to the house, Blake tried very hard to keep the images out of his head. He knew he'd be forced to confront the reality soon enough, and he needed to brace himself for the task ahead. Once he reached his parents' front lawn, however, distraction served in the form of the man attempting to pull himself down the steps. He wasn't doing a very good job of it, Blake noted with some satisfaction, as he watched him eventually slide bumpily over the maple boards.

Grasping the wounded man's ankle in an iron grip, Blake hauled him back up the stairs and through the front door. He continued dragging him until they reached the dining room, and then he leaned over to yank him up onto his feet. Without any hesitation he slammed the man onto his wounded back on the hardwood table, eliciting a sharp exhalation of pain.

Blake quickly gathered a few supplies, and proceeded to duct-tape the intruder to the table, arms and legs spread-eagled. Now that he was immobilized, he was faced with the daunting task of caring for his family. Not that he would be doing them much good at this point, beyond providing them with some level of dignity.

Ignoring the man squawking at him from the table, he exited the house through the kitchen door and walked across the back lawn to the garden shed. He found a shovel and some drop cloths he and his dad had used the last time the two of them had painted the bedrooms. Blake found he had a hard time swallowing as he thought about the memory. It had actually been a lot of fun, though neither he nor his dad had been any good at it. The most they could have said was that they hadn't coloured outside the lines, but it was far from a professional job.

He stood in the yard a moment to catch his breath and try to get a lid on his emotions. When he saw the vegetable garden, however, he almost lost his mind. This was how his family had been surviving. He'd already known that. But he also knew that there would have been plenty of food in the pantry from last year's harvest. Everything was pickled, preserved, or canned, because his parents always grew way too much food for the three people who had been living in the house still. They even gave half of it away to neighbours, or traded for things they didn't grow themselves. There was no way his family would have been starving, and if those asshole cannibals had even bothered to look, they would have seen plenty of food to be had. Instead they had chosen to kill his family. Apparently they had developed a taste for human flesh and vegetables just weren't enough to cut it.

Blake began to dig a square hole in the back yard. Somehow it seemed more appropriate to him that his family all be buried together, rather than placed in individual holes. Occasionally he would hit rocks with the blade, but they were always fairly small ones that he could easily dig out. He would use them as markers when he had the time to carve something on them. Before he could do that, however, he needed to make sure the men who had done this were all dead.

More than anything, Blake wanted to head back into the dining room to start in on the interrogation, but his father, mother, and sister could not wait. Hopefully the wounded man wouldn't expire in the meantime, but there was no help for it. Instead of focusing on that, he lost himself in the sound of the repeated scraping of the shovel against the dark soil.

It was starting to get dark by the time he was done with the digging. He could see the solar lanterns coming on inside the house, making him grateful for his dad's tendency to plan ahead for situations such as this. Of course, he likely hadn't planned on anyone coming in to the house to kill and eat the three of them. Which begged the question, why hadn't his dad simply shot these people on sight? How had this group of men even come close to the house without his father blowing their heads off? He was former armed forces, too, and he would not have been casual about the safety of his family.

Blake shook off the thought for the time being. Hopefully he would have some answers soon, but he had to get on with the grisly task he'd set himself. He took the drop cloths into the house, and tossed them on the floor beside his dad's bloody form. There was a knife beside his flayed arm, that had obviously been used to slice away chunks of the muscle. His empty stomach heaved at what had been done. He couldn't even bring himself to look at his mother and sister yet.

Putting off the inevitable for a few minutes, he started hauling out the bodies of the six intruders who were already dead. There was swampland across the road that would make for a well-deserved burial ground, but for the time being he would just let them sit in the yard. There was something he wanted to do with those bodies before he permanently disposed of them, and he also wanted them identified by his captive.

Finally he could no longer delay the gruesome task he had set himself. Blake unfolded the drop cloths beside each of his family members without looking directly at their bodies, but that was the end of his reprieve. He moved his father over to one of the cloths, stretching him out straight on it. Nearly choking on his grief he rested a hand on his dad's hair and kissed his forehead.

"I'm sorry I didn't come home sooner, dad. Together we could have stopped this. I know it. And you would all still be alive. I know you wouldn't have wanted me to leave my post, but there was no post left. I've known it for weeks now, and yet I couldn't bring myself to leave. God, I wish I had!" His tears fell on the silvery hair beneath him, even as the rage built inside his heart. He used the rage. Moving his mother and sister onto their respective cloths was the hardest thing he had ever had to do in his life, and the anger was all he had to help him.

He kissed his mother and sister goodbye as well, saying a few words of apology to each of them that he hadn't been there to protect them. His eyes skipped away from their wounds as he covered each of them in turn. Blake wished he could do more for them, but he understood the value of what few supplies remained in the world. Sheets and fabrics would soon be rotting, and nothing new was being manufactured. He couldn't afford to be wasteful, even if his current mindset meant that he didn't much care how long he survived. At the very least he needed to stay alive long enough to rid the world of the vermin responsible for killing his family. The remaining survivors didn't need to be forced to deal with them.

Blake carried his family members out to the backyard, one at a time, leaving his sister's slight frame to the last. He lowered them into the deep hole in the same order. When he climbed out he debated on whether or not to offer a prayer for their eternal souls. He was angry enough that he didn't think God deserved a tribute, but he was a good son who had respect for his parents' beliefs. He wasn't even sure if what he chose was appropriate for a funeral, since he'd never attended a religious burial, but he began to recite.

"The Lord is my shepherd; I shall not want. He maketh me to lie down in green pastures: He leadeth me beside the still waters," he uttered, his voice hoarse. It took every ounce of the strength he'd developed during his time in Afghanistan, to finish the remainder of his prayer. Blake picked up the shovel when he was finished, loaded it with soil, and forced himself to drop the first shovelful over the bodies of his loved ones.

He felt like he was defiling them somehow, just throwing dirt on them, but he knew it was a necessity. He didn't want the animals getting at them. Maybe in addition to the stones he would etch with their names, he could plant a tree over their graves. If he was still around it would give him something to talk to, almost like he was talking directly to them, because it would grow from the energies within their bodies. At least, that was how he looked at it. He'd certainly never be able to plant anything edible in this spot.

Once again Blake blanked his mind and set to the task of burying his father, mother, and sister. He couldn't allow the movie-clip-like memories of Becky to intrude, no matter how persistent they were. If he did, he didn't know if he could resist jumping back into the hole to uncover her. It wasn't quite the same with his parents. He felt guilty for not being home, but with Becky he was devastated. He was her big brother. It had been his job to protect her from the monsters of the world. Instead of fighting monsters in another country, though, or in another area of Canada, it turned out he should have been fighting the ones that had shown up on his own doorstep.

By the time the dirt was mounded over their bodies, full darkness had settled in. The moon was bright, thankfully, or he wouldn't have been able to see what he was doing. Being this far out from town meant there were no streetlights anywhere, and he wasn't even sure they were working in Mactier. Not all streetlights were solar-powered yet. The yard lights didn't work, of course, since the house itself wasn't on solar either. It was just the bright LED lanterns inside giving off any light.

Blake was grateful he was able to finish, rather than putting some of it off to the next day, because he wouldn't have wanted it hanging over his head all night. As it was, he wasn't likely to get much sleep. He had work to do, and there was no way he'd get the images out of his head any time soon. But he needed to rest at some point, and he wouldn't have been able to do that if his family had remained unburied.

"Hello again, asshole," Blake said with false joviality once he stepped into the dining room. "It looks like it's time for you and me to party a bit. Had to get some work out of the way before it was time to play, of course, but now that that's done we can boogie all night. First of all, I think some food is in order. Not for you, of course, but I need to eat. It's too bad you didn't bother to check the pantry for the food stashed there. It might have saved your friends' lives, and possibly yours."

Blake smirked at the renewed struggles of his captive audience, then spun on his boot heel to grab some food from the pantry. He wasn't the least bit hungry after what he'd seen, but he was going to eat for two reasons. First, he needed to keep up his strength for the evening ahead, and, second, he knew it would drive the man on the table crazy. Not even bothering to see what it was he lifted from the pantry shelf, he did another one-eighty, grabbed a spoon from a drawer in the kitchen, and returned to the dining room.

Plunking his body down on a chair beside the table, Blake unscrewed the top of the mason jar. It wasn't until he'd shoved the spoon in his mouth and his mind was flooded with memories, that he realized he had grabbed a jar of crabapple sauce. His mother was the only person he'd ever known who made it, and the pang in his gut nearly had him choking, despite how wonderful it tasted. He hadn't had anything this good since before he had left for boot camp. He could only be thankful that it was dim enough he didn't think the man on the table could see his expression. He swallowed heavily and cleared his throat.

"Mmm. This is some damn good crabapple sauce," he said heartily. "Reminds me of the stuff my mother used to make. Oh, wait. It *is* the stuff my mother used to make. It's really too bad she'll never be able to make it again because of you and your friends. Yeah, my mother was a damn good cook. We used to have this with pork chops, just like most people had regular applesauce. Well, that and the puff pastries she used to fill with it. I gotta say, you've deprived the world of a really good cook. Of course, you've also deprived me of my fucking mother, you cocksucker!" The last was said in a rough growl.

"Now, it looks as though I managed to nail most of your friends, but I think I'll get to know you a little bit better since we're going to have such a good time tonight. Let's start with your name," he said.

"Fuck you, asshole," the wounded man rasped.

"No, thanks, but I appreciate the offer. Or is that your name?" Not bothering to say anything else, he slid his Grohmann combat knife from its sheath and waved the oddly-shaped blade under the man's nose. When there was still no response he dragged the tip across his captive's throat very lightly. The implied threat was enough for the moment.

"Rob," the restrained man croaked at him.

"See? We're having fun already! Who was it that ran out ahead of you? Not a very loyal friend was he? If he was willing to leave you behind, wounded and all, I mean." When Rob hesitated, Blake increase the pressure on the knife, this time drawing a little blood.

"Ritchie," he gasped. "He'll be coming back for me, don't you worry. And when he does he's going to eat your fucking eyeballs."

"Why would he come back? I'm sure he thinks

you're already dead, after all."

"He's my brother. He'll be back," Rob said smugly.

"Right. Because he was so interested in your wellbeing as I chased him through the bush in the other direction for so long. Yeah, he was pretty determined I'd say. To save his own ass at any rate. Who were the rest of those assholes?"

"Just some guys we used to go hunting with. Well, one of them was our cousin, Steve, but the rest were just buddies." Blake prodded him for every detail he could get regarding the full names and former addresses of the men he had shot. He wanted information, just in case anyone came looking for a family member or friend. Among other things.

"How did you get into the house?"

"The girl was in the garden, and Steve pulled a knife and used her as a shield. The old guy wasn't gonna shoot through her, which got us in the door. He let Rob have his shotgun when Steve told him he had to or he was gonna slice the girl's throat."

Blake let him continue to talk, and he could picture all too easily how they had managed to subdue and then kill his family. First they had shot his father with the shotgun, which had also resulted in the broken glass sidelight when some of the shot missed his dad and gone through the window. After that it had been child's play for them to use the knife on his mother and sister. The only relief he got from learning the details, was that it had apparently happened pretty quickly. Their suffering had been over fast.

A number of hours had passed since he had taped Rob to the dining table, so he went to the old-fashioned well to draw some water. He drank deeply before returning to the house. He dribbled some water into Rob's mouth. He wasn't sure how long he was going to keep him alive, but if he didn't hydrate him the choice would be taken from him. With that in mind, he decided to take a look at the wound in his back. There was no way it had hit his lungs or major organs, or Blake was pretty sure he would have been dead by that point. He moved a light close, released the tape on one wrist, and yanked Rob over onto his side. He had to slice through the ragged, blood-soaked t-shirt to see the wound.

From what he could tell, and he wasn't a medic, the angle of entry was so steep that it had just shattered a couple of ribs and lodged beneath another one. It explained his difficulty moving, and the fact that he was still alive. Breathing probably didn't feel very comfortable, either, which gave Blake a modicum of satisfaction. He dropped Rob's shoulder back on the table, making the man gasp. The sound was followed by a wheezing moan.

"Probably shouldn't have killed my family,

then," he remonstrated as he re-taped Rob's wrist. Blake stood there contemplating his options for a few minutes, before covering Rob's mouth with more of the duct tape. He didn't need him to call out information to his brother, should the coward decide to come back to find out what happened to Rob.

Grabbing the shotgun from the living room, Blake headed upstairs to the hallway window. He would need to sleep at some point, and now was as good a time as any. He just had to make sure he had the high ground. It would give him plenty of time to wake and respond to any intruders. He'd had lots of practice sleeping light in Afghanistan. Some bumpkin in butt-fuck Ontario wasn't going to get the drop on him. And this time there was no young girl they could use for cover.

Blake got a solid hour's sleep before he awoke to a thump. The sound repeated, and he realized it was coming from the dining table, rather than outside. Leaving the shotgun in the hall, he used his hands to slide down the banister rails, rather than using the stairs. When he got to the bottom he pulled his Browning from its holster before confirming his suspicions. It was just Rob attempting to pull free of the tape, but the effort was costing him a great deal of pain. He stalked over and ripped the tape from the guy's mouth.

"What's the problem, dude? Not a comfortable enough bed for you?"

"Fuck you," Rob snarled in a raspy voice.

"Wow. That's truly generous after my first rejection, but I'm afraid I'm not interested. Now what seems to be the problem here?"

"I wanna dance, of course. What the fuck you think, man? I want outta here!"

"Ah, I see. Well, I'm afraid we've got a bit of a difference of opinion here then, because I believe you should stay right where you are. Seeing as I'm all hale and hearty at the moment, with a pistol at the ready, I think I'm gonna win that argument. But seeing as I'm awake now, we can finish our little party. Got a couple hours left before dawn, and I've got this here jar of crabapple sauce to finish."

So saying, Blake dropped into his chair again and grabbed the jar. He started shoveling the food into his mouth. Rob's eyes shifted to the spoon every so often, so Blake knew he was probably pretty hungry. Well, now was as good a time as any, he figured. He placed the half-empty jar on a side table and cautiously headed outside to the bodies on the lawn.

He felt around until he managed to grasp a lifeless arm. He pulled out his knife and used it to slice away a large chunk of flesh. If Rob was hungry, he was going to have to make do with his usual fare.

"Here ya go, asshole," Blake said, as he dangled the raw meat over Rob's mouth. "I couldn't tell ya who it came from since it's pretty dark out there, but suffice it to say it's not one of my family members this time. You wanna eat? Well, this is what you get now."

Rob looked up at the meat in distaste, but bit off a chunk of it anyway. Apparently he was so used to eating human flesh, that the fact it was a friend, or possibly a relative, of his didn't faze him all that much. Blake shuddered in disgust. There were other ways to eat, he knew. Especially when someone had experience hunting. There was no excuse for what they had done to his family. He turned his head and waited until Rob was finished eating. He replaced the strip of tape over Rob's mouth, then went outside and poured some of the water from the bucket over each of his hands in turn, rinsing off the blood.

The sudden snapping of a twig caught his attention. Out in this neck of the woods it could be anything from a raccoon or skunk, to a full-grown bear, but in this case he was pretty sure it wasn't a forest creature. The noise had come from the other side of the house, so he knew he couldn't be seen where he was. Blake decided to head back into the house and go upstairs for the shotgun. At least Rob wouldn't be able to warn his brother.

By the time Ritchie came through the front door, Blake was pointing the shotgun down the stairs directly at him. Out of the corner of his eye he could see through to the dining table where Rob was frantically trying to signal his brother, but it was too late. Blake pulled the trigger, and Ritchie fell to the floor in shock before he'd even had a chance to see who had shot him. He was still alive when Blake reached the bottom of the stairs to lean over him.

"You and your friends really shouldn't have fucked with my family, man. I'm gonna take you out to my front lawn to bleed to death, slowly but surely. You can join your friends and your cousin out there. Then I'm gonna slice off a piece of you for your brother to eat." Blake grabbed him by the hair and pulled until he'd managed to take out the trash.

A sharp pain in his head had him reeling. He stumbled over what he assumed were Ritchie's legs. As he fell toward the ground, he pulled his knife from his sheath again. Twisting, he blindly thrust the knife upward. A heavy body fell on top of him. When no more pain was forthcoming, Blake shoved the body away. Beyond sick and tired from the whole ordeal, and dizzy beyond belief, he changed his mind about drawing it out. He used the knife on Ritchie to be certain there would be no one left to try to kill him.

When he got to the dining room he soon realized how Rob had managed to get free. He obviously hadn't been paying close enough attention to his free hand when he'd checked out his wound. He must have managed to unwrap his other wrist, or at least mostly, just waiting for his opportunity to pull the rest of the tape free. It was a stupid mistake that had almost cost him his life, and for all he knew it still might. His vision was blurry, the part that wasn't fading to black, and he felt sick and weak in addition to the dizziness. Worst of all, all he could think about was his family. Now that the danger was over, he was left with nothing but his grief. Instead of dealing with it, he just let the blackness wash over him.

ↄ ᙣ

He couldn't remember why he was walking along the road when the car swerved to avoid his staggering form. In fact, he couldn't quite understand what the woman from the car was saying to him, except that she seemed to be gesturing that he should follow her. Unable to think what else to do, he blindly dogged her footsteps as she walked backward toward the vehicle.

She handed him food and water, and at one point asked his name. He couldn't bring himself to speak, though he was grateful for her help. Like a lamb to the slaughter, he did as she suggested and sat in the passenger seat of the car. When she parked the car, however, he listened closely to what she was saying. Her tone didn't match her expression, so he decided to follow her when she got out of the car.

He had to stay pretty far behind her to keep her from noticing his presence, so when he heard the alarming sound of a gunshot, he couldn't reach her right away. When he came on the scene of the two women, there was a stranger standing over her with a gun in her hand, facing away from him. The woman who had just given him the food and water was on her knees, with blood pouring out of her mangled arm.

Not thinking twice about it, he reached up and snapped the other woman's neck, letting her drop on the ground in front of him. Now he had to find some help, and he didn't even know where he was.

Thanks go to a very special man I thought I'd never find (one who understands and encourages my crazy writing state, and loves me anyway). Geoff, you're one in a trillion…at least. I'll love you until the end of time.

ABOUT THE AUTHOR

Rain Stickland, though raised on a farm, has been writing since the age of twelve when the fever took hold and never truly dissipated. Despite two decades of interest in off-grid living, she was only recently introduced to the vast world of preppers. Her interest kicked up a few notches, however, during the Northeast Blackout in 2003, when the world went dark for millions of people, some for weeks.

Her novels, Tipping Point and Ground Zero, books one and two of the Tipping Point Trilogy, are available on Amazon in paperback and Kindle. Salvage Rights, the third and final book of the trilogy, will be available in late summer, 2016.

Called the Canadian Tornado by friends, she's written and published nearly 400 articles on a wide variety of topics, including everything from stem cell transplants to the care and feeding of cats, dogs, and ferrets. She lives with her daughter and boyfriend in Ontario, Canada. You can find out more at www.rainstickland.com.

Rain's Facebook:
facebook.com/CanadianTornado/
Rain's Twitter: twitter.com/RainStickland
Join Rain's mailing list:
mailinglist@rainstickland.com

Truth, Part One
by Marlin Woosley

It's Not Over Until It's Over

In Less Than a Century

In the twentieth century, the New World Order seemed little more than a conspiracy theory, boasted about by extreme right wing nut jobs and quietly feared by leftist nuts. By the end of the twenty-first century it had come to full fruition. Sovereign nations, what was left of them, existed in name only. Nearly all of them were led by puppet governments, bought and paid for by the wealthiest of the world's ruling elite.

Global warming had been brought to heel but not until hundreds of thousands of square miles of land mass had been replaced by swelling oceans. The city of Miami was the first to become a man-made reef as the seas consumed the peninsula that was called Florida. Left homeless by receding shorelines, hundreds of thousands of people succumbed to starvation, pandemic, and exposure.

Banksters pursued those that they could find, for mortgages past due on homes now in the new Atlantis. Debtors prisons were brought back into practice for a new but racially diverse institution of slavery. These prisons, privately funded for profit, were little more than a reincarnation of the nineteenth century southern American culture of masters and overseers.

Throughout the world there were more prisons than employment. Incarceration, for the pettiest of crimes, was more likely than finding a job. The consumerism of the twentieth century was gone for lack of workers paid well enough to purchase basic needs, much less frivolous wants. Military service was the only steady means of income to common people.

Though it might seem that, with such a consolidation of power at the peak of the global hierarchy, there would be no wars requiring soldiers to fight. The Mideast, however, remained as volatile as it ever was in the days of Western meddling and regime change. The country previously known as Iran had never given up its economy to a central banking system. Allied with Russia, they had grown as a sovereign world power in their own right. As they reclaimed all of ancient Persia and many Arab lands, they brought back stability that the West had destroyed.

For the Persians and Russians, fiercely holding onto their culture and power in the world, there was no end to wars. A combination of patriotic propaganda and imminent starvation kept up a steady supply of young idealists who were willing to sacrifice their lives for the lies of the Ruling Elite.

An Existence, Nothing More

There was a knock on the door. Without waiting, two staff members barged into the room. One laughed and turned to the other, who was a trainee.

"See I told you what he would be doing. You can count on it. He won't wear clothes unless he leaves his room, and this time of day you can count on him spanking his tired old monkey when you walk in."

The second woman's eyes widened and her jaw dropped.

"If you know that he does this then why don't you wait for a reply before coming in?"

"Doesn't matter; he won't stop. Especially if he's close. Look!" She pointed as the old man's body convulsed and climax erupted onto his belly and chest.

The trainee's face reddened with embarrassment as the other woman cackled in her amusement.

"This one is nothing. We used to have one in here that go would at it all day without getting the cannon to fire. I never checked but it seemed that he should have had calluses on it.

"This old codger used to bone his wife on a regular basis before she died. From the moans and screams that could be heard from outside the door, it was obvious that she was loving it."

"Oh my! Tell me that you didn't..."

"No, of course not. I didn't interrupt that. Some of the staffers did though. Any two old farts that could enjoy the horizontal mamba as much these two did, deserved to be left alone as far as I was concerned."

The old man stared blankly as if not cognizant of the conversation. The staffer ran warm water in the bathroom sink. Then she wet a washcloth, wrung it out and tossed it onto his belly.

"Clean yourself, Frank, before that shit drips off of you and all over the bedding."

He complied but his face was still that of someone not there.

"Time for your shower, Frank." The woman took one of his arms to guide him to standing position.

"One thing about Frank is that you aren't

bothered with undressing for a shower. You have to dress him for meal times, though, unless we're short-staffed. Then we bring his tray to the room. He wouldn't mind going into the common areas naked but we can't have that. He did it a couple times right after his wife died. We were able to convince him that he had to stay in his room if he didn't want to wear clothes."

When the shower was nearly finished the woman lifted gently under Frank's arm to stand him. He waited patiently as she parted his cheeks and scrubbed between them.

"Don't forget this part with anyone. Some them either have slight leakage problems or they just don't make proper use of toilet tissue. For those with no control at all, we use disposable briefs."

"How long has he been zoned out like this?"

"As soon as his wife died. Before that you couldn't have wished for a more happy and outgoing couple. When she died, it was as if he closed off the world."

After he had been toweled dry, the old man doddered out of the bathroom, without prompting, and dropped into his rocker recliner. He touched the tilt button. When the chair tipped, he settled into staring at the ceiling.

Because the old man was fresh out of the shower, the staffer covered him with a sheet from the bed to avoid a chill. The two women left the room, closing the door behind them.

THE NOTIFICATION

The old man looked up and toward the sound of a knock on the door. Why they ever bothered to knock totally escaped him. They always barged in before he replied anyway. When his wife was still with him, their intimate moments were sometimes interrupted without apology.

Excitement warmed him when the door opened only slightly and he heard the voice of his grandson. calling out softly.

"Grandpa."

He stood, took his robe from the rail of the bed and put it on.

"Yes, Nathan, come in."

The two men embraced. Nathan was smiling as usual, but the young man's eyes told of a truth being held back. The old man dismissed the thought. The relationship between the two men was solid. The younger would come forth with the message soon enough.

The introductory conversation between the two men was brief. The strength and intimacy of their relationship did not require many words. Their unspoken communication could not be discerned by an observer. It was as if they were one when they were near each other.

The old man was actually Nathan's great grandfather. A centenarian now, he was well into the autumn of his life when the boy was born to the old man's widowed granddaughter. Both the boy's father and grandfather had been lost to senseless wars.

One war could not be over without the neofascist imperialists sending armies in to save another population from the bliss of their generations-old simple existence. It was always done in the name of human rights, but, if truth be known, the armies marched to benefit of the neofascists' wealthy puppeteers.

They sat down to a game of chess. The skills of the game had been lost to generations of electronic entertainment on hand-held devices but the old man loved the game. He taught the grandson to play when he was a young boy.

There was another knock at the door. The door opened and a staffer stuck her head into the room.

The old man froze with his hand on one his knights. His previously alert face went blank.

"Okay, Grandpa, that's the knight. This could be a good move but do you remember which way a knight moves? Take your time. Think about it." Slowly, the old man moved his knight into a position that forced Nathan to retreat his rook.

"That's so cool that you take the time to

stimulate your grandfather like this. He is so lucky to have someone like you."

"Thank you!" Nathan smiled. "Except when he had to be away, he was always there for me as boy. It's only right that I do the same for him now."

"Yes, but most of the others have no one who cares. You are a gem. I wanted to see if you were going to stay with us for supper. We can either bring two trays to the room or we can dress your grandfather so that you can both come to the dining room."

"What do you think, Grandpa? Do you want to go out to dinner or eat here?"

The old man starred at the chess board without a response.

"I could run out for beer and a carryout pizza if you'd prefer a change?" Nathan smiled at the staffer and winked. Then he said, "Tell you what. We'll come to supper but you won't need to dress him. I can do that. What time?"

"Six o'clock sharp."

"Great! We'll be there a few minutes before."

"Okay, thanks! See you then." She was gone behind the closing door.

The two finished their first chess game, and left a second game standing uncompleted while they went to supper. The meal would have been boring with the old man's facade of being zoned had it not been for the other residents and staff who knew and liked

Nathan. There was plenty of conversation around him as the old man stared blankly at his plate while he consumed his food.

Upon returning to the room, whatever was bothering Nathan had to come out. The skills of the two men were evenly matched for the most part. After having won two games and the young man showing no sign of conscious engagement in the third game. The old man paused. His grandson had left himself wide open for a checkmate.

The old man took the box from the side of bed where he had laid it and began to put away the worn pieces.

"What are you doing? The game isn't over. Are you tired, Grandpa?"

"No more than might be expected of any old soldier who has survived four wars. Tell me what is bothering you."

The young man hesitated as if about to say something. In silence, he assisted the old man in putting away the chess pieces. He averted his eyes. The old man sensed Nathan's discomfort but knew that he had to press toward the cause.

Nathan put the chess game into the cabinet where his grandfather stored his few belongings. He stood by the cabinet glancing back to his grandfather. He could not hold a gaze into the old man's eyes. He stood, staring toward the door, needing to speak but words would not come.

"Do you need to leave?"

"No, it's just… It's just that…"

"Nathan, sit down, please."

The young man complied but still looked away from his grandfather's eyes. The old man had endless patience, especially when it came to his grandson.

"There is obviously a concern on your mind. I have taught you, and I know that you have practiced, that it is best to confront your fears lest they consume you. I am an old man with memories that you can only imagine. Nothing that you might say is likely to shock me."

Nathan's hand fidgeted with something inside of his jacket pocket. He looked into his grandfather's eyes but, still, he could not speak. The old man glanced to the distraction of the fidgeting hand. It was then, without words, that he knew. The truth from one man's eyes to the other.

Knowingly, the old man held out his hand. "May I have it?"

With only slight hesitation, the young man withdrew a small vial from his jacket and held it out to his grandfather. Two distinctly different tablets were contained in the vial. The vial was sealed and marked with two six-digit numbers. Nathan had been advised by the authorities that it was his grandfather's time.

Centenarians were quite common among the

wealthy in this century. With genuine, quality healthcare for themselves, rather than so-called medicare from profit-generating medi-businesses, the wealthy were living productive lives up to a century and a half long. The ruling elite took excellent care of themselves. Their servants were likewise well cared for, until they outlived their usefulness. Euthanasia had become common practice for the elderly or infirm. Like worn out farm animals or racing animals of the previous centuries, those without wealth or health were put down when their time came.

The old man, a veteran of four wars, had married up in the social hierarchy. His wife's family had moderate wealth and status. She once told him that she had a distant kinship to the Rothschild Family but that wasn't anything spoken about to just anyone. At any rate, her status bought her a natural death and long-term care until the very end. With her gone, however, the state took what remained of her estate, and the old man had been waiting for the system to process him out.

His service in four wars had bought him a little more time. Though wounded many times, he had managed to come away from those wars with limbs attached and his mind sound. He was more fit, for his age, than the state would ever acknowledge or that he had shown since his wife died. That mattered little, though. Commoners were harvested at the discretion of the state for benefit of the state.

The solution to caring for crippled soldiers had been the catalyst, generations before, for the now-common practice of euthanasia. It started quietly, with families left to believe that their soldier relative had been mortally wounded. With the increase in battlefield deaths, coupled with diminishing numbers of returning veterans requiring rehabilitation, it became obvious what was happening.

The state eventually acknowledged that there had been some wounded soldiers put down rather than treated for severe battle trauma. Soon after this disclosure, the dutiful media began to tout the benefit of battlefield euthanasia, over the shame of being dependent on others for basic needs and care.

Now there were no longer poor, useless souls missing limbs as a result of their misguided patriotism. There were no mentally disturbed veterans wandering homeless on the streets of the cities for lack of proper treatment. Those things were in the history of the previous century. Over time euthanasia became as accepted as the cruelty toward domestic animals that were used for food.

Nathan's anxiety dissipated as he watched his grandfather's calm acceptance of what was about to take place. As the old man looked at the vial in his open palm, the finger tips of his other hand slipped under his shaggy hair to touch a spot on the back of his neck, just below his hairline.

"Were you able to get the other items?"

Nathan nodded and dug a small cylindrical package from his inside jacket pocket. He held it out to his grandfather. The old man emptied the package and examined its contents.

"Can any of this be traced back to you?"

"No. I took all of the exact precautions that you told me to."

The old man nodded his relief. Frank had not shared any more information with Nathan than what he absolutely needed to know. Nonetheless, if his grandson was found out to be assisting him, his time would also be expired. Fearing for his grandson's safety at this point, the old man sent Nathan home. The young man left, never expecting to see his grandfather again.

The Interruption

Frank didn't want an interruption of what he had to do next. There would be shift change of the staff soon. The leaders of the two shifts would make rounds together. He leaned back in his recliner, naked and uncovered as usual, and forced himself to doze until after the shift change.

He was sleeping somewhat soundly and showing a nocturnal erection when the door to the room opened quietly. Two staff members, one male and one female, looked in upon him. At the sight of the old man's erection, they grinned at each other. The woman stepped over to the recliner and, with her finger tip traced the center ridge from the back of Frank's scrotum to the base of his erection and down the length of his penis. His penis convulsed as her finger slid off of the tip.

She giggled and stepped back. Frank's deep breathing shifted to a conscious mode as he stirred. Grinning even bigger, the woman shooed her co-worker back out of the room and she followed. The magnetic door latch closed without a sound.

As Frank came out of his sleep, he suspected what had happened. It gave him concern that someone would be back when the shift change was complete. A staffer had occasionally come into the room on the nocturnal shift and fondled him. When he stirred awake the person would dart away but often returned later. Each time he stirred, the encounter ended. The trouble was that he didn't have time for games tonight.

He set a contingency plan in his mind and went back to sleep with his mental alarm clock set for one hour. The hour was only half past when he sensed that the couple had returned to his room. Frank kept his eyes closed but did not try to feign sleep.

A small hand was fondling and massaging him.

The female presence was strong in his senses before her hair fell across his face. He became fully aroused as she cooed and purred into his ear.

The cooing continued as two hands massaged his pectorals and gently pinched his nipples. It wasn't long before Frank knew that there were two of them. The man, he suspected from behind his closed eyes, was giving him fellatio.

Frank was purely heterosexual but the woman's scent and her gradual intensifying of stimulation soon brought to a climax what the man was doing. The two left the room as quietly as they had before, with the exception of an escaped giggle from one of them.

Frank dozed for a few minutes, but was awakened by the cooling semen that had drizzled onto his belly. At least they wouldn't return again tonight. Frank was losing darkness.

THE DECEPTION

The midnight teasers had cost much-needed time, but there was no way of knowing how many days Frank had left. It had to be tonight or maybe never. With the pills and small package in hand that Nathan had brought to him, Frank went to the bathroom and sat on the commode.

The several tasks that Frank had to perform must

be timed perfectly. He opened the small package. There was a compact bloodless scalpel, a relic to modern times but functional for the need at hand. It had probably been surplus from one of the earlier wars when there were actually attempts made to save the lives of wounded soldiers.

There was also a tiny clamp of approximately the same length as the scalpel. Last, there was a tiny gel capsule. It contained the minimum of liquid suture required to seal the wound that Frank was about to inflict upon himself.

First, Frank swallowed the two capsules which had come in the separate vial. There was no turning back now. Next, he touched the back of his neck just below his shaggy hairline for his mark. With the scalpel his other hand, he parted the flesh, careful to measure depth with his thumb and forefinger firmly pinched around the blade. Removing the scalpel, Frank pressed the slightly-opened clamp into the incision. Again he measured for depth, but this time he pressed a little deeper than the incision.

Satisfied that he had hit his mark, Frank locked the clamp into place. He took toilet tissue and folded it over in several layers. As his bowel released some of the contents of his colon, Frank caught the dropping in the tissue. With his free hand, he pulled the clamp from the incision, bringing a tiny chip with it. He pressed the chip into the feces, released the clamp and dropped the wad into the commode.

Digital chip implants became a practice for identifying domestic pets in the twentieth century. It didn't take a genius to realize that, with the wrong government and a little demagoguery, the practice could eventually expand to include humans.

Chip implants became law as a result of the fear of terrorists posing as immigrants. Thus, no consent was required and the actual purpose of the chip had evolved toward sinister benefit for a neofascist government. Thanks to the dumbing-down of the populace, and controlled media broadcasting, few of the common people knew the ramifications of being fitted with a chip implant at birth.

Fortunately for Frank, his was an early version of the chip. It measured and reported body temperature and was assigned to Frank's DNA code. Modern versions identified the body tissue into which it was embedded, as well as the individual's DNA code. In addition, the modern chips were planted much deeper and nearer to the brain stem.

Frank put the projected end of the gel capsule on his wound and squeezed it gently into the tiny laceration. He put all the items, including the vial, into the cylinder, capped it and pressed it deep into his rectum. Washing his hands, without rising from the commode, Frank dried them with toilet tissue that he also used to wipe himself.

A monitor alarm brought the two staffers who had visited Frank earlier. They found him in a rather undignified position that resulted from going unconscious while naked on the commode. His paling skin left little doubt to the staffers that Frank had expired. There would be no heroics anyway. By the time individuals made it to this sort of care facility, they were allowed to die without intervention attempts.

The woman looked into the commode, and, seeing contents in the water, flushed it. "He shit himself to death." The two grinned at each other over her dark humor.

"Let's get him stretched out before he locks up in that position. We'll never get him into the cooker all kinked up like this."

"He's in a good position for one thing, though. Don't move him yet." The man left and returned with cotton that he used to plug Frank's rectum.

"You don't really need to do that. He's going straight to the cooker, as soon we get the go ahead, you know."

"If ever you have one of these blow shit all over you while you're moving them, you'll make sure to plug the next ones that you move. Guaranteed!"

They stretched the body out without benefit of a prop under the head. This forced the mouth wide agape from the slackened jaw. Any color that might have indicated life was completely gone from the cooled skin. Half-slit eyelids revealed sightless eyes.

The cooker, to which the staffer referred was a hybrid cross between a standard mortuary cold chamber and a cooking oven. Bodies were seldom preserved in this facility. Most of the deceased were cooked to the point that the flesh was falling from the skeleton. The roasted remains were taken to a processing facility for separation of hard tissues and soft tissues.

Soft tissues were processed into food pellets for common people. Hard tissues were ground up and used for fertilizer at the corporate-owned farms. Nothing was wasted.

Confirmation that Francis Warren Sanders had expired came into the main desk from the agency that monitors chip implants. Drop in body temperature, as read by the chip, was all that was required. His remains were ordered to be prepared for final processing. The two staffers placed the body into a large pan, hefted it to a cart, and wheeled it down the hall to a small morgue-like room.

There were two compartments built into the outer wall. Outside, the compartments had doors that could be opened for removal and transfer to the final processing facility. The cart was level with the compartments so little effort was required to load the body into one of them.

A timer switch was above the compartment door. It had only two settings, HOT and COLD. One of the staffers turned the switch to HOT. They walked away, indifferent to what would happen next. It was how they had always done it.

There was individual purpose to each of the two capsules that Frank had taken. The first was to give him the appearance of being dead. The second, on a timed delay, was the antidote to bring back consciousness. The cooker was warming but not yet uncomfortable when Frank regained consciousness. If heat had still been fossil-fueled, he would have suffocated almost immediately.

He felt around the door at his head for the grave bell latch. This early model of cooker had been designed with an emergency escape. Unable to locate the latch, he felt around the opposite door with his foot. The latch flipped easily. Frank kicked open the door, and slid out into the cool, moonlit night.

The service gate of the fence surrounding the area was latched but not locked. The moment that Frank stepped up to the edge of the street, a hover cab was by his side with an open door. The driverless vehicle sped away the second that Frank's naked butt settled into the seat.

There was clothing for him in the hover cab. He dressed and wished for a weapon. Frank couldn't shake the feeling that something was wrong. Nothing to do now, though, but wait out the ride.

TRUTH, PART TWO
by Marlin Woosley

FACING THE END

SEEING THE CHANGE

Frank Sanders looked out over the landscape as the hover cab glided toward a destination unknown to him. The world had changed more than he had expected it would, in the time he and his wife had been put out to pasture. Her wealth and status had afforded comfort and care to her end. Having only married up in social status, Frank lost his wife's privileges upon her natural death.

He had managed to escape the euthanasia that was the demise of most commoners in these times. Now, trained soldier that he was, he calmed himself into crystal-clear thinking. He had no idea what he might see when the cab docked and the door opened. He had to have his mind prepared.

Passing over a city, as the sun broke over the horizon, Frank could see much of what was below. The remains of what was formerly a network of ground transportation infrastructure lay in ruins. In the previous century it was used beyond capacity, and then allowed to deteriorate into uselessness for lack of funding, or the labor to maintain or rebuild it.

The evolution away from wheeled transportation made the roadway system obsolete anyway. In some areas, bridges had purposely been destroyed to contain hordes of starving populations and the pandemic that they would spread throughout the clean world.

There was little of the known population that wasn't under control of the neofascist Ruling Elite. The ruins of the previous century were quiet and left to waste. What hadn't been lost to neglect and destruction, deteriorated with the help of vegetation and wildlife, as nature reclaimed the asphalt, concrete, and steel of cities and roadways, back into the earth they had nearly destroyed forever.

The view below changed into another world of lush green farms. The boundary from wasteland to farmland was separated by a river with a high levee on the green side. Frank could only imagine the misery of the slaves that were forced to toil for food that they would never consume.

The diet of this controlled population was of the food pellets made from the garbage of the elite, and the carcasses of their own fellow slaves, as they outlived their usefulness in their designated service to the state. The slaves knew no better life as the rule of the world had evolved over the generations before them. Their great-grandparents had been forced into slavery by debt, and the lack of means to reduce it.

The dumbing-down of the working class had begun with the propaganda broadcasts of the corporate-owned media. This was enhanced with the rants of so-called elected leaders who were, in fact, shills for the ruling elite. Their skilled demagoguery kept enough of the people from seeing the truth, that those with eyes were silenced by the ignorance of the masses.

Frank had sensed something was amiss when he boarded the cab, back where he had faked his death. It occurred to him now, while skimming above the modern and well-maintained world below, that there was no doubt. He was in trouble.

THE WELCOME

The view of farms was soon replaced by other

greenery. Well-maintained parks and golf courses came into view. Beyond these playgrounds, were high-rise dwellings of the wealthy. Single family homes existed only in the ruins of the wastelands.

The wealthy had moved toward greater efficiency of their privilege for themselves. Only those at the very peak of hierarchy had the means to maintain vast estates. The army of security and technology networks required to protect them, was beyond the reach of citizens at the other levels of wealth.

A population of malcontents still held out in the wastelands and plotted revolution. This riffraff of human origin seldom ventured outside of the wastelands. When they did, it was in reconnaissance teams that were fearless in their resistance to security forces if discovered. The notion that there even were reconnaissance efforts made the fear of large attacks real in the minds of the emasculated citizens.

In addition to being fearless, the soldiers of these small teams could not be broken to tell of their strongholds of other sensitive information. No amount coercion, whether physical, mental or chemical, could crack their individual defenses. They were extreme warriors.

The high-rises gave way to a view of skyline reminiscent of the old capitol, before its destruction by the extreme weather conditions of global warming. The ruling elite knew all along that climate change was real in the 21st Century. They had delayed any reaction to the inevitable catastrophe in order to reduce populations to a more manageable count, via natural disasters. There were miscalculations that resulted in some unforeseen collateral damage.

The hover cab docked on the rooftop pad of one of the taller buildings. A lone person stepped out of the penthouse, and crossed the pool area toward Frank. The smiling face was so familiar to Frank that he should have been at ease, or even elated, for seeing it. The context was all wrong, though.

Frank's warning sensors red-lined. Nathan Sanders, his great-grandson, should not be there. The very fact that he was, meant that both of them were in serious danger.

Frank's eyes scanned as much as he could see without giving up his awareness by an obvious turn of his head. There were people beyond the glass doors of the penthouse but Frank could not make out who they might be. Nathan's warm smile faded with the sense of the concern that radiated to him from his grandfather's warning look.

Frank quickly put on a fake greeting smile to relax his great-grandson. He needed a few more seconds to assess his situation. Reading the reaction, Nathan put his smile back on too. The facial cues had been read already. They were surrounded by security guards with weapons ready.

Another man, also familiar to Frank, came out of the penthouse and walked toward them. He motioned security to put away the weapons. With a disingenuous smile, he spoke a greeting to Frank and held out his hand in a gesture of friendship.

Frank accepted the gesture, but only in order to feign trust. The odds were not at all in his favor at the moment. Worse than being outnumbered, there was no escape. Then there was Nathan, who could read his thoughts, but had never been tested in a combat situation.

FOR FUN OF THE CHASE

"Cut through the bullshit, David. What do you want?"

David Bachmann had served with Frank's son in the second Persian war. He had never been able to prove it, but Frank had a good idea that Bachmann had been responsible for his son's death. If not, he could have at least prevented it.

"In time, Frank, in time. First, I have to tell you that your escape was absolute genius. The way that you played it out for so long, by acting like a demented idiot after your wife died, is to be admired. You are a true soldier. You had everyone fooled, right up to the point that they turned on the roaster to make dog food out of you."

"It wasn't good enough if I'm standing here looking at you now." Frank's tone was even. He was not going to give up any clues as to his thoughts.

"Come inside, Frank. Let's get out of the heat."

As they walked, Bachmann continued.

"The truth is, Frank, that your plan was flawless with only two exceptions. I especially loved that part when you flushed your micro-chip down the shitter in a turd. We never would have thought to trace it to the treatment plant, had it not been for the two flaws that you missed."

Frank's face remained emotionless as he looked into the Bachmann's eyes.

"Your big mistake was the lack of a body when you left, Frank. Did you really think that, when they came for your cooked carcass, there wouldn't be an immediate investigation and manhunt? Seriously?"

Frank decided to play along a little. "I wasn't exactly in a position to find a replacement, now was I?"

Bachmann grinned.

"I like that, Frank. No, you weren't. Especially since you have a strong aversion to murder. Without that conscience, you might have secured a temporary replacement cadaver."

"So, are you going to play this out all morning, David, or are you going to tell me what else I did wrong?"

"Nothing, Frank," Bachmann said smiling. "Absolutely nothing, but you could never have known that our reach had extended much farther than you would have imagined in the old days. You see, your boy, Nathan, took every precaution that you told him to take. It wasn't enough, though. We were on to him right away. Then we tracked him to you. We monitored his visits to you, and the rest was easy to figure out even before he made the pass to you."

"Okay, David, you've had your glory. Now, like I said to start with, cut the bullshit. What do you want?"

THE DISCLOSURE

Frank had little patience for David Bachmann's cat and mouse game. He only wanted to know what kind of a situation he was in. Then he could tell Bachmann to fuck off so that he would unknowingly disclose more than he wanted to Frank to know. He knew Bachmann well enough to know his buttons to push. Of one thing Frank was certain. He was to be used for some sort dirty work while Nathan was held hostage.

Bachmann related to Frank knowledge of an insurgent force in the wastelands that was gaining in numbers and quality of weapons. They had been able to secure a sizable cache of modern weapons, from raiding government armories near the perimeter. They had been able to steal weapons without a single casualty to the government's soldiers, or themselves.

"Not your style of war is it, David? You like a body count?" Frank couldn't help releasing some sarcasm.

"Very funny, Frank. It's worse than that. One of the reasons that their ranks are gaining numbers is desertion from our own ranks."

"How could that be, David? Your soldiers are guaranteed food pellets in their bellies, a soggy sleeping bag when it rains, and battlefield euthanasia if they get wounded. What in the world could the enemy offer them to desert? Except maybe hope of a life in which they can control their own destiny?"

"It's a good thing for you, Frank, that you're in a private setting or I'd have you tried for sedition."

"You aren't going to do shit until you tell me what you want, and I decide if I'll do it. Now, will you get done with the story-telling and say what you want of me?" Now Frank was playing the cat.

Not intimidated, but nonetheless sensing impatience on the part of Frank, Bachmann explained. They had sent in agents disguised as deserters on two separate insurgent raids onto army posts. It was unknown if they had had any success, or if they were dead. Their micro-chip implants detected animal DNA, and were moving about randomly within an undeveloped area of the protected territory.

Bachmann wanted Frank to infiltrate the insurgents to gather intelligence, either on his own or with the existing agents, if they were alive.

"And exactly how am I supposed to get there, David? Are you going to send me in a fast attack hover cab painted hot lime green? Then I could jump out wearing full army combat gear and say that I'm a deserter. Better yet, give me a lifetime membership for REI so that I can get some rich man outdoor gear in a lot of bright and trendy colors. I'm sure that will fool them! Then it will be a short life on the REI membership! Well here's your answer. Fuck off!"

Now it was Bachmann who was out of patience. Nonetheless, he expected this reaction. Frank knew that this was not the final word but he also was not going to rollover easily.

A tall mature-looking woman had been paying close attention. She stepped forward as if she had something to add. Bachmann signaled her to stand down.

"I'm going to give you overnight to rethink that position, Frank."

Bachmann ordered that Frank and Nathan be

taken away for a night in a cell.

NO NEGOTIATION

The two men did not know exactly where they had been taken. Frank was thankful, however, that they had put them into the same cell together. Nathan was a trained soldier, but had not been hardened by combat. Not knowing what they might have to endure, Frank did not know how well Nathan could stand the test.

They were given an ample helping of food pellets and water in the late afternoon, and early the next morning. Nathan's army training paid off here. Nathan had enjoyed more palatable nourishment while growing up in the privilege of social status inherited from his great-grandmother. He ate the crude meals without protest in order to maintain strength for the unknown that was to come.

By mid-morning of the next day, Bachmann summoned Frank. Nathan was left in the cell. Without asking if Frank had reconsidered, Bachmann introduced him to Dot. She was the woman who stepped out to speak on the day before. She was to be Frank's partner.

Dorothy Goldman was about ten years younger than Frank. In spite of the obvious signs of her age, she looked superbly fit. Women much younger than her might envy her form.

Dot's gray hair was cut short. There was some turkey wattle on her neck. The gray-blue eyes set into her weathered face had the glow of a twenty-year-old.

With a sincere but knowing smile, Dot held out her hand to Frank. He took it.

"I understand that we're going to be working together."

"You'll need to explain before I acknowledge that," Frank replied.

Dot told him that she was a double agent. Her mission was to get him into the insurgent group, establish him as a trusted member and return to Bachmann with an update.

"What do they need me for if you can get in so easily?"

"We need a permanent plant," she explained. "The insurgents know that I'm a double agent, but they think that I'm working for them. I've led them to some of the weapons that they have been able to gain for raiding armories. What they don't know is that the weapons will be electronically jammed when they need them most, in the heat of full combat."

"I don't like it, and now I don't think that I like you. I'll take a pass. You can go ahead and dispose of me if you want. I won't do dirty work like this."

"It's not that easy, Frank."

Bachmann nodded to his security men, who surrounded Frank and escorted him to the door. They took him down the hall to an elevator, and up a few floors. Stepping out into open air from the elevator, a crowd could be heard. They were in an arena.

THE PERSUASION

Frank was escorted to a club box. Bachmann and Dot soon joined them.

"I don't have too much more to say but there is something that I want you see, Frank. A few things have changed since you've been away. Watch."

Bachmann nodded toward the arena. In a mix of ancient Rome and contemporary electronic games, there was a combat contest about to happen on the arena field. Overhead and center was a four-sided Jumbotron-like screen televising the action to give the crowd a close-up view.

"Watch this one game and then maybe we can talk some more, Frank."

A man and a woman stood ready in the center of the field. They were both naked and without armor. They had choices of various blades, bludgeons and shields available in racks near them.

There were two more combatants, one stood at each end of the field. When zoomed into on the

Jumbotron, they looked to be neither human nor beast. In fact, they were a genetically modified cross. Also, both naked, the only thing certain was that one of them was also a male, and the other also a female.

The crowd cheered as the game began. The man and woman had little chance. Their adversaries were brutes who were only angered by the minor wounds inflicted upon them by the humans' weapons.

The only relief for the man and woman came when one of them was able to gain points by inflicting substantial but nonfatal wounds on a combatant. The referee would knock the combatant out with a stunning shock to the collar that it wore. Within less than a minute, however, the combatant was back in the fight with a vengeance.

The couple fought valiantly against their impossible odds. Microphones had been installed on the collars of the combatants so the sound of each bone they broke in their victims could be heard on the stadium sound system. The crowd roared approval with the sickening sound of every snap and crunch.

When too many bones had been broken for the man and woman to even retreat, much less fight, they were tossed into the air for the pure thrill of seeing if their tortured bodies would move again after impact with the arena floor. When they could no longer even utter a moan, they were dragged to a huge stone in the center of the arena. Gripped by their feet, they were flung against the stone to smash their heads like pumpkins in a final and fatal blow.

Frank was sickened by this brutality, and the crowd that cheered it on. He had a good idea where this was going but refused to show emotion. He thought for a moment about simply killing Bachmann where he sat. His goons would be on him, but not soon enough to save Bachmann.

As the field was readied for another fight, the Jumbotron flashed an announcement that the next contestants were about to be chosen. The camera panned slowly down the line-up of naked candidates. Even though he was expecting it, when the screen filled with Nathan's naked form, Frank felt a punch to his soul.

THE AGREEMENT

Frank turned to Bachmann. "Alright asshole, I'll do your dirty work. First, get my grandson out of that line-up and by my side. Do it now!"

"You're not in a position to be giving orders, Frank." Bachmann sneered.

"And you're not going to be in need of oxygen if you push me any longer. I'll kill you where you sit, and hear the dying squeals of the coward you are, before your goons can take me out."

Whether Frank was capable of what he threatened, or not, didn't matter. He had put a horrible image into Bachmann's mind. The confidence left his face just long enough for Frank to know that Bachmann would comply.

"Bring the boy here now," he barked toward his guards.

Without speaking, one of them was gone and came back with Nathan, still naked, in less than five minutes. Now the attention was on Frank and Bachmann. It was uncertain who was really in charge.

"Alright, Bachmann, Listen closely. Don't even think about trying to counter this offer. I'll run your mission but not until I know that my grandson and his mother are safe and cannot be found again. He will advise me when he and his mother have reached sanctuary. It will take less than 24 hours unless your goons interfere. Then and only then I will leave with your agent. It's that simple."

"Yes, but..."

"Just do it, Bachmann! Get my boy some clothes and show him to some reliable and untraceable transportation."

THE BOND

With Nathan safely on his way, Frank turned to Dot.

"If we're going to work together, we have to trust each other. That will be a stretch for me. How do we get started?"

"Mutual disclosure, one layer at a time."

"Like an onion? There will be tears then, and don't expect to reach my core. There are limits."

"I like your candor, Frank." Dot smiled. "First, we need some privacy. Let's get out of David Bachmann's lair."

Bachmann sat erect as if about to protest.

"Save it, David. I know the evolution of your Patriot Act over the decades much too well. Privacy is difficult enough anywhere in the world now. It's plain impossible in your jackal's den."

Bachmann offered a government vehicle, which was immediately declined by both Dot and Frank. Their impromptu, mutual agreement was a promising start. The two took a public taxi to a location that Dot commanded to the vehicle once they were in with the door closed.

The taxi docked in front of a hotel. Dot passed her palm across the scanner at the hotel entrance. The outer door opened and closed behind them. Almost immediately, the next scanner flashed an intrusion warning.

Dot pressed her open palm onto the scanner.

With one finger of her other hand she tapped a sequenced code between her spread-open fingers on the scanner. The inner door opened into the hotel lobby.

At a kiosk inside, Dot requested a suite for two. She caught the look on Frank's otherwise poker face, at her request for only one room.

"Nothing to be concerned about, Frank. I can handle myself with or without consent."

The suite was one large room, with a kitchenette, table and chairs, sofa, and one king-sized bed. In the corner near the entrance to the bathroom was a hot tub surrounded with clear glass walls.

"I'm sleeping in the bed," Dot told Frank. "You're welcome to join me there as long as you don't roll around much, kick, or wet the bed." She grinned. "Or if you'd rather, you can take the sofa. Remember what I told you if you join me in the bed, though....with or without consent."

It was midday. Dot ordered room service. After eating she wasted no time in laying the skin back off of the onion. She went over the general logistics required to get to the insurgents. For fear of attack, the insurgents didn't stay long in one place. Once she and Frank were close, the insurgents would find them.

THE PLAN

Given Dot's experience in the wasteland and her description of the terrain that they would be going into, Frank deferred, for the most part, to her ideas on equipment and supplies. They would make the bulk of the trip in a medium-sized cargo craft. This craft was large enough to carry the four mules that Dot wanted to finish the trip.

A hover craft of any sort would get them where they needed to be but Dot did not want the attention that it would draw along the way. Mules would draw more attention than she wanted, as well, but the animals might have bartering value if needed.

Dot did not ask if Frank could ride a saddle mule. It was enough to know that he was a veteran of the Persian Wars. Any soldier of those wars could ride a horse, mule, or camel, as well as he could drive a tank or truck.

Dot looked at Frank with doubt when he added powder-fired weapons to her list. They were heavy, require frequent reloading, and gave away a combatant's position with their noise. Frank insisted on four of the hand-held versions with dual-holster shoulder harnesses.

The list of needs was sent to Bachmann with instructions to have everything at the airfield by midnight. They gave no mention of when they would be departing. Best to keep Bachmann guessing or trusting his assumptions.

"What about your grandson?" Dot asked.

"He has made it to the sanctuary."

"Good," she nodded. Dot did not question how Frank seemed certain of this fact. She had heard of his reputation of telepathic communication with those whom he had a close relationship.

Dot ordered room service again for supper. Both agreed that it was best to lie low for the night. No doubt Bachmann's dogs were sniffing about, and it was best to let them wonder.

After eating, Dot stripped naked and tossed her clothing into the launderer porthole near the bathroom door. She turned to Frank.

"Do you want to put your things in here before I start it up?"

Frank nodded, stripped down and tossed his clothing into the machine. The two lounged together in the hot tub, for a time, before going to bed early.

Frank opted for the comfort of the bed over the sofa. It was hard telling what he might have to sleep on for the next few weeks. Best to enjoy a good rest when he could.

THE DEPARTURE

Dot was the first to awaken. She turned on the room lighting but set it dim. It was not that she worried about waking Frank as much as she did not want to alert any of Bachmann's watchdogs.

Frank was up and drawing fresh coffee in the kitchenette when Dot came out of the shower, toweling her short hair.

"Coffee?" He asked.

"Please, and black is fine."

Dot hung the towel across the back of a chair and grabbed their fresh clothing. She laid Frank's things out on the bed, and dressed herself. Frank brought the coffee to the table. Dot thanked him as she drew the steaming cup closer and took in the aroma.

When Frank finished a shower and was dressed, Dot had a hot cereal breakfast ready with fresh fruit. They ate and headed to the field.

The cube craft was loaded with the exception of the mules. They were stabled on the far side of the hangar. Dot and Frank looked over the supplies. Everything was as they had requested.

Frank was especially impressed with the powder-fired weapons. There were two .357 revolvers complete with four speed-loaders. Two .45 ACP semi-automatics were hung in shoulder harnesses for carry under each arm. There were spare magazines for them and plenty of ammunition in both calibers.

Other than two security people, no one was in the hangar. They loaded the mules, secured the craft doors, and headed out before they had to deal with Bachmann. As Dot eased the craft up to the hangar door, it opened before she called up the code. They were gone into the early morning darkness.

The wisdom of a Texas country boy that Frank once knew in the army echoed in his mind, as Dot held the craft at low altitude. *The higher up you get on a limb, the more people can see you and want to take a shot at you.*

They arrived at their destination in good time. They had the mules out, saddled and packed well before sunrise. Two mules were for riding. Only one was needed for packing but the fourth might come in handy.

Dot set the solar-powered camo shield on the cargo craft before they left. The craft was tucked away but the camo blended it with the surrounding terrain. Only someone who knew the area well would realize that something was amiss.

As they were riding, they made no effort to conceal themselves. Dot explained, however, that there was the possibility of being discovered by a renegade band before ORINO found them.

ORINO was the largest and most organized group of insurgents. The name stood for Our Revolution Is Not Over. For the most part, these were good, hard-working people who just wanted a real government back, with a reasonable redistribution of the wealth. Their issue was with excessive greed rather than wealth.

Some of the renegade groups were impatient hot

heads that had splintered off from ORINO. There were a few gangs, however, that were no more than ruthless thieves and murderers without conscience. Like 19th century Comancheros of the southwestern territories of the United States, they were dangerous beyond the imagination of even the most seasoned warrior.

They had no reason to hurry the mules. Wearing them down could be detrimental to a running escape should they be chased. Still, they were putting ground behind themselves in good time.

CONTACT IS IMMINENT

Frank was concerned that some of the terrain they passed through was prime for being ambushed. Dot assured him that it was best to stay low until they were closer to ORINO territory. If they showed themselves too much in the open, they were more likely to be over-powered by larger numbers than themselves. Her point was proven soon enough.

By midday of the second day on the mules, they came to a vast clearing. It was flat ground without much vegetation. The deteriorating ruins were evidence that the area was the remnant of an oil refinery from the days of fossil fuels.

They crossed the clearing without event, but Dot warned Frank that even if no one had seen them before, she was certain they were being watched now. It had taken most of the afternoon to reach the cover of forest again. They had not set a full camp on the previous night, and even with their slow pace the mules were showing the wear of the trip.

Frank took care of the animals while Dot set up the camp. He freed them of their burdens of packs and saddles. Then he hobbled the mules in an area near a stream, where they had access to both water and grazing. Frank would never hobble horses. Unlike mules, they could be easily excited into panic. A horse that panicked while hobbled was, almost certainly, a horse to be put down.

Dot found a small package in the mule pack and carefully removed the protective bag. She adjusted the camouflage setting to automatic, jerked a tab on the small bundle, and tossed it. The pop-up tent settled onto the ground complete with sleeping gear inside for two.

Dot pulled another tab, and opened an extension to the shelter space for storage of their other gear. Last, she set the shelter climate control to provide comfort for two people in combat-ready dress. The camouflage blended so well into the surroundings, that Frank nearly walked into the shelter when he returned from taking care of the mules.

They talked about the possible events of the next day, as they ate the last of their fresh food. They had enough condensed combat rations to sustain them for several weeks if needed. Dot expected contact with ORINO by tomorrow. In that case, the remaining CCR would be given to them for use in their recon patrols.

They agreed to break camp at midnight. There was still enough daylight when they retired to give a 360-degree view of the campsite from within the pop-up tent. The skin of the shelter was designed to be see-through from the inside.

Before bedding down, Frank removed the hobbles from the mules and tied them onto a stringer within view of the shelter. As much needed sleep took the two into guarded rest, they were acutely aware that all of the sounds from the surrounding woods were not of nature. Dot assured Frank that the perimeter monitor built into the pop-up tent would give them ample warning, in the event of a breach.

WITHOUT WARNING

The moon was not full, but it provided the light Dot needed to find her way to the rendezvous area. She was certain they would make some contact by midday. It came sooner.

It was barely dusk when Frank's saddle mule went down. The stink of burnt flesh, from the wound in the mule's chest, permeated the air. On the ground almost as quickly Frank was from his downed mule, Dot identified the threat and returned fire.

One shot into an oak tree neutralized the threat. She held focus on the spot where the sniper had fallen to the ground. Frank's eyes scanned the area around them for others.

With no movement evident where the attacker had gone down, Dot approached cautiously. A young woman, probably still in her teens sat with her back to the tree trunk and her weapon semi-ready. Dot drew her weapon to fire but the young woman was still.

As Dot moved in closer, the woman's clouding eyes made it obvious that the spirit was leaving her. Breathing had stopped and the heart was on its final beats. Satisfied that the separation of soul and flesh was complete, Dot moved in and took the weapon.

"Any idea who she is?" Frank had tied the remaining three mules and followed her.

"No one that I recognize. She was probably with a renegade band. As young as she is, it's a good guess they may have sent her solo, on an initiation mission, to prove her worth before letting her into their ranks. They could have been who we heard in the woods last night."

With the exception of closing the dead girl's eyes, they did nothing with her body. Dot was confident her people, renegades or not, would come for her. Most important was that she and Frank were not there when they did.

They doubled the pack load on one animal, and Frank put the dead mule's saddle on the now-unburdened animal. The single pack mule would still do well with both loads. They had loaded each mule with only half of what they were capable of carrying, when they started the trip.

Dot was mounted. Frank was about to mount when he saw the vague outline of a weapon drawing a sight on his companion from the same oak tree. Likely, it was the spotter for the downed sniper.

No spotter was needed at this close range but the skilled pairs seldom separated. They became joined at the hip after some success with the long shots together. Whoever he was, he got off a round that took Dot off of her mount in the nanosecond before Frank's shot knocked him from the tree.

Frank ran to Dot. She lay motionless and face down. Her charred clothing smoldered around her wound. Without Dot, Frank's position had become complicated, maybe impossible. It would take every bit of his experience in four wars to even survive, much less accomplish the mission.

Editor's Note: To be continued in Perfections, *coming soon...*

Just a regular guy with a head full of stuff waiting
for paper.

Marlin's Facebook:
facebook.com/Marlin-Woosley-Author-Page-
125995674252918/
Marlin's Twitter: @MWoosley_Writer

Primary Service
by Jill Taggart

"Home is the place to be safe, to hope, to grow. Home is everything. So why do I feel so empty at home? After all, isn't it all good?"

Blue: 57392 looked at the small screen in her hand and, after a moment's pause, hit delete. After all, it was just some kind of vague feeling, nothing she should worry Blue: 85206 about.

She looked around her home and involuntarily shivered. She had been doing that lately and she didn't know why.

Her home consisted of four walls painted hot pink…someone's idea of a calming color, a metal bed bolted to the floor with a thin mattress on top, a sink, one table also bolted to the floor along with an unbolted chair, a cleaning cubical, a food cabinet, a separate cabinet to hold her three mandatory blue jump suits, and a waste disposal unit. The wall opposite her bed glowed with the Wall-Com device that had no controls and was always on.

That was her home and she had lived here for as long as she could remember. She had never been inside anyone else's home but she assumed they were all the same. She knew from her schooling that she was special; that she, along with the rest of the Chosen Ones were descended from the lucky few who had escaped from a war-torn Earth and been saved by the Corporation and that, one day, her descendents would find another planet on which to live. Perhaps, if she was lucky, that planet would be found during her lifetime and she would be one of those who would colonize it for the Corporation.

Five, as she thought of herself, put her hand-held Com Device down on the table, stood up and stretched. Her short, blond hair and green eyes complimented her slim body, but she didn't know it. In her 18 years of life, she had never seen a mirror and had no idea what she looked like.

The Wall-Com rang.

A mechanical voice purred, "Blue: 57392, it is time for you to fulfill your Primary Service to Wendko International, Ltd. Please report to the Center for Future Design."

Her heart pounded and she broke into a sweat.

"Now? So soon?" she said, hoping she had not said it aloud.

"You have ten minutes, Blue: 57392."

She had always known this day would come. She had been trained for it. She knew it was her Primary Service and for the good of the Corporation and the Ship. Of course she owed her life to the Corporation, as did everyone on board the Ship, and so part of her was glad that the waiting was over.

But she was still scared. She was about to meet one of "them" for the first time. She had seen pictures, of course, it was part of her training, but face-to-face was different.

With a great deal of anxiety Blue left her home and walked through the blank, white corridors of the Ship passing others on their way to work or to their homes. She spoke to no one, she smiled at no one and no one spoke to or smiled at her. Some of the people passing by she knew, most she didn't, but she found herself wondering about them. That girl with the red hair, was she coming from work or going to work? Had that tall girl who looked so angry just come from the Center for Future Design? Blue hoped not. There was little socialization on the Ship. The Corporation assigned one Friend and three Acquaintances to each person and that was it. Even speaking to a person not in your Official Assigned Circle was discouraged by the Board of Directors. Unless, of course, it was for business purposes or the obligatory basic education and then only a bare minimum of contact was acceptable.

As she stood in front of the door to the Center for Future Design, Five took a deep breath. Her courage faltered and she almost turned and ran. But there was no place she could hide on the Ship, so feeling a strong sense of imminent doom which she shoved down into a deep, hidden place so she could ignore it, she reached out her hand and on her third attempt she managed to touch the glowing pad next to the door. The door slid open without a sound and, trembling slightly, she entered. The door slid closed behind her and she found herself in total darkness.

As the room slowly brightened she saw It standing in a corner opposite her. One of 'Them.' A male. The first she had ever seen. And he looked every bit as nervous as she felt.

This room was slightly larger than her home but no calming hot-pink here. These walls were bright orange and the bed, while still bolted to the floor, was big and looked soft. There was no other furniture of any kind.

The Wall-Com flickered.

"Blue: 57392 and Yellow: 19640 please commence the breeding process. You will have one hour starting now." Soft music filled the room and the lights dimmed slightly.

Five's courage deserted her. She turned and pressed the glowing pad next to the door, her only thought: escape. The door remained closed. She took a deep, calming breath. *I have been trained for this work*, she told herself. *I must not let the Corporation down. It is all good. It is all good.*

Across the room the male turned his back to her and began to remove his yellow jump suit.

Exactly one hour later the Wall-Com flickered into life again.

"Blue: 57392 and Yellow: 19640, you have fulfilled your Primary Service to your Corporation. Wendko International, Ltd. thanks you. Please return to your respective Circles."

Five hurriedly put on her blue Social Circle jump suit and, without once looking back at the male, left the Center for Future Design. The male, in his yellow Social Circle jump suit, left by his own door across the room from hers.

Not one word had been spoken between them.

Five felt strange. The breeding process had hurt at first, but she had been taught to expect that. The important thing was that she was fulfilling her duty, completing her assignment, and supporting her Corporation. Nothing else mattered.

And, after all, it was all good.

Time passed and for awhile nothing changed. One day was like the next and like the day before. Five texted to her Friend about the breeding process, and Blue: 85206 texted back that she, too, had been called to perform her Primary Service.

After a month had passed, Five realized that she had, indeed, been successfully bred. She was relieved of her usual work and required to follow a routine specifically designed for her.

When she reached nine months, Five delivered a new worker to the Corporation.

The new worker was cleaned up, inspected, numbered, and removed to the Development Center where it would stay until it reached the age of three years. During this time it would learn language and be tested to determine its health and its future work for the Corporation. If the worker was determined to be healthy and sound it would be removed to its permanent home and schooling would begin. At the age of ten the worker would commence the work it would do for the rest of its life.

Five was instructed to recover and return to her regular duties within a week.

She did not know if she had given the Corporation a female like herself or one of 'Them.' A male. Nor would she ever know.

The day she returned home from the Worker Delivery Center, Five sent a text to Blue: 85206. She hadn't heard anything from her Friend since leaving for the WDC to deliver the new Worker, but she knew that Blue: 85206 was supposed to deliver her Worker the same day as she. She sent several texts and still nothing came back. Finally Five texted one of her Acquaintances asking if she knew where Blue: 85206 could be.

The answer came back quickly.

"She failed in her Primary Service. She was damaged during the Worker Delivery Process and rendered useless for future breeding so she was discontinued. Perhaps you should request a new Friend from the Social Procurement Office."

Five felt a twinge of sadness at the loss of her Friend, quickly followed by fear for herself. Then she decided she would probably be safe. After all, she had already been bred successfully once and if the new worker turned out to be sound, she would be bred again.

Meanwhile, still feeling tired from the delivery process, she sat down on her bed and watched the Wall-Com which was showing a video of the Ancients. Old women, some looked to be as old as 50, strolled through trees in a gentle, misty rain. This was something, the narrator said, that used to often happen back on Earth.

Five found the trees and rain to be interesting but the old women were strange and frightening to her since she had never seen one before. On the Ship no one was old. Blue had never thought about being old before and briefly wondered why women got old on Earth but not on the ship. She felt that something about that was wrong, but she didn't know what.

After a while her eyes grew heavy and she slept.

ᏨᎽ

Evan Woodbine, CEO of Wendko International, Ltd. sat at his desk looking over the latest actuary figures. He was disturbed because the numbers for new workers were down slightly. He needed at least 642 births a month just to stay even with Exhavode, Inc. and last month production had fallen below that number. Not far below, nothing to panic about, but something needed to be done and done now.

Mr. Woodbine thought it was possible that his new assistant, whatever his name is, might have the right idea. New Kid, as Mr. Woodbine called his assistant, said that production could be increased if the males and females weren't kept strictly separated except for direct breeding purposes. It was a radical idea and one to perhaps consider, but Mr. Woodbine was afraid of the chaos that might result. He remembered all too well the riots of 2087 that had completely destroyed Conohist, Inc. and the wars that resulted.

Of course, war was completely normal and expected between the Corporations. But war was certainly not acceptable within a Corporation. That was treason and exactly what had happened to Conohist. But now that his war with Exhavode, Inc. was almost 24 years old with no sign of a let-up, the breeding program had to increase somehow.

What to do? What to do?

Mr. Woodbine tapped his fingers on his desk and

glanced out the window at the top of his enemy's dome way off in the hazy distance. He could just barely see it as a small pimple on the horizon. He supposed that Marc Holderin, CEO of Exhavode, could see the top of his dome as well. The land between them was barren. Brown earth filled with deep holes, the result of the bombs that the two corporations had flung at each other several years ago. Now, of course, bombs were no longer used, phased out in favor of the hand-to-hand combat that Mr. Woodbine and Marc Holderin both preferred.

He glanced down at the battlefield between the two Corporations. The war was going well...both sides taking causalities at a good pace.

Mr. Woodbine briefly reflected on the history of his corporation. He had inherited his CEO position from his father who had inherited it from his father. Rumor said that Wendko had once been in business, that they had produced things called 'automobiles' and that they went to war with Exhavode over a substance called 'oil.' Mr. Woodbine was glad that this was all in the past, he could not imagine having to produce a thing that was dependant on another thing that someone else owned. Much better to simply produce the things that you needed and forget the rest. And these days what he needed was workers he could turn into fighters. So, bottom line, what was needed was more brood-mares and more breeding.

He glanced out the window in time to see a contingent of his fighters mowed down by the superior forces of Exhavode. He sighed heavily.

New Kid is right about one thing, he thought. *The workers must never find out that they are actually on Earth. At least not until they are sent into battle. That would lead to rebellion.*

ଓ ଚ

Five recovered and returned to her usual work within a week. She was glad to be working again, but, deep inside her secret self…a self she had only recently discovered…she hoped that the Ship would land someday so that she could stand outside and feel that thing called rain. And see a real tree. And maybe even grow old.

But for now, it's all good.

Jill was born in Hollywood and raised in the wilds of Laurel Canyon in the hills high above Los Angeles.

She wrote her first story when she was around five years old. Something about a pixie and a buttercup as she recalls. Science-Fiction called to her in her teen years and she wrote many short stories in this vein. One of these stories was published in a Perry Rodan book and later in three different anthologies. *Final Victory* was a short-short shock story about the end of the world.

She's had a checkered career, or several checkered

careers…As Jill Taggart, she was one of the first female radio talk-show hosts with a show in Los Angeles called, *Male Call*. Also won an Emmy for Sound Effects Editing some ten years later…that show was *The Day After* and was all about nuclear war and the end of everything. About the weirdest job she's ever had was crawling through air-conditioning ducts in high-rises to clean them! The things artists do to stay alive!

Since she is one of the few pre-war babies…someone born after the Great Depression but before World War II, and there are only about 3 years worth of them…she remembers the war. Jill lived through this time of uncertainty and she still finds it both terrifying and fascinating. This was a period of unbelievable world-wide tragedy. It was also the time that America burst onto the world stage as a major world power. And it was the time that women gained enormous strength both personally and in the work place. And that is what her first novel, Cold Canyon Drive, is about.

Jill now lives in Oregon, enjoying the rain and the cold. And the trees. And she is completely owned by cats. Her husband calls her a Cat Enabler!

Find Jill on Facebook at:
https://www.facebook.com/jill.daubery

ONLY ONE WAY OUT
by Traci Sanders

I need another blanket. The room is frigid and reeks of cleaning products. I want to open my eyes but one is swollen shut, thanks to his famous right hook, and the other is reluctant to make an appearance because I can hear *him,* playing the concerned husband role flawlessly, as usual. He should be a pro by now; he's gotten plenty of practice. Those who are fortunate enough to not know Daniel like I do, think he's the model husband. My scars and bruises tell a different story.

Thanks to this ventilator, he can't tell if I'm breathing naturally or not. *Could this finally be it?*

I hear the doctor say, "I'm sorry, Mr. Shaw. Tanya suffered severe head trauma when she fell down the stairs."

Ha, fell down the stairs. That seems plausible,

right?

Daniel will never tell the truth, that he dragged me by my hair to that staircase and then shoved me down the stairs when I tried to fight back—or so I let him think. He probably intended to "teach me a lesson" a bit longer that night. *Sorry to have to inconvenience you, darling, but for once I was in control.*

His voice is further away now and I squint to see him talking to the doctor in the hallway, but I'm careful to not let him see me.

"When will she wake up?" he asks, faking concern.

A few moments of silence cuts the air between us until the doctor says, "The chances of her waking up are almost nonexistent. I'm very sorry."

Through slit eyes I watch my tormentor rub his face and turn around in a half circle. Then he turns back to the doctor and asks, "What's the prognosis?"

"Well, she won't have much of an existence, even if she wakes up. She'll feed from a tube for the rest of her life and will need round-the-clock care."

Another long silence and then, "What's the alternative?" my self-serving husband inquires.

"We turn off the machines and let nature take its course." The doctor sounds even more saddened by these words than my own husband.

I close my eyes quickly when Daniel turns in my

direction. For a moment, I think I see a tear attempt to meet with his cheek. *Was I wrong? Does he actually care?*

My heart races as he walks toward my hospital bed, and I pray he can't tell that I can actually breathe on my own.

His next words are like ice through my veins.

"Let's do it."

So cold. So callous. So ... him. *I made the right decision.*

Dr. Davis calls for a nurse to come remove my ventilator and turn off the beeping robotics. I cringe inside as I orchestrate the breathing patterns I've rehearsed many times. To my dismay—yet relief—my husband doesn't even wait until it's over, and walks out of the room. *Coward.* But at least he's gone.

Dr. Davis stands beside my bed for a few moments to make sure I'm really *gone,* and to make sure Daniel isn't coming back.

Still too afraid to open my eyes, I hear, "Thanks, April. You can go now. I'd like a moment alone with my patient," and the nurse walks out of the room.

The sound of a door shutting, followed by blinds being closed, signals me to finally open my eyes. I feel a familiar hand on my cheek. But this one is soft and loving.

"You took a hell of a beating this time, babe,"

Dr. Davis says.

Through a raspy voice I ask, "He's gone?"

"He's gone," the doctor replies and plants a soft kiss on my lips.

"Thanks for the help, Travis. I never would have made it out without you."

His voice adopts an angry tone. "I just wish that bastard didn't have to do this to you."

"It was the only way, sweetheart. He would have killed me before he let us be together," I reply in a tired, shaky voice.

A soft knock sounds on the door and my heart pounds. A smiling face greets me and I relax.

"Hi, April. Thanks for everything. You were a star," Travis says to the nurse.

"Yes, thanks April," I add.

Travis hands me a wad of cash, which I stuff into my pocket, and a bag of clothes, which he stuffs under my sheet.

"I'll meet you at our place in three hours, okay? Just as soon as I finish my shift."

"Okay. I love you," I reply, and kiss him again, still not believing I've made it this far.

April covers my body with the sheet and I assume the position as she prepares to wheel me out of the room.

Voices whiz by us as the bed rolls along the hallway and into the elevator. *Almost there.*

I'm doing fine until a certain voice shakes me to

the core.

"Excuse me, is that my wife? Is that Tanya under there?" *I guess he didn't leave after all.*

A pain radiates through my left arm and spreads into my entire body as my chest tightens and I moan. I hear his voice again. "That's my wife! That's my wife! She's alive!"

Then I hear April shouting, "Crash cart! Someone get me a crash cart! Sir, I need you to back up. Security!"

The pain is unbearable—emotional and physical—and the fear is immobilizing. Images flash through my mind like a movie reel, a horror movie. Visions and memories of him slapping me and throwing me against the wall. The burn of his angry touch sears my skin.

"We're losing her!" April shouts, and a multitude of panic-stricken voices ring out all around me.

The voices get softer, more distant, and then fade completely.

I was right. There was only one way out.

Traci Sanders is a mom of three, seasoned child care provider, and multi-genre author of parenting, children's, and romance titles. In addition to books, she writes poems and songs. In fact, she can write about pretty much anything as long as she has a topic.

To date, Traci has released seven titles and is working on eighth book, her third romance in the Love Hurts series, "Cowboy Tears." She is also the founder of the Readers Review Room online where authors can submit their books for honest feedback and reviews, and readers can find their next great read from those site.

Traci is a huge supporter of Indie authors and features them on her blog quite often, along with a segment for authors titled "365 Days to Write Right" where she offers daily tips on writing, publishing, marketing, and more.

Follow Traci on Facebook at:
https://www.facebook.com/traci.sanders.399
Find her on Amazon at:
https://www.amazon.com/Traci-M-Sanders/e/B00BA9VUUY/

PASS THE SALT
by Jennifer Stewart

"The first time I punched my sister was in a fight over the salt."

We were on a river boat, sailing up the Nile. Adam sat on the other side of the table from my cousin Rose and kept his eyes on her face. He had no expression on his—poker face, I guess. He reminded me of Harrison Ford at his most deadpan wooden. I can never tell whether he's a really good actor or just deadpan wooden. Same with Adam sometimes. Was he putting on a show, or was there just nothing going on? I never figured it out, and I grew up with him, too. My parents were Catholic, and he was orphaned at six. Catholics love rescuing. So Adam came to live with us. I was five.

I remember that day as clear as a bell.

My parents used to own a farm that had a small

dam where you could swim. My father could fly-fish but I could never get the hang of it. Anyway, that day I was wading in galoshes, catching tadpoles. It was winter. The air was wet with thick fog that hugged the valleys. I didn't hear or see him approach. I don't know how long he stood watching me.

"Hallo, what's your name'?" he said. I got a fright. I jumped backwards, losing my tadpoles and almost my balance.

"Felix. You made me lose my tadpoles," I said crossly. "Who are you?"

"Felix? That's a funny name for a girl," he said.

"I'm sick of people saying that," I retorted, "and you look Jewish."

"What do you know about Jewish?" he scoffed.

"Lots," I said. I didn't, of course. I had just read about different nationalities in our encyclopedia at home. And something about the description of Jewish people seemed to fit with this boy.

"Can you fly-fish?" he asked.

I scowled at him.

"Do you want to learn?"

I never had up until that point, but suddenly I did. He told me we were adopting him. It was like we were of one mind right from the start. We walked back to the house together. He chanted my name over and over, "Felix, Felix, Felix." I kind of liked it.

I never found out what happened to his parents. Catholics also love secrets, maybe even better than they love rescuing. It's better that you don't know, darling. It seemed like my parents knew, but they wouldn't tell me or him and he was much more persistent than I was. You see, he couldn't remember anything. Big blank. At some point in his memory he had a mother and a father, and a home and toys and a life, and then came this blank, after which he didn't have any of it. Big mystery. So he wasn't really my brother. But he did really punch me.

Michael looked away from Adam. At me.

"You let him punch you?"

I nodded.

"I don't believe it. You just sat there and let him do it."

"Of course I did. It hurt, but not that badly. And then I broke his nose."

Michael and Rose laughed. Adam grinned at the memory.

"So when was the second time?"

Adam transferred his deadpan look to me. "When she wouldn't pass me the salt." He was lying but I said nothing.

"You'd think she would have learned," said Rose, laughing. She was Michael's girlfriend. Adam and I were kind of together but not in that way. We just never hooked up with anybody for long, either of us, and in between disastrous love affairs we hung out together. People got used to us. Kind of brother and sister and maybe something else one day.

"Who needed to learn?" I replied. Adam shrugged his shoulders, and we said it at the same time. "Both of us."

"You still do that," said Rose, "saying the same thing at the same time. Anyone would think you were twins." For a moment she looked sad.

Adam was oddly Jewish-looking. Oddly because he wasn't Jewish—it was just something about the set of his features which triggered off an idea that somewhere along the line a forebear had said his prayers in the synagogue. I wasn't the only one who had mistaken his nationality on first meeting; lots of people did. As for the rest of him though, the stuff on the surface, he was as Scottish as they come: tall, big build, blue eyes, and blazing red hair.

"What happened?"

Rose sounded vaguely bored, but I knew she wasn't. She had a talent for watching people covertly from behind a vacuous mask she could assume with ease. Times like that, she seemed dead-beat stupid, and it fooled most people. But you could never be sure with Adam. Not in those days, anyway.

It was a strange moment. Something happened between the two of them which I couldn't put my finger on, though I knew she was having him on, and that he probably wasn't falling for it. She emanated a sort of low-keyed animosity, like the vestigial growl of a wild cat that doesn't want to eat its prey, but doesn't mean to let anyone else come too close. She didn't make a sound or move a muscle; it was just something I sensed behind her deadpan face. Adam sensed it too, I could see that. It could have been a tussle for power, I wasn't sure.

It was our first lunch on the Nile cruise. Unbearably hot, the temperature close to forty degrees, even in the restaurant. Most of the other diners had gone up onto the deck. Waiters lethargically moved around, clearing tables slowly, almost randomly, interspersing their work with languid comments. Sweat dripped down my back. I looked out through the window across the river to the bank. The air seemed white hot. A man on a starved-looking fawn-colored donkey galloped along the shore for a short while, as if he was playing at Lawrence of Arabia racing across the desert. He let out a series of whoops, which came faintly across the river, then for no apparent reason suddenly reined in, and sat totally still, watching us move away. A couple of children ran up to him, calling out, but he ignored them. A group of palm trees took their place as the boat slid up the Nile, then gave way in turn to sand banks. White sand, white light. No movement of air.

Adam held Rose's attention with silence for a while, but for the first time in all the years I'd known him, I thought he miscalled the shot by a fraction of a second when I felt, more than saw, the tension in her subside as she lost interest. She pushed her plate away, and stood up.

"I'm going up onto the deck."

"Don't you want to know what happened?" said Adam lazily. I saw that I'd misread him in thinking he'd lost the tussle. You can't lose if you don't engage. He wasn't playing games. He was just letting her be. His voice was level and his look friendly, but impersonal. Still, he didn't mind showing that he was amused at her reply.

"About as much as you want to tell me." She smiled. Nothing vacuous in it, though.

I leaned forward, dipped a napkin in a glass of water and mopped my face and neck. It gave me a few seconds of respite from the heat. Adam watched me, laughing at my discomfort, being totally at ease himself in the heat in his khaki pants and white cotton shirt rolled up at the sleeves. He relaxed back in his chair and picked up the salt cellar. It was one of those cheap glass ones; octagonal, with a bulbous silver screw-top. He rubbed his fingers around it. I could see he was pressing quite hard by the whiteness of his fingernails. It was the only thing that gave him away. The rest of his body was still. A waiter hovered with intent to clear the table, but moved off reluctantly when Adam shook his head. He put the cellar down and looked up at us.

"We were ten. It was a huge family gathering…" He paused, looking inward. "Christmas. Anthony was sitting opposite me." Anthony was another Catholic orphan. We got him when Adam was eight and I was seven. I hated him at first sight.

Adam snorted in amusement at the expression of distaste on my face. I looked away. All the waiters but one had left. He slouched on a chair by the door, eyes closed, hands hanging limply by his side. A couple of flies buzzed round his face. Without opening his eyes he waved them away, then let his hand drop to his side again. A boat similar to ours passed us going down-river. I kicked off my shoes and poured tepid water down my gullet.

"Felix liked a lot of salt in those days." Adam picked up the salt cellar again, and sprinkled a few grains on the table. Put a finger to the salt, and licked it off. He grimaced, rubbed his finger and thumb together, looking at them, then wiped his hand on his trousers in a dismissive gesture. I took over the narrative.

"Anthony didn't, but he always kept it next to him, making sure it was out of my reach so I'd have to ask him for it." God that was irritating. "Anyway, as usual I was annoyed and asked him to please pass me the salt. He totally ignored me. I asked him again, this time loudly and without saying please. Everybody stopped talking and turned towards me to see what the fuss was about. My mother opened her mouth. My father raised his hand to her, to stop her from saying anything, but in any case Anthony got in first.

"He said no. He spoke loudly, turning the corners of his mouth down and pushing his chin out aggressively," I said, feeling the heat rising in my body at the memory. "It was the rudest anyone had ever been to me in my life. But it was more than that. He was wielding power over me."

"I thought she was going to kill him," said Adam. "She got up and marched around the table."

"Blood was pounding in my ears," I said, "I wanted to eliminate him. Forever and ever and ever. Pound him to a bloody pulp."

Michael looked a little nervous but Rose laughed. It penetrated my rage. I realized Adam was watching me like a hawk, his eyes piercing. He put his hand out and touched my arm reassuringly. I settled down. Leaned back.

"Jesus," said Michael to me. "So how did that turn into Adam punching you in the face?"

"He had a kind of mocking smile as he sat stock-still, watching Felix come towards him," said Adam, "only moving his eyes. I think he expected her to just make another demand once she was standing in front of him, and actually I don't know what I meant to do, but I got there first and my fist shot out and—crack."

"You misfired and broke Felix's nose?" Michael didn't get it.

I laughed. "No. He punched Anthony. I was furious with Adam because I wanted to do it. Adam and I got into a fight. That's when he broke my nose."

A burst of laughter from Rose. It had a throaty quality. I could see it turned Adam on. The waiter sat up with a start. Glared at us. I beckoned him over, and handed the glass and napkin to him. He muttered something to me in Arabic, and shuffled out.

"Blood everywhere, total mayhem," I said. "My mother screaming about poor children and charity and all that crap. Nobody worried about me but I didn't care. My father collared Adam and me and sent us off to our rooms. He didn't actually congratulate Adam, but I knew from the way he gave us a shove that he thought it was pretty funny."

Adam continued. "Anthony always thought that our parents preferred me. He resented me and them for it. Actually our mother doted on him, there was nothing he could do that she wouldn't forgive, or find some excuse for." A shadow passed over his face. "It wasn't enough for Anthony that she loved him so much," he said. "In fact he hated it, but he manipulated her for his own ends. He was always rude to her, as if she was his slave or something. He didn't dare try to manipulate Dad, though. Anyway, that night with the salt cellar was the first open acknowledgement of war between Anthony and Felix. And me."

I shivered. Adam spoke in a relaxed and quite neutral tone, but I felt something sinister I couldn't define.

"And?" Rose was still amused and interested enough to have relinquished her mask. She scraped a chair out, turned it around and straddled it, crossing her arms on the top of its back. Adam sat forward, and slid the salt cellar around, making a figure of eight pattern.

"His nose healed, but he wouldn't back down about the salt. It was odd," he said as he turned to me. "You never once remembered to come down early to the table and get there before him so you could claim that salt cellar." He flicked the one he was holding.

I didn't understand it either. Anthony's power over me wasn't limited to the salt. "He was anal about it, completely obsessed. Only with me, of course, not with anybody else. He never said no again, but he just wouldn't let it go. I mean he wouldn't stop playing his stupid game. I always had to ask him."

Adam arched his back and stretched in the chair.

He glanced at Rose, who held his eyes. Saucy. He half smiled.

"So Felix gave up salt. One morning she came down to breakfast and had this look on her face. I can't tell you," Adam looked at me, laughing, "how much pleasure I got from watching him squirm when you didn't ask for that damned salt. He didn't want to lose face, of course, by showing that he noticed or cared. But I knew, and he knew I was laughing at him. That fraction of time made up for all the frustration I'd watched you suffer at his hands. It was probably the..." he glanced at Rose. "One of the most intensely pleasurable moments I've experienced to date."

So they were lovers. Some kind of strange game playing out between them of pretense that they didn't care. I wanted to die. That wasn't who Adam was! I hated Rose in that moment. It was shock that I felt so strongly. I glanced at Michael. He didn't seem to have noticed anything. How could she have Michael and want Adam? They couldn't be more different.

I didn't understand how Adam could ever have fallen for her. She was a prime manipulator, obsessed with emotional power, and if Adam had recognized it in Anthony why didn't he see it in her? I asked the question but I knew the answer. Rose was just unbelievably beautiful. She was tall and slender, with dark hair, a wide mouth, and an energy which could make her glow. When she wanted, she could seduce anybody. I never knew a single person who was able to resist her. Even I couldn't at first when we met. I wondered how it would pan out. That story of his about the salt and power hadn't exactly been about nothing.

Rose smiled at him. "You don't hate Anthony any more, though." It was a statement more than a question, but Adam answered anyway.

"No." He spoke slowly. "We don't hate each other now."

I never understood what happened there. But at some point Anthony and Adam made peace. I hated it. Anthony's power games just didn't bother Adam any more. I didn't know even then, that day on the Nile, what he'd done to get over his anger, and to establish equilibrium within himself, but whatever it was, it worked. It drove me crazy. Everybody hated Anthony, except for Adam. His pathological control obsession meant that he was always playing a game, always looking to get the better of whoever he was with. He was a nightmare. Exhausting to be around. I couldn't stand him as a kid and as a man he was worse. Except for that one period...

"Where is he now, by the way?" I asked. I'd completely lost touch with him.

"Anthony?" Adam said casually. I noticed something happening between him and Rose. A quick glance. Conspiratorial? "We'll see him tomorrow. He's joining us for two days."

"What?" I shouted. "Why didn't you say anything?" I jumped up, my chair crashing over. I didn't want to ever have to see Anthony again. Ever!

"I didn't ask him," Adam said, eying me coolly. "I just found a fax—dated the 25th. When was that, last Tuesday? It was at reception. I picked it up on my way in here. He wanted to know why the hell I wasn't checking my e-mail, and said he was going to join us in three days. I didn't even realize he knew I was on this trip, let alone with the three of you." Adam shrugged his shoulders and smiled apologetically at me to soften the blow. "Sorry."

I slumped down in my chair. "What the hell. Maybe I could find an assassin here to do away with him." Maybe I would.

"So I finally get to meet this Anthony, face to face," said Rose casually. I didn't answer her. I got up and walked up onto the deck.

We didn't get the opportunity, though. None of us ever saw him again—alive, that is. Adam got a message at six-thirty that evening from Anthony's business partner saying he'd been found dead in his upstate cottage at dawn by the cleaning service, which, given the time difference between New York and Luxor, was midnight the previous night for us. He'd been dead for a while.

It's one thing to want to kill somebody. It's another thing when somebody else does it. I was shocked but also kind of relieved, but it hit Adam like a grenade exploding in his face. Michael was out of his depth, and Rose? I couldn't read her. I persuaded them all to at least complete the day here and decide later what we were going to do.

The Valley of the Kings is on the west bank of the Nile, the bank that signified death. Appropriate. We were there months after that horrific massacre of tourists, and all along the sky-line snipers were posted at regular intervals. The strangest feeling came over me, as I emerged from Tutankhamen's tomb, and looked around me at the monolithic rocky desert mountains which housed the tombs of so many dead Pharaohs. The four of us were alone. It was quiet. Eery. Anthony's death preyed on all our minds, for different reasons. In all the years I'd travelled to Egypt, it was the first time that I felt the history-laden silence sink into my bones. Death will do that to you. Even the death of somebody you hate. We sat together on a wall and time just stopped. Nothing around us stirred, no movement of air, no creature to be seen. Just the three of us; ancient tombs of ancient people; the walls of the valley rising sheer. My eyes travelled up to the top. Silhouetted against a deepening sky, motionless snipers.

I shuddered. My mother would be devastated at

Anthony's death. She'd want to have the funeral at home. She'd want Adam and me to be there.

Morning shifted to afternoon, and afternoon slipped into evening. We were making our way back to the boat. The tranquility was shattered by someone shouting in the distance, down the road. Judging by his voice he was coming towards us, but we couldn't see him at first, until he rounded a bend. It was like being in a movie: he rode a camel, and was waving a piece of paper, shouting something unintelligible in Arabic. As he came round the final bend where the road opens up into the valley he saw us, and got even more excited. I realized he wasn't speaking Arabic at all, but was calling 'Misteradam,' over and over again. As he came closer it was obvious he recognized Adam. I wondered where from. He slowed down, hesitant, then stopped the camel. I saw he was from the boat. Adam walked quickly towards him.

Unaccountably, a shiver ran down my spine as the man handed the paper over—another telegram? The thought ran through my head that it was from that bastard, he wasn't really dead, he'd been playing a sick joke. Adam must have read it through three or four times before he dropped his hand to his side, let go of the paper, turned his back on us and walked away down the road. His feet crunching on the dry gravel road as the paper fluttered to the ground. The Arab sat motionless on his camel. I walked toward him, picked up the telegram and read it. I felt like a thunderstorm broke inside me.

I looked at Rose. "The bastard committed suicide."

Some emotion I'd never seen before swept across her face: I couldn't define it, it wasn't pain, but it wasn't joy, either. She didn't say anything, just looked at me. Her body was still, tense. She looked at the paper I was holding. I crumpled it up, took a deep breath and looked around at the sky-line of this mournful place.

"Suicide," I said again.

Rose let out a primitive wail that tore itself from her core. It echoed against the cliff walls. I glanced up instinctively to the skyline, and saw snipers move. Rose collapsed in a dead faint. Michael caught her before she hit the ground. White faced.

But it was Adam's reaction that surprised me the most. That night he came late to the dinner table. It wasn't only his face that was pale, but his whole being. Grieving for a man who he thought of as his brother, whose manipulations he saw, understood and never judged, and who he had come to love with his own intensely personal brand of generosity. I was torn. I hated seeing him in such pain but he knew better than anybody else how much I hated Anthony, and it wasn't just about what happened when we were kids. I wasn't sorry he was dead. I didn't say I was glad but I didn't have to. Adam knew. He knew why, too.

So it surprised me when he touched my arm and leaned close. "I need your help."

"What do you mean?" I felt dread although I didn't know why.

"I mean that I know he didn't commit suicide."

I sat bolt upright and glared at him. "No." Please God, not this. "Adam," I leaned forward and put my hand on his arm, shaking it, "You have to let him go. He did commit suicide, it's just the kind of thing he would do."

Adam looked away from me and stared out over the Nile.

"Adam!" I raised my voice, insistent. "*Look* at me."

His eyes met mine. I was shocked again at the desolation in his eyes—in his whole body. His skin was pallid, he looked angular, as though he'd been at death's door for months. I took a deep breath. I could see he was sure. I felt a knot of tension form in my stomach. Dread.

"Why then?" I asked. "Why do you think he didn't commit suicide? Are you saying he was murdered?"

"Yeah. That's what I'm saying. I know he didn't do it. It's a gut thing."

I felt a wave of anger wash over me. Even in his death Anthony was creating havoc. Would he ever leave us alone? But it was no use fighting Adam on this. His gut feelings always led him to the truth. Actually, although I didn't want to admit it to myself, I also had a gut feeling that something was wrong, though I couldn't put my finger on it. Would Anthony really have committed suicide? I wanted to think that he would, as a final sadistic act of manipulation, knowing he would haunt Adam and even me for the rest of our lives. But I wasn't sure.

So I gave in. "Okay. But I don't know what we can do."

There was a moment of silence as Adam looked at me, and I saw our kinship in all its depth. "Thanks" he said. He took a deep breath, exhaled and leaned back in his chair, closed his eyes. "God," he said quietly. "God, I'm exhausted."

I was afraid this would dredge up what had happened to a couple our parents knew. It was a time of horror for all of us, but Adam took the brunt. He was the one who found them. Supposedly a suicide pact; he shot her, she shot him. I never believed it. Bernard was an anal, repressed and frustrated man who beat up on his wife Edie. They came round for drinks one weekend just before Adam went on a holiday to Spain and I was getting ready to go to university. Bernard was drinking heavily and Edie was wearing the proverbial dark glasses and a scarf. I asked her if everything was okay. She skittered away from me.

"Fine, everything's just fine, Felix." Her hands

fluttered in the air helplessly as she tried to wave away the shadow that crossed her face at my concern. I didn't know what to do. She had never let me in, and though I was sure she was covering up for Bernard, how could I help? Besides, I was scared of him.

So I did nothing. I went to university early and put it to the back of my mind. Adam went to Spain and I didn't hear from him for a while. He phoned one night. He'd come home. Our mother was worried about Edie because she hadn't seen her for a while. Adam went to visit. They were both dead. The police pronounced double suicide, and closed the case. But I never believed it. Adam just flat out refused to talk about it, though; I never understood that. Now we had another suicide that was probably murder. And closer to home.

I might as well tell you why else I hated Anthony. Adam wasn't the only one who forgave him. I did too, for a while. He went through a period where he seemed to change. I thought it was Adam's influence. He became charming and entertaining and the life and soul of a party. He seemed *happy*. Then he turned his charm on me.

If Adam hadn't rescued me I'd have gone the same way as Edie.

In the morning, I woke up before dawn. Adam was already on deck. He looked as if he hadn't slept. I hadn't much, either. We stood at the railings watching the bank slip by slowly. It was quiet and should have been peaceful. We were heading towards the Old Cataract Hotel where Agatha Christie wrote *Death On The Nile.* I wanted to stay here forever, with Adam. I wanted Anthony to have never been in our lives, but since he was, I wanted him to stay dead, be buried and forgotten, as he deserved. I stretched, feeling old, and as if my life as I'd known it had disappeared in a flash and would never return. Never is a pretty irrevocable concept. Death I can handle but 'never again'?

"I don't want to do this," I said. "I don't want him to poison any more of our lives."

Adam didn't reply for a minute, then he said, "It's weird, isn't it?"

"What? That it should have happened just before he was coming here?"

There was a fraction of a second before he replied. "No." He leaned over the railing, looked down into the water. "That it should have happened at all. After all these years. I wonder who killed him."

"I don't know. " Why had he hesitated?

"And you don't care." His voice was flat.

"No, I don't. And you know better than anybody else why. What's weird is that it didn't happen sooner. He lived in a shadowy world. He hung out with people who were far too powerful. He was a power addict."

Adam nodded. "He did. He was. You're right." He half said to himself, "I wonder if I can request an autopsy."

It irritated me. I shouldn't have said I would help him. What could I do anyway? What could either of us do? "Even if you find who did it, will it change anything? Will it? He's dead. And it's because he lived a corrupt and crooked life and a million people hated him. You're probably the only one in the world who didn't."

I knew what Adam was going to say before he said it. "That's why."

"We're from South Africa, we're in Egypt, our brother was murdered in New York. We don't know a fucking soul there." My temper flared again.

Adam muttered something. I didn't hear him. I let it go.

"I suppose you want to fly to New York straight away."

He shrugged. "We can only get out of here on a flight from Luxor tonight. So we've got another day of temple-hopping." I didn't like that he had already checked without talking to me but I let it go.

Rose came up on deck. I'd forgotten her reaction to the news of Anthony's death and was shocked at how fragile she looked. There were dark rings under her eyes. Her pale skin was almost luminous. I glanced at Adam. He was staring at her as if trying to reconcile something. She wouldn't meet his eyes.

She stood next to me at the railing. I put my arm around her. She flinched when I touched her and pulled away. My eyes shifted to Adam. Still watching her. There was something in his eyes. Betrayal? Fear? Protectiveness? I'd never seen anything like that before in him. He got a grip though, as Michael joined us, tense and unhappy. Whatever was wrong with Rose she hadn't told him; she'd simply locked him out.

"Are you guys coming down to breakfast?" he said, trying to sound normal.

Adam patted him kindly on the shoulder. "Sure. Let's go and have breakfast." The two men walked off. Rose half turned to watch them go. I tried to read her but I couldn't. Was it grief? For *Anthony?*

"Fuck off, Felix," she said and walked off after the men. I stared after her. Something about her reminded me of somebody. I couldn't put my finger on it. I almost wished that somebody would take her out as well. She could RIP with Anthony.

I skipped breakfast.

When we docked we were driven to the mortuary temple of Queen Hatshepsut. None of us had anything to say to each other; each of us in our own worlds, although I sensed something had been said between Rose and Adam. I went off to be by myself. Just me and the spirit of a Queen. Hours went by as I walked through the death temple. When I came out I saw Adam and Rose arguing heatedly in the shadows of the colonnades. I walked towards them, wondering where Michael was.

I wish I could have stopped time at that point.

It was Rose, I was sure of it. She killed Anthony or had him killed. But Adam took the rap. He flew to New York and handed himself in, confessed to hiring somebody to do the dirty. They offered him a deal if he would rat on the guy who hired him but of course he refused. He got thirty years. I moved to New York to be close to him. I couldn't get him to admit that he'd had nothing to do with Anthony's death. Our mother refused to visit and she didn't believe me when I said Adam was innocent. Dad came out once a year until he passed away. He didn't know what to believe but he still loved Adam like a son. Rose disappeared. We argued about her a lot at first, then I put all my energy into looking for her. Last month I discovered that she had gone back to Egypt and was a resident at the Old Cataract Hotel. She didn't have much money when we knew her. Anthony did, though.

Adam will be out in two years. We're going to do that trip along the Nile again, just the two of us. We can rebuild our lives together. But I don't want Rose to be a part of it. Yesterday I booked a ticket to Egypt and a room at the Old Cataract Hotel. Rose is in her seventies now. She was at least ten years older than Adam. She's changed, judging by the photographs I have of her. She looks so old and shriveled. I've also changed. I doubt she'll recognize me.

Jennifer is a writer, screenwriter and script editor. She has adapted one story into a fabulous coming-of-age big-budget screenplay for a US producer, and has worked as head writer and script editor for a South African production company (and is currently script editor for another). Additionally, she has co-authored two scripts and written one original, all of which were made into TV movies. She has two thrillers destined for Hollywood and six screenplays in development. She is now working on the novel of one of her thrillers and a memoir.

Jennifer plays piano, acoustic, and electric guitar,

and sings jazz standards, adult contemporary, and some of her own songs. If that wasn't enough, she sketches, paints, reads American crime novels, loves TV series like *Rizzoli and Isles*, and constantly vows to go to the gym tomorrow. She never vows to give up chocolate. She's crazy about President Barack Obama and First Lady Michelle Obama who she thinks are way ahead of their time. Jennifer lives in Cape Town, South Africa, but feels she's pretty much always in a New York state of mind.

You can find Jennifer at her website,
jennifer-stewart.com
Join Jennifer's mailing list at:
info@jennifer-stewart.com

SCARE TACTICS
by Rain Stickland

MARCH

It was just supposed to be a scare tactic to help Kelly get back on track, but it was too late to turn back now, and Geraldine listened as the gasping breaths slowed. Then they stopped. Up until that moment she'd been able to reassure herself that they could always back out. It didn't have to be permanent. Now it was, and the corpulent flesh ceased its heaving evidence of life as soon as the rasping breaths ceased. Kelly was dead. They had really done it, and now the real work would begin.

APRIL

Immediately upon entering the cabin they were

renting for the next two weeks, Melanie began retching.

"What is that smell?" Her voice was muffled by the hand she'd clapped over her mouth, and had a nasal quality. Jim couldn't be certain it wasn't attributable to the folds of flesh constricting her airways, though. Melanie wasn't exactly svelte. Of course, that's why they were here. She needed to lose more than a pound or two. He had only managed to talk her into it by telling her there was a five-star restaurant at the resort. It was true, but there were details he had left out in order to get her here. Blaming her weight on a thyroid condition wasn't going to do her any good this time.

Melanie tried to back out of the room to get away from the stench, but her vision went dark before she could retrace her steps.

JULY

Amy arrived the night before the other girls were due. She kept tossing and turning, and there was that smell beneath the damp. Despite the odor Amy was starving. She always was. Her thoughts zeroed in on the giant ring of pepperoni she'd brought. She'd probably end up eating the whole thing by herself before her friends got there.

Not bothering with the light, Amy tripped on a warped board and slammed into the floor with her knees. She cursed a blue streak that would have made her boyfriend cringe in embarrassment, and then hobbled over to the wall switch. When she crossed back over the floor she saw something gleaming in the cracks that looked like gold.

Not one to pass up personal gain, Amy tried to see what it was that was shining so brightly. It had to be gold, because anything else would likely have tarnished in that kind of dampness. The overhead light wouldn't penetrate far enough for her to really see, though, so she dug her tiny flashlight out of the purse she'd left on the coffee table, and directed the beam into the half-inch crack.

It was a ring, with what looked like a very nice stone set into it. She wasn't too concerned about how it had gotten down there. She just knew she was going to figure out how to get it. As she moved the beam of light, however, bile spurted up her throat. That was a finger inside that ring.

"Looking for something, Amy?" She yelped and struggled to her feet.

"What are you doing here?" The laughing response only confused her.

"Same thing as you. I need to lose some weight."

"But, you're not fat." She frowned. What was going on here?

"I don't recall saying that I was. I said I needed to lose some weight. About 250 pounds of it." He laughed again, and Amy got a sinking feeling.

That's how much she'd weighed at her last doctor's appointment.

"You came all this way to dump me? In the middle of the night?"

"You could say that."

"But, Jim..." Before she could complete the sentence she saw the axe in his hand. Nothing but a gasp came out as she watched him start to swing it back in an arc she knew without a doubt would embed the blade in her skull. She was too stunned to move, and wouldn't have had time anyway. Just before the axe head reached the top of the arc, Jim's chest jerked once and the axe slipped in his hands. In surrealistic horror Amy watch the sharp edge crease his cheek on the way down. Then she noticed the blood staining his grey shirt. She inhaled sharply when she saw the woman standing behind him.

"Geraldine?"

"I'm guessing you have some questions." It only took about fifteen minutes for Amy to hear her out. The brevity was a blessing, because her gaze kept going back to Jim's body. He hadn't died instantly. His heart had stopped pumping blood, of course, what with the hole Geraldine had managed to put through it with her Glock, but it took some time for his brain to realize there was no more oxygen coming. Considering the fact that he'd tried to kill her, and for no better reason than not liking the extra fat she carried around, she was content to let him die. Slowly.

"I guess we'd better head out," Amy said, unsure what exactly they should do about the situation. She grabbed her purse and headed for the door, but then she paused.

"Was there anything else before we go to the police and get all this cleared up?"

"Just one more thing." Amy just had time to register the knowledge that she was about to die, before Geraldine pulled the trigger. Then Geraldine laughed. She was getting good at this.

A FORGOTTEN ESSENCE
by Danicka Winters

In his excitement, Jana'aro had forgone the cardinal rule of concealment. After days of watching, charming her so she would end up at the entrance every day, he'd grown reckless. Still, with what he intended it wasn't likely to matter. She stood amongst the corn, staring at him in shock as he rose up through the doorway, his pheromone vents opening along the sides of his leanly-built body, until he was at ground level and towering over her. His memory charms had made her forget him, over and over, until they met once again and he lifted them. She always told him that wasn't what she wanted, and he'd denied her every single time, but no longer.

The net of pheromones enclosed her fear-frozen body, triggering the release of her memories, along with a riptide of hormones. She gasped from the rush of pleasure. Scylla fought the weakening pull valiantly, however, her anger strong enough to overcome even his most potent lures. For a while.

"You did it to me again! You're messing with my brain. It's a complete violation! You have no right to choose what I am allowed to remember, Jana'aro. I tell you what I want, and you consistently take away my choices. No more. This is the last time I will allow it. We either move forward or you make the choice to forget about *me*!"

"*Scylla...*" The word vibrated within her body, shooting warmth and pleasure deep into her belly. He could speak to her audibly, but he chose to do this to her instead. She wanted to be furious, but knew she fought a losing battle, the weakness in her being stronger than her anger.

"God, don't. You know I can't..."

"*Exactly.*" Despite millions of years of evolutionary divergence, certain physical attributes hadn't completely changed in either Humans or Kirala. In moments Scylla found her body wrapped around his. Her arms and legs covered some of his vents, however, causing a backwash of pheromones into his own body. Inability to release them heightened his sensitivity. Soon she would know how that felt, and he throbbed with pleasure at the knowledge.

When Jana'aro finally released her from the prison of her pleasure, he pinned her with his gaze.

"You will come with me now, and see. There are steps to take." She shuddered again at the effect his words created inside her at a skeletal level. He led her through the entrance.

She had expected darkness, yet there was light everywhere. After many twists and turns, well below the cornfields above, they arrived at what she could only assume was a desk. The Kiralan seated behind it looked up at her, and then stacked some wooden cubes together.

"Welcome to Immigration and Naturalization. Please have a seat and we can get started on your forms. You will be given a chip that will explain everything you need to know about assimilation into Kiralan society, including your rights, abilities, and responsibilities once your latent gifts have been activated." Scylla nearly choked, but managed to answer the questions as they were put forth. *Gifts? What gifts?*

"Now, Scylla'ara, please stand up so we can complete the process. Jana'aro, if you will?" Scylla stood. In seconds she was gasping for breath as her body and brain were flooded with unexpected changes, though none of them felt strange or wrong. It was all she'd been meant to be.

"Is the seed dormant or active?" Scylla drew a blank.

"What seed?"

"The one you currently carry, of course. It is the only acceptable reason for immigration. You carry the beginnings of an offspring." Scylla couldn't speak, but glared at Jana'aro. She felt sick, and now she wasn't even certain of the reason for it. *She was pregnant?*

"I activated it just before I brought her here," Jana'aro said. Scylla was furious. Even though a small part of her wanted to celebrate the news, she wouldn't be letting him off the hook for this one.

"Do you mean to tell me I'm pregnant? Without my knowledge or consent?"

"Not really. You simply carry a seed for the moment. That will change shortly," he said.

"Oh, God. Why didn't you tell me? Or ask me, for that matter?"

"I assumed you were fully cognizant of the process of procreation, Scylla. You're not a child," he admonished. She was stunned. She had no idea how he expected her to know anything about cross-species procreation, when most species on the planet could not breed with any beyond their own.

"How could I possibly know, Jana'aro? You're the one with knowledge of both species, not me."

"Obviously I do not possess such knowledge, or I would have realized you wouldn't understand. You have nothing to worry about, Scylla. Yes, we have mated, and will soon produce offspring together. However, it is not you who will become pregnant. I am the one who will carry our child." His vents opened again, emitting the pheromones necessary to extract the seed. In response the newly-formed vents in her own body automatically produced a similar cloud. Instantly she was plastered against Jana'aro, repeating the mating ritual, forgetting that anyone was still in the room with them.

"Thank you for your service," Jana'aro said as soon as they had finished. He left the room. Completely at a loss as to where Jana'aro had gone, Scylla flushed when she saw the immigration officer still standing there.

"*My name is Cifa'aro*," his voice vibrated to her, as he opened his vents.

Danicka likes to write mostly horror and erotica, and she often combines the two. She likes to say she enjoys making people shudder and shiver at the same time. She wishes she could blame her horrid reading habits throughout her formative years, but if nothing else she does prefer to take responsibility for her own beastliness.

Born in Toronto, Ontario, Danicka has lived all over Canada and currently resides in Ontario with her own twisted menagerie. You can find out more about her on her website at danickawinters.com, but be warned. It's strictly eighteen and over!

Danicka's Facebook is here, should you so desire:
https://www.facebook.com/Danicka-Winters-1668430693410587/

THE STRANGER
by Jennifer Stewart

She was a woman of the night and I don't exaggerate when I say she was strange. I'm not talking about mildly unusual; she was much more than that. There was something about her which defied all description.

I had always fantasized about spending most of my waking hours when it was dark. I was fascinated by the mystery that cloaks the world when the sun has gone to bed; I could see it having an effect on the nature of people in a way that fascinated me. They were out of their normal element; they became prey to the workings of their darker side. I know what you're thinking; dark means evil. Maybe you're right, or maybe it's the part of us we don't want to admit to. Whatever it was, I was obsessed with it. Rules which usually apply in daylight, when the world can see you and you it, somehow fade into insignificance, overpowered by this other. This intangible. That's the part that I was drawn to. Unconstrained, I thought, surely a person would give voice to the truth of their soul. A truth that they and everybody else might not like. But isn't truth better than a sugar-sweet fantasy? I've always wanted to believe it was. And I've always hated rules.

There was something, too, about the shadows of night which gathered themselves to my imagination back then. Daylight felt unsympathetic. More than that, it was glaring, intrusive. Chiaroscuro seemed like it would be paradise. I spent hours day-dreaming of being like a cat, sleeping during the day, finding a warm spot to curl up into myself, and at night waking up to prowl. I never talked about my fantasies but sometimes I thought I could see people reading my mind. Or maybe they smelled my longing. Sometimes I realized they could read my mind. I could see the thought forming in theirs that it wasn't natural, this love I had of the dark. That there was something wrong with me. I was weird, twisted inside. Whenever it happened a primordial scream would erupt within me. I can't begin to explain what it felt like to hold it in.

The Stranger shared my sentiments, I know she did. I knew we were kindred spirits the first time I saw her.

Some people are super-religious and they think that when you die you go to heaven if you've been good and to hell if you've been bad. I've always been amused at that, since nobody can ever really agree on what good and bad are. Other people say that at the moment of death your life is like the explosion of Adolf Miethe and Johannes Gaedicke's flash powder, potentially harmful in large amounts, soon extinguished, leaving something that has to be processed before it can be an image and then that's all there is. Your life leaves no trace beyond a tiny trail of smoke, a vague smell and pictures that might or might not be true about you in people's memories. All that's left of all that was is a vessel of a body that has no use other than as food for worms.

Others swear that at the moment of your death your past inches slowly across the retina of your soul and of your mind. That it takes centuries to do so and then suddenly, for no reason, halts, leaving you trapped in a moment from which there will be no escape. Ever. That's what infinity is, they say. I'm not so sure about that. How can you describe infinity when your only tools are finite words and images?

I've never been sure of what will happen when I die but every time I board an airplane I can't help speculating, and this time as the plane's engines screamed on takeoff I wasn't dead but my life did flash before my eyes and yet at the same time everything stopped. How can you have movement and dead stillness all at once? I was trapped in a moment of time that felt as if it would never end. I felt a darkness come over my soul as we soared into the clouds. A sense of inevitability, of being drawn to a final moment that had always been waiting for me. The thought went through my mind; who knows how long we're preparing for death? We notice it at some point, usually right at the end, but maybe the how and the why of it has been orchestrated years before that, coming towards us with certainty for a long time. Not from birth, just from a certain point that we don't pick up on.

At first everything in me revolted. The more my imagination ran riot, the louder my inner protest was. What was the point of everything if we didn't have any choice ultimately? It was early evening. I watched the sun disappear as we settled into cruising speed and a calmness came over me. Maybe it was just the knowledge that my fate was out of my hands completely, whatever the ultimate truth was. I had a window seat. I peered out as the sky grew dark and the stars glittered. That dark went on forever. It scared the hell out of me. I shrank into myself, but I couldn't tear my eyes away. It was so beautiful!

I've been afraid of the dark ever since I could remember and have hated myself for it. I craved it but couldn't tear myself away from light. It was torture! I've never liked people very much, either. I always wanted to be a writer, and as a child I was. I filled my universe with the words that I couldn't say out loud. On the outside I was neat and tidy and well-mannered and quiet but on the inside my world was a riot of protest and colorful, rebellious expression. I didn't like flying and I still don't. And I've never given much of a damn about food or drink of any sort either.

Yet here I was, on a plane bound for a foreign town in a foreign country, on a continent I had never visited, with an assignment; the food and drink culture through four seasons in Trondheim. Where there is no light for months!

My father, a great sensualist, was a large fleshy chef with a booming baritone and a grand temperament. He loved food of every kind; he had travelled all his life and tasted every possible dish under the sun, I'm sure—which was obvious from the size of him. He had had a string of restaurants from a young age. I don't know if he enjoyed the food or the bullying more. Nobody dared stand up to him! If ever a person was racing towards his own demise it was him. Heart attack was written into his fate, I had no doubt. He would be torturing and bullying some poor sous-chef for imagined imperfections in a dish which he would be stuffing his mouth with as his heart just rebelled and stopped.

My mother, who I'm sure never, even in her wildest moments, whispered the word 'sensual' to herself, was a food critic of the worst sort. The word that springs to mind when trying to describe her nature is vinegar, except that vinegar, used judiciously, can add great texture or subtlety to a flavor. And also you have a choice in what type to use. My mother, however, had no subtlety or variety in her personality or peculiar brand of critique. She was just nasty through and through. She knew exactly what point to stick her razor-sharp knife. Then she would twist it. She loved hurting people! It was her way of having an orgasm. Nothing she ever tasted ever pleased her in the slightest. She boasted about how many dreams she had shattered, how many hopefuls she had destroyed. She was as feared in restaurants around the world as my father was! And she had a critic's vocabulary that could fill a library of encyclopedias. It was her outlet for a monstrous creativity.

How did they ever fall in love and marry? God knows! She was physically beautiful. That much I can say. Perhaps he wasn't always a glutton for other people's punishment. Maybe her beauty cast a spell on her soul and he couldn't resist. And she loved having power. He was putty in her hands at first, I suppose. Well, whatever adverse fate drew them together initially, it wasn't long before it evaporated. Neither of them had any restraint in articulating their ever growing mutual resentment towards each other, always expressed in culinary metaphor. Each in their own way had a highly customized venom manufacturing capacity that was reminiscent of a self regenerating and permanently exploding shrapnel bomb. From the time I could crawl I found my way into small dark cupboards. Later I would lock myself in them. The dark became my refuge and yet my prison because no matter what I did I couldn't block the screaming. So in time I developed a terror of and a craving for small spaces and the dark.

Understandably, as a child it was a long time before I uttered a word and I came quickly to hate food and drink and to think of them as a necessity that verged on intolerable at times. I would retch at the sight of food on my plate. Often at night I'd wake up in a cold sweat and vomit my guts out.

But once I found words and learned how to write them, they were my refuge. When I was seventeen my parents died in what I must presume was an mutual attack. I've been told that I was present, that the evidence suggested they stabbed each other violently and repeatedly. That the walls were covered in blood and they lay in pools of it. But I remember nothing of it and I never saw their bodies when I recovered consciousness. One day they were my torturers, the next day they were gone. You'd think it would have been a relief, and in some ways it was. But they left huge debts so I was forced to go out and earn a living. Not surprisingly, I became a journalist and worked as a war correspondent. Throughout my life the world has provided plenty of subject matter for me to cover but I have never left Africa.

There was still no shortage of work but recently war had started to get to me. I felt the same way about it as I had always felt about food. I couldn't look at any more dead bodies, tortured children, ravaged cities. All the violence, and the pleasure in it, reminded me of my parents' savagery. One day I quit in the middle of an assignment. No big rebellion, no noisy slamming of doors and shouting *fuck you!* I just got on a plane and came back home. I deleted my email accounts, got a new phone. Started a new life. I had some money saved up. I'd had enough of the world and being forced to write what everybody else wanted, forced to witness what only heightened my inner torture.

I started writing a novel.

It was harder than I thought. I'd lost my fluency from all the years of being somebody else's word-slave. So my money ran out long before my book was finished. Those were dark days. The only thing that stopped me from ending my life was the thought that I might meet my parents on the other side if I died being such a victim. It's funny, the things that inspire you. So one day, I took another job. A food and drink assignment in a dark, cold, inhospitable country. Was this part of the end, or part of the beginning? Maybe in being forced to live in such darkness I'd get over my fear and spend the rest of my life giving true expression to my soul. But it was terrifying. A whole season without light!

I wondered if somewhere my parents, may their acerbic souls rest in peace, were fighting about what my approach to critiquing food would be.

I was born and raised in Southern Africa, where there's always plenty of heat, where autumn and spring last a few days if you can discern them at all. Where winter means sometimes having to wear a jersey or a jacket, and the days are a couple of hours shorter than they are in summer. I've never understood how Scandinavians can handle the soul-suffocating winters where the dead of night encroaches until day hardly exists. And the cold. Jesus. I had never made any real friends throughout my life but there was one person who quietly stayed around in the background. He didn't intrude, but he didn't go away either. He had moved to Trondheim and he's the one who got me the job.

He said to me "It's the beauty, the poetry, the stillness of that night, the promise of light. It's the sadness of autumn; the fierce fight you have to put up to survive winter; the thrill of spring, when you explode with joy; the madness with which you drink in every last drop of summer sun and warmth. You'll never understand until you live here through four seasons."

I took the job and he invited me to stay for a year, promising me he wouldn't intrude or get in my way. I wouldn't die of exposure or wither away from light starvation, he said. I didn't know what else to do, so I took him up on his offer. Or that's what I told myself. The truth is, I was tired through to the core of me. Tired of myself, my life, my past, the way my brain worked. Tired of my fears and memories. Too tired to fight anything. He suggested I arrive in summer, but the thought of making that slow, surely excruciating transition to darkness sounded terrifying, and if I waited too long I thought I might just wither inside so much that I couldn't make any choices at all. And I didn't have any money! Rent was due. I could either pay it or buy a ticket out. If I stayed I wouldn't have money for food. It's funny how you can hate something all your life and then suddenly realize how much you need it. I wondered if I would ever know a time where I wasn't caught between a rock and hard place.

I booked my ticket to leave in a couple of weeks. I would arrive a month into winter in a town whose name is derived from an old Norse word meaning home of the strong and fertile. I wondered about the fertile part, thinking it probably didn't refer to

Trondheim citizens' reproductive capacity. There was no end to the things I wondered about in those days. The night before leaving I packed my bags marveling at my stupidity. Why not just get a job at home? What was I doing? Going to a strange culture, strange place, living with somebody and entombed by season dark just so that I could do the one thing I'd hated the most all my life—eat.

The next day I rode out to the airport in trepidation, with a constant mantra screaming in my head *it's not too late to cancel*. But I took my seat in the plane, albeit with my heart in my throat, wondering if I'd ever see Africa again. It felt like prescience. I tried to shrug it off and when nothing untoward happened on the flight and as the plane descended—it was dark of course—I was slightly reassured. The lights down below were pretty; this looked like civilization. Maybe I would survive.

It was warm inside the airport, of course it was. My friend met me at the gates. I was surprised to actually feel relief at something familiar, although another part of me shrank away *don't come too close.* I don't know if he saw it or not, but he just ignored it and chatted away as if we were two normal life-long friends. He made it kind of easy. I was tired from everything from the flight, so I let go. When we walked out of the airport the cold punched me in the gut. But oddly, it was kind of refreshing. My friend laughed the rest of my fears away as he bundled me into a down jacket. I felt like a suited-up astronaut but at least I was a warm one.

"You're going to love it," he said as we marched along, "a bit of dark never hurt anybody." A shaft of white hot rage scorched my soul. It shocked me; I hadn't felt anything like it since before my parents died. I stopped as an image flashed across my memory's retina, too fast for me to grasp. Interpreting my hesitation as reluctance, my friend grabbed my arm and pulled me along.

Again the rage.

But I acquiesced, sensing again that forces were at play in my life, drawing me towards some inevitable destiny from which I would never return.

My innocent friend took me on a night tour of the old parts of Trondheim and despite the darkness in my soul, or perhaps because of it, I was instantly enchanted. Wooden buildings from a bygone era lined wharves of the river that wound through a town a thousand years old, their reflections vaguely reminiscent of Venice. I felt all my pre-conceived notions of this cold, dark country slip away as we walked for a couple of hours. The thing I'd always fantasized would happen if I faced down my fear of the dark, did happen. My imagination caught fire, and although I suspected part of my excitement was just from the novelty of my experience, I also knew I'd been moved in a way that was more profound and that the darkness in my soul was somehow being fed.

Did I imagine it? Did my friend glance at me strangely when he bid me goodnight having extracted a promise from me that early the next morning, long before dawn, I would visit Bakklandet?

I stared at him. His expression mutated to pleasant but I felt the rage again. Mine, not his. Or perhaps it was the reverse. He walked off whistling softly to himself. Again an image flashed across my retina. A face? A body? I couldn't hold onto it.

That night I didn't sleep; imagination unlocked, fingers flying. All thoughts of preparing for my assignment consigned to hell, the very idea of food a poisonous blight. Instead, the plot of my novel consumed me, taking a dark turn, with threads going back into the Middle Ages where religious fervor was mixed in with superstition. Where kings were gods and queens were murderers.

All the while a voice in my head warned me not to visit Bakklandet and enticed me to satiate my curiosity, taking me back to days when I would seek out the dark and know the intoxication yet pain and imprisonment of it once locked away.

At four in the morning, nerves on fire, white hot and jangling, I bundled up warmly and made my way to Bakklandet with its wooden houses dating back to the 16th and 17th centuries and streets as narrow and winding as they were in Medieval times. It had snowed in the night and the streets were covered in soft white. Strangely, the lightness of it appealed to me, perhaps because it accentuated the darkness elsewhere. Not a light was on, doors were locked to intruders, windows stared blankly at me. There was not another soul in sight. And yet I could feel somebody's presence. A dark kind of presence with which I knew I would have a kinship, if it revealed itself. Human? I didn't know. Apart from it, I could have been walking through a ghost town. Those old buildings whispered to me as the crunching of my footsteps echoed in my ears.

The darkness began to fade. I felt a deep sadness for this world I had craved but been terrified of for so long. As it folded into itself it left me with profound regret for all the years I had wasted in my desperate attempts to block out the truth of who I am. But strangely, my regret was mixed with gratitude and awe at how life had brought me back to myself. I had imagined I would experience the pleasure of dark and evil thoughts and actions in embracing darkness, but I hadn't expected to feel this seed of hope, of renewal.

I wasn't just embracing the darkness of the world around me or the darkness in my soul, I was becoming the darkness. The relief was immense. No more fighting within! No more resistance. I glanced at a large window to see the true me reflected.

And that was when I saw her. Time stopped and so did I. Rooted to the spot I stared at her reflection smiling—grimacing—as she flew at me, believing I hadn't seen her. An old crone now, but as bitter and acerbic of spirit as when I was a child, hatred flashing in her eyes. Was it my mother? Was she a figment of my imagination? Was she the *ghost* of my mother, returned to remind me of my years of torture and so help me stay locked in the darkness forever? Was she enemy or friend? Was she real? I whipped around, heart pounding, mouth open in a shriek that seemed to make no sound. Then I felt my hands around her throat. Her scream pierced the fragile silence, bouncing off the walls in echoes that had no ending. The old crone struggled, surprisingly strong, but I had found myself and slowly, with infinite pleasure, I began to choke the life out of her. My mother had taken pleasure in destroying people. She had taught me well.

Then there was chaos such as I had never experienced. People shouting and shrieking, sirens screaming, lights flashing, hands clawing at me, howling in my ear, somebody hauling me off the old crone, yelling at me "Stop! What are you doing?"

Everything went into slow motion. Sounds warped. My life flashed before me in a series of vignettes with excruciatingly intimate detail and stopped at my father lying on a floor in a bloody pool, my mother standing over him, knife in hand, panting. And I the seventeen year-old who was still trapped in childhood staring from the doorway. Then I turned and ran for the cupboard where I locked myself up, hoping, praying, that she hadn't seen me. But then how did she die?

As the truth slammed into me I stared horrified at the old woman as she was wrapped up, moved onto a stretcher and carried off. I realized she looked nothing like my mother. She was just an old woman. I felt somebody behind me. I turned and stared at my white-faced friend. Did I see a flash of white hot rage?

I couldn't tell. Was it his or mine? Was I still imagining things? Was I trapped in that moment of infinity?

The next thing I knew was that somebody was shaking me, not violently, but insistently. I opened my eyes. A child stared at me with relief and jabbered something incomprehensible but not unkind. She tore her jacket off and covered me with it as best she could. Her hands were somehow warm. I felt the heat travel to my frozen heart. Snow was falling gently, shrouding the world in soft white. The light was ethereal. The little girl ran off, looking back to reassure herself that I was still moving one more time before she disappeared around a corner, shouting out her incomprehensible kindnesses to me.

She returned with her mother, who helped me sit up and wrapped me in a blanket. She dipped a piece of bread into a cup of warm milk to my lips. Instinctively I turned my head away but she insisted, the little girl peering into my face, also insistent. So I ate. And then I drank. I looked around. There were no signs of a struggle. No sirens, no shrieking or screaming. I lay back down in the woman's embrace, not sure if I was alive or dead. All I knew was that the food and drink had tasted good and the ethereal light was welcome.

DISORDERLY EATING
by Jill Taggart

Sam lived in the city. He married his wife, who was not at all pretty, because she was a good cook. Sam liked food. Enjoyed food. Gloried in food. Sam was fat.

"What's for dinner?" Sam would shout every night when he came home from work.

"Swiss steak," his wife would answer. Or sometimes, "Pot roast." Or maybe, "Turkey and dressing."

One night Sam came home and shouted, "What's for dinner?"

"Fried chicken," his wife answered from the kitchen.

Sam sat down at the table and looked at the chicken, and it seemed to be looking back at him. He could almost see it walking around covered with feathers, clucking to its friends, and he couldn't eat.

Sam had grown a conscience.

"I don't want to eat anymore meat," he told his wife, "or any fish or fowl."

"How about eggs? asked his wife.

"Especially not eggs."

Sam lost weight, but he ate lots of vegetables, and he loved vegetables.

"What's for dinner?" Sam would call when he came home from work.

"Asparagus and yams," his wife would answer. Or sometimes, "Tomatoes and turnips." Or maybe, "Carrots and rhubarb."

One night Sam came home and called, "What's for dinner?"

"Broccoli," his wife answered, "and baby peas."

Sam looked at his plate and saw the broccoli waving in the breeze, allowed to bloom. He saw the young peas snuggled securely in their pods, and Sam couldn't eat.

"I don't want to eat any more vegetables," he told his wife, "No leaves or roots or seeds."

"How about bread?" asked his wife.

"Especially not bread."

Sam lost a lot of weight. He grew thin, but he drank milk and ate cheese. And Sam loved cheese.

"What's for dinner?" Sam would whisper when he came home from work.

"Milk," his wife would answer, "and Swiss

cheese." Or sometimes, "Cheddar cheese." Or maybe, "Muenster cheese."

One night Sam came home and whispered, "What's for dinner?"

"Milk," his wife answered, "and Monterey Jack cheese."

Sam looked at his dinner and saw a baby calf taken away from its mother. He heard the calf crying and saw the mother struggling to keep her child, and Sam couldn't eat.

"I don't want to eat any more dairy products," he told his wife, "no ice cream, or milk, or cheese."

"How about...," his wife started. Then she was silent. She couldn't think of anything else.

Sam became very thin. He stopped going to work. He stopped walking. He stopped standing.

One day, Sam stopped altogether.

BURN

by Rayven McCoy

The world burns... Right before my eyes, the entire world is burning.

A fire that had originally been many, had now become one giant monster, and with its roar it licked and greedily consumed *everything* in its wake, while perfect puffy clouds of toxic chemicals blocked out what was once the sky.

I can only laugh now at the spectacle before me. My scalded flesh has ceased to really *feel* the burn anymore; no, at the moment it was more of an *expectation* of heat—a sense of horrible humidity and impending torture, but no longer was it the agonizingly brutal searing away of my largest organ, the protector of all my gooey insides.

My nerves had scorched away along with my vocal chords as I had screamed at that excruciating pain, and now there was a kind of cold numbness left.

I could no longer smell my hair and skin, either—likely because my sinus cavities were charred away with everything else—and for these small favors I was thankful. At least I wasn't screaming and vomiting all at once—now *that* was a painful experience, if not exercise—while choking down smoke as I tried to breathe that unmistakable odor…that disgusting, gut-wrenching, and putrid stench, of human hair and flesh. It was hard to say which had been worse, really; had it been the pain, the helplessness of feeling—as well as seeing—my skin melt, clumps of it literally falling from my body? Was it that fucking *smell*, (which had seemed to last *forever*). *Or*…or was it the *reaction* from it all; had it been the *totality*? Now *there* was a nice multiple-choice question! I laughed again, something like a frog croaking who'd swallowed some culvert full of shards of glass, nails, and concrete, chased down by carbon monoxide, of course.

Why would I be laughing at this moment in time? You might ask yourself that, or you may just figure I'm quite insane by now, or that it's some strange neurological reaction, (call it a survival mechanism in this shit world now turned to ash, and well, shit), and that may be true; in some parallel dimension, where everything that *could* possibly happen *has*, including my death; a 'place' where every possible scenario had played out, along with my subsequent behaviors and emotions, I'm sure it was *very* possible that I was not just laughing, but *hooting* with full blown hysteria or crying my eyes out with some form of regret. However, in the here and now, in this reality—the one I perceive, the *only* one that matters—that's simply a great veneer, a charade. I am *not* recording this to lie *or* to mind our recently departed society's ideas of propriety, after all; nor am I the posterity kind, either (that would be filled with all kinds of untruths, of course). No, I am recording this for honesty's sake—call it my lifelong good deed and first real article; facts aligned, research done, and as objective as possible.

So, now, stuck in a cave I finally wriggled into as that futile house of cards we so gullibly called reality and the world sweltered to the ground, and even farther down, broiled into the very core of the *earth*, (yes, up in smoke, too, if you insist) I had fashioned a pen out of some remaining twig-paintbrush; ah, desperation. Now, well, *now*, I was using my own ample blood supply on the walls. Another laugh bubbles up as I imagine this is what human ancestors once did—at least *they'd* had either an animal or foe they could murder for the job, giving them *plenty* of ink without the pain, (even if it *was* simply recalled). As it is, I must be careful and ration, I suppose—as if it matters now, anyway, but I *would* like to get all of this down…

Now you might suppose I'm some despicable psychopath—or just an evil bitch—which *may* be closer to whatever the 'truth' is, but that matters naught to me, especially right now. For one, I saw this coming—I *had* seen this coming for *so* many years the only surprise was how *long* it had actually taken for the chips to fall! The fact was, most of us had at least *acted* as if it *could* happen—and not so long ago, absolutely *would* happen, if you believed American news. Oh, those pathetic 'preparations' of generations past—like kids curling under their desks would ever help a blast like this, but it gave that most important of all drugs, *hope*. Those gestures of frightened people spurred on by war and propaganda meant to mislead, and ironically, also convince us of our brute strength, and above all, *righteousness* against any and *all* opposition.

The enemies are always the same (have always *been* the same), just with slightly different faces, spewing their similarly autocratic and 'evil' ideological rhetoric in a myriad of tongues. Add to that our color-tinged speech and spin-doctoring giving *them* their own brand, and us our brand new bigotry—back then it was 'the Reds,' those Bolshevik fucks. Later it would be (and this truly made me laugh in my situation) cave dwellers with their harems, tons of kids, and unlimited resources—oil or heroin, it was all the same, it all amounted to money to buy convoys, bombs, and of course hidden factories where they could dedicate their 'best and brightest' to methods we had long ago perfected. Hairy, dirty men on television, full of the bravado only the 'holiest' of wars could bring, would boast of their machetes (and how many Allies had been decapitated by them), car bombs, IEDs, and of course their own people so intoxicated with fanaticism as to kill themselves to inherit a heaven of virgins, (they used to call that type of warrior 'Kamikaze' back in those 'Red days'). On a side note, I always wondered why in the *hell* anyone would want that many fucking virgins all scared and inexperienced when they could have 'sluts,' (that term is not derogatory to me, of course, I love sluts), or those who at least *enjoyed* sex, of course.

Ah, America; home of the kind-of-sort-of-*somewhat* free and the *brainwashed* brave—cowboys with no couth, but full of ass-kicking grit just the same! Not that we were any dumber or exceptional, not that much more ill-advised or corrupt than any other country; we just *loved* our mixed messages and oh-so-sly misinformation and chicanery—and everyone else seemed to, as well, and we were *so* good at it, we'd used it at *every* chance; the old Razzle-Dazzle, if you will—from the White House to the court house. Well, that was gone, now—immolated into a heap of smoke and ash; maybe, just maybe, some bones of engineering, industrial, and architectural brilliance had survived, and maybe even some fragments of good old calcium, chock full of marrow-deep-DNA for the next whomever to study whenever.

But, you see, to me, this was almost a *relief*; it was *finally* over, or so it seemed, except for one...*tiny*...detail—and you *know* the devil's in those details—those oh-so-tricky clever scientists had been wrong, *dead* wrong, because here *I* was, *quite* alive, huddled in a cave as the world vaporized before me and I practiced art and lit with my fucking blood. Now, this begged *many* questions, which all flew through my still overactive brain regardless of blood loss. But perhaps the most important at this second was just who *else* had survived this cataclysmic pissing match of nuclear proportions that had been some 80 years in the making? More analyzing led to *why* I— and whoever else—had survived, anyway? Better, maybe, was that itchy, niggling little question that kept pinging around in my likely somewhat exposed brain pan: *Was* I truly still alive?

PART 2

As I write, sitting in this amazingly apropos (and epically poetic) reminder of our not too distant past, when we were far more honest as beasts rather than 'altruistic' global policy-makers, I chuckle again; that utter demolition in flames just a yard away. What a room with a view!

I am using the nicely pooled, albeit charred, blood on my side to write, and watch the show: 'The end of the world' (thank you R.E.M., it is indeed 'the end of the world as we know it,' and I *do* feel fine). Now, I admit, it's hard to rationally convince you that the entire planet was literally blown to smithereens—especially by such antiquated deadly weapons we were always blathering about not using, and especially not letting others have—but I *know* it was; all gone, all acid rain and ashy weekends at Gamma Ray Beach, okay? We had *known* the gamble we were taking, we knew the losses, the risks, the possible rewards, but like most egocentric, addictive games, we'd rolled the damn dice anyway. So, for honesty's sake, whether you like it or not, *everyone* had gotten what they deserved, and further, *every single* one of us had played our part to perfection, thank you.

This brought me right back to the worries, though; see, I knew I *was* alive, (we'll get into that in a bit; better, in human skin), and that meant presumably there were others. Just this once *assume* would *not* 'make an ass out of u and me,' because, logically speaking, I *knew* there *would* be others, and that brought another question: Just what in the fuck *did* all this 'survival' in this type of conflagration so designed to kill *everything* in its path *mean* exactly? I don't like things I don't know or cannot figure—hell, you don't live this long in this whacked existence without learning a thing or two, and so my mind was spinning.

That Hell that was still engulfing the world around me now crackled at my 'doorway,' offering light to write, and *warmth* (I chuckled again at that)...this whole scenario was some fucked up time-travel special: A Cro-Magnon caricature of an early Grimm's tale made manifest by Industrial Aged WMDs.

I made a decision then, to stop fucking around— and this is a hard task, given my fundamental *nature*, you see. Back to that complete honesty, there are things which will clear quite a bit up for you; now, whether you *choose* to believe or not, of course, *is* up to you, as usual. Moreover, it may just also release *me* from the bonds of eons—secrets (kept by me and mine) so unwanted in this human realm as to be only hinted at through things like faery-tales and fiction, mythology, religion, and ancient allies in secret societies that form their own legends.

So, as I gather up my now interestingly-colored viscous life force—which had become quite a palette of colors, like blackish brick red from soot in places to brown in others where the iron was beginning to oxidize and dry, along with the deep darkest vein wine to the lighter oxygenated arteries, I perceived how colorful we all were on the inside *and* on the floor, where my plasma was beginning to separate. It occurred to me that I was taking too much time; call it the procrastination of a writer or the trickery that comes to me oh so very naturally. I also couldn't help but think of all those poor monks locked away in cement dungeons, scribbling their truths in one form (and tongue) or another; was I now to be ascetic? Well, certainly it seemed so— why did I have a sudden fascination for the truth, for revelations to you? Well, call it being in this mind and body too long; here it is, there are no more opportunities to 'make right' and suddenly I'm confessing trade secrets? Hmmm, well, the psychology on that one could fill up a chapter, but I digress...

The facts are that I don't actually *have* to tell you shit and you *certainly* don't have to believe it. I can be as honest as I've sworn to be (not exactly my essential nature), and that may *still* be futile; again those holy men come to mind; how many of them were deemed mad in the end? On the other hand, I *could* wrap this up in some baroque fiction that you *would* buy, hook, line, and sinker, and it would *all* be lies. What an interesting realm this place is...or should I say was? Even now, at the end of perceived time and existence, we still have choices—free will—and yet what a curse, too. I sighed, thinking of all the minute details that had led to this moment...The Design that was the base of everything—the Puppet Master—and decided to start there.

PART 3

It truly doesn't matter *what* book you choose to believe; which set of papyrus set into motion long ago that you choose to study—they *all* tell a very similar tale of what you may call 'the beginning,' or, if you like, 'the poetic and prose ramblings of early scholars trying to explain their world via religion.' Back then, it was mythology...oh what good old days, when gods (with the 'little g') were as human as the humans they guarded, victimized, loved, hated, raped, exploited, and, most of all, demanded from them their restitution for this behavior. Back before duality there was no true good or evil; there were simply the gods, the warriors, the humans...not simple, but definitely more to the point, then; Zeus and Ares were rapists (quite frequently, I might add), and their preferences were extreme, to say the least! Gatherings in the names of those 'fun loving gods,' like Dionysus—later to be known as Bacchanalian feasts in Rome—were legendary; ripe with orgies, drink, dance, and no judgment as to what your own sexual preference was, really…well, as long as there weren't too many girls on girls—the guys had to get theirs, of course! Really, it was one large bonfire wherein all of your wildest fantasies played out, music, wine, sex, and hedonistic fun, including blood sports, of course. Much like sex, drugs, and rock 'n roll, what can I say? Why is it every damn generation thinks their way is somehow *new*?

Back then, the closest one could come to 'evil'—and it was never termed that, really—were 'Trickster gods,' such as Loki (oh, he's a devil, that one), or Pazuzu—now made famous because of the movie, *The Exorcist*. He was considered *unlucky* for the people, as well he should have been. Look, if you live in the desert and some south wind kicks up a sandstorm in your direction, well, that isn't going to be too cool, right? It did not mean he was hated; he was merely an accepted—albeit unfortunate—part of Mother Nature as a whole. I could list all of them, but surely you get my point. There, in the desert, were also the Jinn, other little devils with enormous power trapped in this or that container, able to grant any desire, but much like later texts would describe deals with the devil, you could never actually get your wish as it was always tied up in loopholes, subtext, and addendums—things not said nor thought of at the right time…So, tricky, right, but evil? Nah, not evil, not even *close*.

The Persians believed in duality, as did the Zoroastrians, which led right to the Jewish people. One God, no matter how wrathful in the Torah (or should we say now the Old Testament), was a loving parent, and must be feared—or respected; He must show discipline, etc., and from there all the previous tricksters became evil, for surely there had to be evil for there to be good, and vice versa, right? Sure. Even I can buy that one. But we've been painted so wrong for so long—and we have almost as much P.R. as the Big Guy!

Let's start with this: Being created *first*, the first children to watch, enamored and in utter awe as the universe forms and life begins, there is no replacement for that; changing the makeup of an angel is akin to a zebra changing its stripes, ok? I must say, as I write this, I find it hard to explain in human terms, and I have lived among you all for millennia, now! You humans, you think you know love because of that gray crinkled matter and those deep seated feelings in your chest, but you should take it from me, even the *strongest* of your loves is *petty* compared to what we know.

A *good* mother (and I must stress this as I have seen this abuse more than even I can take, and I'm supposed to be the opposing side), holding her child for the first time—that flood of oxytocin that rips through all else as she realizes what she felt for her mate, the father, her friends, lovers, siblings were simply faded photographs against this enhanced purity. That, my friends, is love; it is the closest analogy I can give you, anyway. When she tucks the babe in, makes sure it is fed, has every possible need met, and still wants to do more, still aches with a desire so strong to make this child never suffer and only prosper—that is, on this realm, the only true love, and still, it is just a glimmer of what is Above, in The Design.

Picture that there was a Design set in motion, oh, about 15 billion years ago—in your time, that is; we have no time, that is a human construct, and far too difficult for me to explain. Imagine, now, that at the tiniest level of the so-called 'void' before the 'Big Bang,' the Design was there, and 'aware' (again, having to use your language, well, this is for lack of a better term), and that all that was set in motion was completely predetermined in many realms, worlds, and the multi-verse. I hope I haven't lost you; in the vastness of our universe (or multi-verse); only those in the study of Quantum Mechanics and Theoretical Physics seem to be able to grasp these ideas.

When it comes to destiny, people tend to get itchy, and I really can't say that I blame you—the thought that no matter what you do, it will land you right where you were always meant to be, regardless? Yeah, that's another topic open for debate since The Design guarantees, and in fact, banks on, Free Will. Well that seems contradictory, no? Well, it's not; it's actually a *paradox*, and theoretical physicists *love* them because it is then that they know they're onto something. For instance, most of you believe we will be able to travel through time someday—traversing to and fro through a dimension unlike the other three in many ways, not the least of which is the fact that humans have no true comprehension of it and how it works; there is still many hypotheses and theories that seem to fit as well as the last; again, is this a human construct, as it seems to be tailor-made for living entities with intelligence? There's the thought that time is more like a line of photographs, both constant and yet changeable, or even better, it is an illusion, (of course that goes right along with human construct), and biologically speaking, *every* living thing on this rock has inner clocks all over their body, in its very fundamental neurology, (from the circadian rhythm to the pulse of the heart, there are nerve bundles that literally throb with this so-called time).

This field is filled with paradox—ah, the mysteries of the universe abound, and why? Because at the tiniest level of the Quantum Foam are the sub particles of sub particles—there is chaos within order, and (if you wish for adventure, have the guts to explore, and enough fearlessness to believe it won't drive you insane) still farther down the rabbit hole, more order within chaos within order... Poor old ingenious Einstein; he saw the order, the elegance, what he believed to be the 'face of God,' and yet when he discovered what he perceived as utter chaos, it killed him.

From what I've seen, you all have these preconceived notions about what 'God' looks like and how 'He' must be, how wonderful to behold, and when someone comes along that can really test you on that, you become downright wrathful, if not depressive—you lose your faith, you question everything you'd ever been taught, which is what you should have done in the first fucking place! Why does it always take some strange kind of science or miracle for you people to get your heads out of your literalist asses? Had it ever occurred to you that part of The Design was to have the scholars be men, so that 'God' is always a 'He,' or that It predestined it all, so that you *would* have a choice? You *choose* not to listen; you choose to blindly follow some crazy ass with a few degrees (if that) stomping and crying behind a podium whilst put upon a pedestal—well, there's your free will and choice, kiddies, have you enjoyed them? In Catholicism, 'Pontiff' literally translates to 'God on Earth,' now in this Christian religion, you believe in only one human incarnation of God, right, and that would be Jesus, so tell me, how does this fit into the rest of what you believe?

I see far less believers than I do sycophants and obsequious sheep—oh the blind leading the blind, all ye of little faith. Has it never dawned on you that The Design is meant to be questioned, regardless of whatever book you're following—in fact, that alone should tell you 'He' wanted you to think; why else would He have put so many paths with so many texts at your disposal? From the beginning of human thought process, spoken legends passed down round the campfire to the learning of writing and stencils in stone, and on, these questions have possessed us and our compulsion is obsession, and why shouldn't it be? Don't you think that, too, is part of 'The Plan?' So, you'll excuse me as I laugh while the world outside still bakes around me and I no longer have any worry about survivors, for I feel them coming, now, my brethren. I was in panic mode when I began; now, as I heal, I am calm and collected, and just a little wary of leaving this place, cave or no. The plus side is that it will probably be taken as the ravings of some lunatic at the end. I can deal with that.

I still wonder if any mortals lived through this shit, and quickly decide any humans out there will be some kind of cannibalistic cave dwellers, à la Wes Craven's *The Hills Have Eyes*. If not now, soon enough. Worldwide destruction can bring out the worst in people.

I laugh again, and my voice is already coming

back; I can again smell that damn potpourri of ash, chemicals, flesh, scalding rock, and of course, my fucking hair. Gross.

If I could, I would strip down to my natural 'birthday suit,' but alas, when 'flung' to this damn place, we were all stripped of our wings, given sex organs—which can be fun, but mostly are a pain, so I actually empathize with you people to a certain degree—and are now stuck in this damn human form, having to perform every vile function that makes you more animal than 'image of God.' Oh, yeah, there's a debate for you—that means your insides, in case you hadn't figured that one out yet; that light or spark of Creator inside all of you? Yeah, that's God, and 'His image,' which *was* written, but again, you've *chosen* to make a mountain out of a mole hill.

Oh, well. I wasn't put here to solve all your problems; you have to do that for yourself. Free will, remember? In that predestined Plan full of paradox, there is still the multi-verse and various realms, ergo your decisions from second to second *do* make a difference. The biggest one, of course, is which side of our dual nature do you lean toward most, and which do you choose?

Given this most recent display, I'd say you're a long way off from your Maker, even though you are quite an important part of The Design. Make of that what you will.

Did you even *want* to know what happened? I mean, you can guess, right? America pissed off the wrong countries, the wrong countries got pissed, weapons were traded and sold via the black market, and, for a while, again we had a Mexican standoff, another kind of Cold War. This one only lasted a few weeks—after all, the internet and social media have engendered ADHD in all of us; you humans have no patience anymore, and so, of course, well, the buttons were pushed.

I should probably mention this happened right after the election of some pompous money bags autocrat posing as a good 'Christian,' and that most of this mess had begun with a Dystopia that put all the problems of America at the feet of all immigrants. This, too, made me chortle with contempt and, well, frankly, incredulity, since all you WASPs are truly immigrants! Wow. So now that I'm thinking about it, if Time Travel can be perfected, perhaps I should write the bastard's name down and some traveler will know better than to let him be elected; but wait, that won't work, will it? Can't change time, cannot change that all-important Design, so…you're fucked, basically. Nope, nothing to be done now but wait, which I can do and have done for longer than your imagination could take you.

I chuckled again at the fact that *all* the media had been pointing at for so long now was bio-warfare, and yet, when the chips were down, we fell right back to those good old nukes we swore we'd never use again. But weren't the bio-warfare warnings—including the hilarious zombie apocalypse—shoved down your throats just a little too much, hmmm? Misinformation, my friends. America tends to personify the traits of Satan, too—it loves saying, "Hey, look over here," while it's pulling some shit on the other side.

Now I smell something different: one of my friends is getting closer, and *damn*, from the stench, they got it even worse than I did.

Oh, did I bury the lede? While writing this, I thought I'd take my sweet time giving you some history, when, truly, you're probably more interested in the future; and yeah, there will be a future. Through destruction comes creation, and yes, I am an anarchist.

The difference is, these changes don't scare me, they *excite* me; I can't wait to see what comes next—it isn't as if this hasn't happened quite a few times…just a cleanup, another Babylon or Sodom and Gomorrah, if you will.

I cough up a bit more blood and spit it at the now dried palette on the floor as I hear a voice that sounds like a nightmare.

"So, what did you think about *this* show?" Azriel asks.

"Well, it was grand, I'll give you that! Jesus, but

you look like Satan's shit, my friend!" I said, chuckling.

"Oh, Loki, will you ever stop playing the fool? Let me in, now; the rest are on their way."

"Of course. Tell me Lilith is still as beautiful as ever, would you? And how is Kali?"

"Those bitches? Are you kidding? Kali was gathering heads left and right—shit, she put the poor fuckers out of their misery! And Lilith? Come on, you know as well as I do that it would take a hell of a lot more than one of our semi-millennial cleanses to ever scald her!"

We laugh together, and in the cave we discuss all that had led to this moment; our memories are photographic and everlasting; we *never* forget. Soon enough, we feel, and *smell*, females, and I get very restless, for if anyone has any clue what comes next and what to do, it will be Lilith.

Perhaps this time, we just might get it right, since the only one who knows the entirety of it all is, of course, The Design. We angels were first, but no one holds 'His' secrets; nothing has the vast consciousness of The Creator, and so, in that way, my friends, we are indeed in the same boat.

About the Author

Typhanei Celeste and Rayven McCoy were born December 17th, 1979 in Virginia, but have lived in Florida most of their lives. Although twins with similar interests, they are quite different and have forged very diverse paths in life. While Typhanei has moved back home to be with their mother, Rayven retains her independence. They can only be seen together when Hell has a cold.

Rayven McCoy will not comment on her alleged torrid affair with the supposed "Dark Lord," but insists she is, indeed, his favorite. She began writing articles at a young age, infuriated at a system she calls "choked with institution and hope for the future." She claims Beelzebub loved her article about legalizing prostitution so much that he has made her his "Chief Writer of the 9th Level." She enjoys sex, drugs, and rock and roll, and continues writing extremely dark stories she categorizes as "New Wave Horror." She claims she is, indeed, a deputized succubus, and that the destroyer goddess Kali is a personal friend. She visits her sister and mother only when necessary and lives in Black Diamond, Florida because it is a vortex of evil. Her favorite philosopher, Nietzsche was not a Satanist and she insists she is not, either, and that Aleister Crowley's magic was simply a physical manifestation of what Albert Einstein appropriately called "Spooky Action at a Distance." She is not a practitioner of the "dark arts," but has researched the Occult and continues to confound her sister by claiming she's not human.

Check out her website to stay updated:
rayvenmccoy.wix.com/newwavehorror
Follow her Twitter at:
https://twitter.com/rayvensblood
Find her on Facebook:
https://www.facebook.com/profile.php?id=1000092
02753610&fref=ts

SOUL MATES
by Jill D'Aubery

Shima and Sekeeta were soul mates. They fell in love the first time they met and, over time, their love deepened into a rich, warm sharing of life.

But that first meeting was something. Shima was a rambunctious five-month-old boy-kitten and Sekeeta was a slightly more demure girl-kitten, just eight weeks old. I brought her to him and explained that she was now his. He looked at the little ball of fluff, laid his ears back and hissed, just to show her who was Top Cat. For her part, she looked up at him with undisguised adoration, dropped her eyelids to half mast, reached up and licked him on his nose. That was all it took. He belonged to her body and soul from that second on.

Being a boy and older, Shima was wise in the ways of the world so he took on the task of raising the sweet, innocent little girl. An easy task as it turned out since Sekeeta worshipped him and tried to imitate him in everything. This led, of course, to many rescues off of roofs and out of trees by the human in the family...me.

Before I realized that they were even old enough, they had produced a litter of five beautiful kittens. Sekeeta wasn't into motherhood...she would nurse the babies then, as fast as possible, leave them alone. Sometimes the kittens were alone for several hours as their mother sat outside basking in the sun, enjoying her day. And the one and only time she thought she'd be a real Mom things went very wrong.

The kittens were just a little more than a week old with their eyes still tightly shut and I was sick in bed. For some reason Sekeeta decided to bring all of her brood in to be with me. One by one she carried in the kittens and deposited them next to me in the bed. *Fine*, I thought, *I'll kitten-sit.* I put my arm around the pile of kittens and drifted off to sleep. The next thing I knew there was a huge commotion with kittens squeaking at the top of their lungs and desperately struggling to stand up. Smack in the middle of the squirming mass of kittens was a lizard somewhat bigger than the biggest kitten. The lizard was terrified, the kittens were hysterical, I was stunned, but Sekeeta was very pleased with herself having just dropped the lizard smack in the middle of her sleeping kids. She sat quietly at the foot of the bed watching her frantic babies and I could swear that she was grinning.

I put the lizard in a shoebox and set it free in the back yard. When I got back to bed a now grumpy Sekeeta was taking her kids back to their nursery and away from the Terrible Lizard Rescuer.

Shima more than made up for his Love's lack of parenting skills. He was a wonderful dad. He was there for the birthing, helped with the cleanup, and spent hours cuddling the kittens and playing with them. Shima took over their training, too. He taught them how to climb, how to hunt, litter-box etiquette and even taught them how to play tricks on their mother. Which they delighted in doing, much to Sekeeta's amusement.

One of the babies was born with a deformed leg. This was the only kitten that Sekeeta showed the slightest interest in. He wasn't strong enough to fight his way to a nipple and when he was not quite two days old Sekeeta figured this out. She would nurse the other four then, when Shima came and took over the cuddling duties, she would carry Toulouse-Lautrec, as I named him, into a different room and nurse him separately. When he was full, she would bring him back and unceremoniously drop him in the middle of a bunch of wriggling kittens. She would sigh heavily and go back outside again...a thoroughly put-out and overworked cat.

Somehow Toulouse thrived right along with his siblings.

Finding homes for the kittens was easy, they were extremely beautiful and I actually had a waiting list. Especially for Toulouse. He was adorable and charming and the first kitten of choice for everyone. I insisted, however, that one of his siblings go with him so that he would have help throughout his life. Not that he really needed help because, though he only had three toes on one foot and no forearm on that leg, he climbed trees, ran and jumped and had a great time. He was just a bit slower than his siblings.

A nice young woman took Toulouse and his sister, whom she named, Monet. Shima was sad to see the kittens leave for their new homes, but Sekeeta, as usual, wasn't interested and didn't really notice that they were gone.

Shima and Sekeeta were very different...Sekeeta was always up for an adventure, Shima preferred the quiet life. Shima loved kittens, even the neighbor's kittens that were constantly breeching our fence to play with him. Sekeeta preferred chasing the neighbor's gigantic English Sheep dog up and down our quiet street. She was only slightly larger than one of the dog's front paws, but the poor thing was terrified of her and she chased him relentlessly always careful to not catch him.

Though their likes and dislikes were very

different, they were devoted to each other. Opposites attract, I guess, even in the cat world.

The two cats slept in each other's arms, they ate together, often sharing particularly tasty morsels with each other, and they were seldom out of one another's sight.

They were remarkably tolerant of my habit of putting food out for the stray animals that wandered through my yard, including the possum family that lived in my attic and the skunks living under the house and the various cats that dropped by for a snack. I called these feral cats "Summer Cats" because they just passed through in the Summer time.

The years went by too quickly. Shima and Sekeeta grew old together and were inseparable for their entire lives. Together they experienced parenthood, their respective "little operations," moving house a couple of times, various dogs and one coyote invading their yard, sickness and recovery, one poisoning incident, getting lost and being found, the joys of Christmas tree climbing, and love. So much love between those two. Shima the gentle cat, Sekeeta the fierce cat. Both wonderful senses of humor, each had enormous compassion for the other, and so strong was their love that, when they reached their golden years, they still looked and acted like kittens.

They were thirteen years old that warm Spring

day. The backyard was bursting into bloom, Shima was snoozing under a rosebush and Sekeeta was sunning herself on the lawn, eyes half-lidded and paws tucked under. The very picture of contentment. A blue jay landed not inches from Sekeeta's nose. She opened one eye and looked at the bird. The bird looked back at her. She blinked, then closed her eye and settled back into her nap. For some reason, best known only to themselves, Shima and Sekeeta didn't hunt birds, never had.

I remember feeling proud of my girl as I watched the bird prance around her paws. Then I looked at her a little closer. Something didn't look right about her mouth. Her jaw seemed to be a little distended. I called the vet, a very nice man who actually made house calls. He came and checked Sekeeta out. Took some blood and said he'd call with the results.

I thought she probably had a bad tooth. I hoped she had a bad tooth.

The call came the next day. "I'm sorry, but she has cancer of the jaw."

My heart just crashed. So many questions, such awful answers, so little time. The vet said that she wasn't able to eat anymore but there is a nutrient paste that can be spread on the roof of her mouth…

"No! Stop, please. I know you mean well, but I can't do that to her. I just can't."

The vet came back that afternoon. I held Sekeeta for a few minutes, just loving her and listening to her purr. She knew. I know she knew. And she agreed.

Shima came in and looked at us curiously. He had always nuzzled me when I cried and he did now. Next he went over to Sekeeta and licked her ears and her face. Then he turned around and, without a backward glance, went back outside.

I held my lovely Sekeeta as she left this world.

It took Shima almost two days to realize that she wasn't just off somewhere. That she wasn't coming back. It hit him hard. He stopped eating. He stopped going outside. He curled up on a big, square pillow on the living-room floor and only left it to visit the litter box. He sat on that pillow and cried. He mewed and sniffled and howled his grief. Overnight he lost the vibrancy of youth that had always defined him and he became an old cat.

The current Summer Cat, a little feral boy maybe a year or two old that I called Springer, had been hanging around for several weeks, mostly lurking behind trees and bushes, darting out to grab a bite to eat then running back to the safety of his bush. Like all the Summer Cats he had met Shima and Sekeeta and they all seemed to get along. A couple of days after Shima retired to his pillow Springer decided to move in. Demonstrating a braveness that he had never shown before, he walked into the house as though he owned it, checked out the kitchen and wandered into the living room. He stopped when he saw Shima on his pillow, then went over to the grieving cat, carefully sniffed him, ran into the kitchen, got a bunch of Shima's food in his mouth and ran back. He dropped the food in front of Shima then pressed his body up against the grieving cat and started to gently wash him.

He didn't leave Shima for days, brought him food many times a day, licked him all over until Shima was a sopping wet cat, and even wrapped his arms around him, holding him for hours at a time...and slowly Shima started to eat again. Eventually he came back to life. Springer had done what I could not...he had touched Shima in ways that only another cat could do.

Springer moved in permanently and, although he found a little feral girl cat of his own and brought her home to live with us, he always took care of Shima and spent at least part of every day just being with the elderly cat.

Shima came back to life, but his joy was gone. He went through his days carefully and every once in awhile I found him poking around in Sekeeta's favorite hangouts. And sometimes, in the middle of the night, when he couldn't stand it anymore, he'd howl his despair. I always found Springer curled up with the elderly boy after those nights.

Five more years sped along and Shima became very old and very rickety. On Thanksgiving morning I was working in the kitchen when I saw

Shima stiffly walk over to the heater and start turning around in circles. I thought he was just going to lie down where it was nice and warm, but he kept circling. After a few seconds of this I went to check on him. He turned his beautiful, blue eyes up to me. One of his pupils was a narrow slit, the other was huge.

I called the vet, but he wasn't there. I finally found a vet that was open on Thanksgiving and bundled Shima into a carrier. There was a wait, of course, but finally we were taken in to an exam room. The vet took one look at my boy and told me he had suffered a stroke. And again I was told about nutrient paste that can be spread on the roof of his mouth to keep him alive for a few more days. And again I could not do that to my wonderful cat.

I held Shima in my arms and he purred as he left to join his love. He was weak but he tried to nuzzle me as my tears flowed and he seemed to be truly happy for the first time since Sekeeta died.

THE NIGHT BUS
by T. R. Wiland

"God damnit!" Casey hissed as she jerked back from the burner. She groaned and held her hand. It was a decent burn. She turned from her prep station and headed for the cold tap.

"Again…?" came a voice from behind her. The girl lowered her head at the accusing tone. Dish stared at her from washing a large stockpot. He was a quiet man with a dark sense of humour and a grin that seemed to take over most of his face; Casey often thought he looked like a piranha. They called him 'Dish,' a nickname from his job title of 'dishpig.' His real name was something Casey couldn't pronounce, nor could many others, so Dish it was.

"You gotta stop burnin' yourself, girl. That is the third time this week! Maybe you should go on the plate if you're cooked, eh?" He grinned widely. He had an accent that was difficult to understand, but he always tried to make a joke, so long as the boss wasn't around.

"Ah, I'm sorry! Just um, tired." She forced a laugh, but it was hollow. She hated this place; she was always tired, run off her feet, and never had a moment's rest. So many times she had fought back tears of exhaustion at the end of her shift. Casey returned to her hand, making sure her burn was cooled sufficiently before wrapping it up and returning to work. She could not deny what Dish had noticed.

"Ferguson!" A loud voice wheezed. Casey froze.

'*Shit*,' she thought; it was her boss, Mr. Irving.

"Ah, yes, sir?" she called rather hesitantly, approaching the irritable little man.

"This is the third time you've had an 'accident' just this week! Are you really so stupid that you cannot even manage to go one night without hurting yourself?!" he snapped. Casey found her eyes drifting to the floor.

"I'm sorry sir, I'm just a little tired—"

"You can't afford to be tired!" Irving growled. "If you hurt another member of staff, or mess up the orders… If you can't do your job, you should go home…!"

"No!" The response came out at once, her hazel eyes snapped back up to look at him. "Please! I won't let it happen again sir! I will make sure I pay attention." She nodded. She would have loved to tell him to go to hell, but he would have fired her on the spot, and she couldn't afford to lose this job. She hated having to kiss ass to make sure he didn't dock her pay. Again.

"See that you do, or it's my ass!" With that he stormed into his office again, leaving the kitchen quiet, clattering pans and trays the only noise for a few moments, before the calls began to sound out again. Casey returned to her station to finish prepping vegetables and such for the cooks and chefs. It wasn't a fancy job, but it was a paycheck, so long as Mr. Irving didn't find a reason to dock her wage. It was his favourite punishment. She decided to keep her head down for the rest of the night, lest he find another reason to pick on her.

It wasn't the first time she had burned or cut herself. Everyone had a minor accident in the kitchen at some point, but hers were becoming more frequent. She knew exactly why; she was distracted, exhausted. She was glad when one AM came around and she could finally clock off for the night. It left her alone with her thoughts as she grabbed her stuff from the back room. At least tonight she had some overtime. It wasn't much, but she needed the money. With this, and her job cleaning houses with her mother during the day, they had just enough to keep their heads above water.

Casey had a lot of responsibility; most of the time she felt like she had been thrown out of the kiddie pool and into the ocean without a life raft. She had her mother, and four brothers and sisters. Her mum already worked two cleaning jobs, one of which Casey was dragged along to, but her health was beginning to fail, and her younger brothers and sisters weren't quite old enough to leave school to work, like Casey had, after her father had died. Life had been tough. At seventeen, she had grown up far too quickly. Too soon she learned that the world, and the people in it, should not all be trusted. She grabbed her bag and hooded jacket from her locker and hurried out of there. She had to get home.

Her mother had a boyfriend after her father passed away. In the beginning, Bill had seemed like a nice guy; he had been supportive when Malcolm died, saying it wasn't fair that such a sweet lady had lost her husband. Casey realised now of course that it was far too soon for her mother to be over her father, but she had needed someone to be there for her... and unfortunately for everyone involved, Helen had chosen Bill. It wasn't long before his true colours were revealed. He had a temper, and liked spending the money he made from his job on drugs and booze, instead of the family he lived with. He was rude, crass, and had made inappropriate comments about Casey. She was incredibly glad when he lost interest and didn't stick around.

The area they lived was much the same, hopeful to begin with, but it quickly went sour. It was to be a development project, a housing boom that was mean to 'revitalise' the community, but after only a few places were built, it ran out of steam. Some big shot had gotten in trouble with the law...or something like that; Casey had never really paid attention to the details. The whole area had just been left. Abandoned like a stolen car. There were some old houses standing empty, supposed to be demolished, now filled with drunken idiots or drugged-up maniacs. Too many times had Casey walked by to see yellow tape cordoning off an area, or woken to flashing red and blue lights in her window.

A car rushing by her awoke her from her thoughts for a moment, its tyres sloshing into a large puddle left by the rain, and soaking her from the knees down. She jumped as she felt the cold before realising what had happened.

"Mother*fucker*! Yeah, thanks for that, asshole!" she shouted back at the car, which of course, never even slowed down. She looked ahead; the bus stop she was trying to get to was just round the corner. She walked quickly, hoping she had not missed the last bus home. Not a long trip via bus, but it would take her a long time to walk it if she had missed it, and aside from that, she was a seventeen year old girl alone after midnight in a shady town.

She wasn't much of a target for potential robbers. Her jacket was threadbare, worn, torn at the sleeves and pockets, a few patch marks here and there. Her trousers were faded, the hems splattered with mud and loose threads. Her shoes were old, held together with rubber bands and duct tape, which did nothing to keep the water out. As she walked, she could feel the rain spitting down, a drop here, a drop there, threatening to spill out on top of her as she walked. The sound of her steps was heavy to her ears, a dull thudding, bringing her thoughts swirling around in her head. Being a kitchen hand was never something she had aspired to. She'd had big dreams and aspirations, like most people in this town, before it went to hell.

She wasn't exactly the top student in her class, but she was above average. She always worked hard, and did well, but her true passion was music. She had always loved the way it made her feel, the way her heart thudded in her chest when a good tune came on, the goosebumps she felt when the note hit the right peak. Her father had taken her to see an orchestra when she was very small, and from that day she had longed to be a part of it. Well, she still did, but she knew those dreams had to be put on hold for now. She'd had all kinds of lessons when she was smaller: singing—which she wasn't completely satisfied with—dancing, and piano—which she enjoyed very much—and her father had taught her to play guitar. Her skills and enthusiasm, however were with the violin. She loved to play, and used to practise every day, for hours on end. It had been her favourite gift. She found herself practising during her lunch breaks at school, sneaking into the music room to use their instruments. There was no way she would risk her most precious possession being damaged. But since taking on two jobs during the week and a Saturday morning route for deliveries, she had barely enough time to think, let alone play. She hadn't so much as picked up her violin in months. She wondered if she would ever be able to play it again.

She pulled her jacket tighter around her shoulders as she neared the bus stop. A solitary street light shone down from above like some kind of safeguard against the night around her, illuminating the empty street—or nearly empty. There was a guy sitting on the bench by the side of the road. He looked like life had gotten to him, too. His coat looked ragged, and threadbare, like it had been patched up many times. He was a bit round in the middle, and his hands were covered by fingerless gloves. As she reached the bench she saw his fingers were stained yellow, probably from a bad smoking habit. His trousers were scrappy as well, and a little too short, as his sock-covered ankles poked out from underneath. All he had for shoes were a pair of slippers that were probably once rather nice. The man looked up at Casey as she approached, and bore her a large smile from beneath his greyed and dirty beard. His face was worn, his skin had a leathery look to it, weathered and battered, but his eyes, a pale blue, glinted in the dim light. They still offered life, and hope.

'*At least someone in this cesspool still has some semblance of it*,' she thought, as she offered him a quick, polite smile in return.

"Good evening," he said brightly, his voice raspy and hoarse like he'd lost it at some point.

"Hi," was all she said. It was awkward; she didn't know what to say to a stranger in the middle of the night.

"Working late?" He had a friendly voice, and she couldn't find anything sinister in the question, so she nodded. "Ah, rough one then?" Again she nodded. "I'm Happy," he told her. This time she stared at this Hobo Santa with an expression that was clearly amusing, as it made him laugh. He bounced as he did so, looking ever so jolly for a man that looked like he might pass out at any moment. "Ahhh yes…I get that a lot. But I am as my name says."

"That's not your real name though…right?" she asked.

"Not the one I was born with, no, but I like this one better." He chuckled, his fat slippered feet tapping away to some unknown tune. "Which bus are you waiting for…?" Casey began to get a little nervous—why was he asking so many questions? Was he going to follow her home or something…? Stupidly, because she couldn't think of a lie, she simply told him the bus route she was after. He nodded, but his expression grew a little downturned at her answer. "Sorry to say, but that bus left about five minutes before you arrived." Casey gasped.

"What?! That's the last bus for hours!" The teenager hung her head, she was in trouble, her mother hated it when she was late home, not to mention her feet were already killing her, and it would take something like an hour before she would make it back. "…Shit…" she groaned. "Well… thanks for telling me instead of letting me stand here like an idiot for ages."

"Gee, I wish I could do more…" Happy told her apologetically.

"It's alright, I guess I'd better head home then. Thanks…Happy…" She offered him a quick smile before hiking her bag up on her shoulder again.

"Oh wait!" He pushed himself to his feet with a groan, reached into the pocket of his coat and pulled out a little trinket. Casey blinked and looked at her hand as his pudgy one pulled away. There in her palm lay a small bell, with a little pink ribbon tied to it. She frowned, looking at it curiously.

"If you ever feel like your mind's in a fog...just give it a little ring." Happy smiled at her in a way that made his eyes crinkle up. Either he was a bit soft in the head, but friendly, or he was dangerous and crazy. Casey just nodded dumbly before hurrying off, every so often checking over her shoulder.

She walked and walked, one step after another, the dull thudding in her ears. She wasn't able to even listen to her music. Her mp3 player had been a birthday gift from her mother, but she'd had to sell it a few months ago. It had broken both their hearts, but they had to have groceries, the twins had needed new shoes, and there was not much else that could earn them any money at the time. Her feet made soft *splat* noises on the concrete as she walked. She was lost in the drumming thuds in her own head and the spit of drops from the sky beginning to fall, slowly. She let out a long groan and pulled her hood up; she knew what was coming. The drops began to fall a little more frequently, a little harder, a little more vigorously. A few drops became a sprinkle, a sprinkle became a shower, and a shower became a downpour. In less than five minutes, a torrent of water had been unleashed upon her head. She could barely see the next street light for the rain, there was nowhere for her to take cover, and her clothes weren't exactly waterproof either. She looked at her watch: 1:22. Still so long to go. Her mother would be furious, and she knew she had to get up early the next morning. She would have to make sure she asked her boss to leave five minutes earlier the next time... Oh, who was she kidding? She wouldn't. She never spoke up to her manager, she didn't practice her violin anymore, what was the point? Nothing would ever change, nothing would be different, nothing would go back to the way it was and now she was stuck in the rain. Casey grit her teeth, and tears squeezed out down her face, mingling with the fat raindrops beating down on her.

At times like this, she missed her father more than ever. He had always been there for her, whenever she felt down; always had a smile and a warm hug whenever she had any troubles. He knew just what to say and how to make her smile. Dad would have known how to make it better. If he hadn't gone she wouldn't even be here. If he was still with her she would be at home, sleeping. She'd still be able to go to school, play her violin; she'd still live in their old house, and she'd still be able to see her grandmother in the country.

'*Dad,*' Casey thought to herself, '*why did you leave me...?*' She choked back a sob, her hand covering her mouth.

Suddenly a light shone from behind her. Casey turned to try and see what was coming, but all she could see were headlights coming toward her through the rain. It was a large shape, a truck...? She frowned as it got closer and she realised: it was a bus! An older one, by the look of it, and an unusual colour, a sort of wine red tone, and smaller than usual buses. She was just beginning to wonder where it was going when it slowed, and stopped right in front of her. She blinked in confusion as the doors opened. At the height of the steps, within the doorway of the large vehicle, stood a man.

"You look like you could use a ride," he called, in a voice deep yet smooth. For some reason, Casey imagined it like midnight blue silk, but she didn't know why she had thought of it. She swallowed her sorrow; she didn't want to let some random stranger see her crying everywhere.

"Where does this bus go?" she cried through the din of the rain.

"Where are you headed?" the man answered. His voice was soft but somehow she could hear him perfectly, as though he were speaking in her ear.

"Uh, Stockport." She held up a hand to keep the water from her face.

"We can drop you there, come in, quickly...!" He gestured for her to step over the threshold. Casey felt strange, like there was some kind of buzzing feeling in the air, some kind of electricity. It was warm, and tingled as she reached out. But the night was cold and she needed to get dry her hands were already shaking.

'*To hell with it*,' she thought, and her hand grasped the metal handrail to haul herself up onto the platform. "How much?" she asked the man, and glanced to the driver's seat. The barrier in the way obscured her view of him; she could only make out a darkened figure. Then the man in white took her attention again, making her focus upon him.

"It would be criminal to ask you to pay, my dear—in this state you simply needed a rescue."

Now she was out of the rain, she was able to look at him properly. He was...different. For one, he had white hair, not just a light blonde, but white as snow; she couldn't tell if it was dyed, his roots were hidden beneath the white top hat he wore. He was a good head taller than she was, clean shaven, with a wide, thin mouth, slanted in a smirk, and a strong jaw. His eyes looked like he was wearing contacts, or maybe it was just the light in the bus, because they looked pinkish. She couldn't be sure, though. She assumed he was coming back from some kind of rich party. His clothes were finely tailored, made of fine material, and nary a spot on him—mostly surprising because he was all in white. The suit was a fresh, almost blinding white, the vest beneath it white and gold brocade; there were gold buttons and accents all over his suit: the cufflinks, the buttons, the pin that held the white silken cravat in place. He looked almost other-worldly, and he reeked of money, but still; offering to pay even a simple bus fare…she didn't like people doing things for her.

"No." She shook her head. "It's not your responsibility, I can't ask you to pay for me."

"But you are not *asking* me, I am insisting upon it. Come." He tapped the driver's cubicle twice, making Casey jump as she felt the bus rumble to life beneath her. The man looped a gloved hand around her shoulders—she couldn't help but think that she had no say in the matter—and she was gently ushered along. She was surprised to find the seats not facing forward, like a usual bus, but set up like booths in a diner, or a train—there were even small tables between each. It was surprisingly warm in there; she might have forgotten about the rain completely, were she not still dripping upon the carpet.

He led her down the centre aisle to a booth second from the back on the right. He said little to her as he shuffled her along, taking a short bow as he reached to take her jacket and bag. The girl looked back at him with a hesitant gaze, the man merely chuckled and grinned.

"My dear, please, you'll catch your death in that. Allow me to be a gentleman and grant you respite. I shall simply hang them to dry." Somehow his posh British accent made it seem as though he could say anything and it would be charming. She wasn't sure, however, and he seemed to catch on. "Ahh, of course, a strange man asking a young girl to undress..." He chuckled and held up his hands. "I assure you, I wish nothing untoward, I am merely helping a hardworking girl get out of the rain. I would not want you to be sick, it would be a shame. Though there is a reason for you being out late; work, I assume...?"

"What are you, Sherlock Holmes?" Casey asked, her hazel eyes narrowing. He merely laughed again.

"My girl, it does not take Sherlock Holmes to see your shoes are held together with duct tape, you look so tired you may as well be a zombie and you have a rather dirty-looking apron sticking out of your bag..." He held out his hands again and took a step back. It was then she noticed a door to another small sort of room, which was strange in a bus. Where did that room go? Why was there a room in a bus? Before she could think of it, the man took her attention again, his large gloved hand thrust out before her. "My name is Alistair Velit'Dantis," he told her. Casey simply blinked once more. There was little she could say; she simply didn't know what to make of all of this. Slowly but surely, her hand extended to grasp his.

"Casey Ferguson," she replied, numbly. Alistair merely gave her a wide smile.

"A pleasure to meet you Casey." He shook her hand firmly but gently. "Now, have a seat, there is a blanket for you, and please, take off the wet clothes. I will be back in a moment."

With that, the man in white disappeared behind the door and left Casey alone. She was starting to get a little worried. What had she done? She'd gotten on a strange bus with some random guy—but at the same time, Alistair hadn't done anything…untoward, as he put it. Maybe he was just being helpful. Maybe it was the fact that she'd had next to no sleep, but she found herself wanting to believe it. She began to strip off her jacket and shirt, leaving on the singlet she had beneath it all. She left everything on the opposite table, including her bag, laid out to dry, then took up the blanket and wrapped it around herself.

As she took a seat, she found herself admiring the interior. Most of it was red or maroon against wood paneling and gold trim. Deep red curtains blocked the outside street, the seats were a soft leather, a rich reddish brown colour, the roof paneled in wood, the tables too were solid—everything screamed quality. She only wished her mother could see this. Her Mother...Casey let out a soft sigh. She wished she could give her mum and brothers and sister such nice things. She wished she had nice things. She wished she had a big bed—room enough to put one—she wished for her mp3 player back and her own phone, she wished for time to play her violin, maybe some nice clothes. That would be amazing...

Casey was staring off into air, but as she was, she noticed something out of the corner of her eye, something bright, flickering. She looked to her right and saw that there was a light peeking out from the shifting curtains, it was a pale light, something about it gave her a sense of nostalgia and comfort. The girl felt compelled to see more. She reached out to grasp at the curtain and reveal what lay beyond.

"Here we are!" A voice interrupted her thought, and the light was gone. She looked back and started when she noticed Alistair was sitting there, a smile upon his face. A hot mug of tea sat in front of her, another in his hand. Had she been so spaced out she hadn't noticed him sitting there? Her face flushed with embarrassment.

"Uh...thanks," she said awkwardly, grasping her cup with both hands and staring into it with the occasional sip. The silence stretched on but either he didn't notice, or didn't care. She could feel him staring at her, gauging her, trying to figure her out, maybe? She looked around, avoiding him, his eyes were too intense, they made her squirm. "Uhm…so…what is this thing? Your party bus?" He responded with laughter to her query and she glanced up with surprise. What was so funny? Eventually he calmed enough to answer her.

"You could call it that I suppose," he said, unhelpfully. "I more prefer to think of it as a rescue chariot."

"So you just go around and pick up people out of the rain? Isn't that dangerous?" She frowned.

"I can look after myself, but I am touched by your concern." The comment made Casey blush— she hadn't meant it like that. He chuckled again, seeing her discomfort. "I find wayward souls, those who deserve more than life has dealt them, and…well, I try to rectify it." The way he said it was both comforting and worrying, but Casey began to feel warmer, a little hazy. It pushed the worry from her mind.

"What do you mean?" she asked curiously, a frown crossing her delicate features.

"I like to grant wishes," he told her.

"What kind of wishes?" His grin only widened.

"Let me show you." He sat up in his seat and gestured to the window she had been looking at previously. "Think about what you wish, something you desire more than anything…?"

"More than anything…?" She looked back into her half-empty cup. Something about the strange man urged her to tell him, but she bit down on the words—it was none of his business! He had no right to ask such a personal question! But…he seemed so…trustworthy? That something about him seemed to call to that part of her, the musical part of her she kept locked up within herself, as though he coaxed it from her with thought alone. "I want…I want to play a show…I want not to have to struggle for money…I want…my dad—" She cut herself off with a sob that threatened to spill over. A white gloved hand rested on hers and she looked up. Alistair was not smiling anymore. His gaze had softened; something about his expression told her he had known loss.

"I understand," he said. "And I want to help you. Here…" He gestured to the curtain again. This time, she looked. "What do you see…?" As he pulled the curtain aside, her eyes widened.

Beyond the bus, the curtain and beyond that window lay a field. No longer could she see the street beyond the glass, but a rolling meadow in a hazy afternoon of spring…she knew this place. The country cottage of her grandmother on her father's side, surrounded by flowers. She looked closer; there were people by the house. Casey gasped as she recognised the people standing there.

"Mum…? Dad…?!" She stared in shock. "How…?" She felt a hand upon her shoulder, and turned to see Alistair smiling. They were no longer on the bus. They stood in the field, surrounded by warmth, surrounded by flowers and sunlight and a perfect day. She heard laughter, and looked to see her younger brothers and sisters playing near the cottage behind her parents. They called to her, waving for her to come closer, to join them.

"Go to them," Alistair told her. Casey looked back at him.

"But…how is this possible?" she breathed.

"I told you my dear. I grant wishes. This is what you want isn't it?" He waved a hand toward the scene in front of them.

"Why me…?"

"You deserve it! You've worked so hard since his passing, you deserve some happiness…! Go on, embrace it!" She felt him nudge her forward. Her parents looked happy, waving her closer, calling to her. She couldn't remember her mother smiling so much, her father seemed so real…but he had died. But how could he have? There he was! He waved at her, grinning like he always used to do. Instinctively, she took a step forward. This was the way it was meant to be. She wouldn't have to work three jobs anymore, she would be able to finish school, play her violin, she could go to music school! She wouldn't have to work in that stupid kitchen anymore, she could hug her father again. It was almost like the past few years didn't happen— he didn't leave them, he didn't get shot. That wasn't him at the funeral. But…wait. She remembered hearing the news and collapsing at school. She remembered standing there at the funeral, silent, as her mother and siblings wept. She'd had to be the strong one, she only had to do that because he died. As she looked on, the scene warped slightly. Her father looked a little paler, she could see a…reflection, of a man in white behind her. Her brows furrowed. Yes. Her father was dead, and her mother had to work so hard to pick up the pieces. Her mother…her sisters and brothers. Without Casey they would be in big trouble, they would run out of money quick, they might even lose the house. She couldn't turn her back on them!

"This…isn't real…" Casey managed. Why did she feel so sluggish?

"It's your dream…" Alistair told her gently, he placed a hand against her back. "And you can live it. Just take this…" He held out a hand to her, and upon it lay a key, an old brass one, tied with a white ribbon. "And you can live it…forever."

"But…what about at home…what will happen…?"

"You will be happy with your family here. Leave your worries behind…" Casey felt strange, here was everything she wanted, her family back, a home to live in, she could see it all there, just waiting for her. But…why did she feel so dull, so hazy? It felt like she were in…some kind of fog.

'If you ever feel like your mind's in a fog…just give it a little ring.' The words echoed inside her head. Slowly, she reached into her pocket, and felt the little metal sphere in her hand. She carefully pulled it out, as though she were dazed or hypnotised.

"What is that?" Alistair asked sharply. Casey held up the bell. "How did you—? Stop!" he cried in a sudden panic. The warmth began to dissipate, along with the haze swarming her mind. Anger struck her—how dare he mess with her head!

"No…I can't. I can't do this. I won't abandon my real family for some dream!" Casey shouted. She couldn't just abandon everything to some dream world, real or not! She had responsibilities to deal with. Her father had always taught her to accept responsibility, she had to look after her family. Even if it was hard, even if it felt hopeless, she couldn't give up. Dad never did, so she couldn't either!

"It's your happiness! Take it girl!" Alistair urged.

"NO! I won't live a lie and I won't be happy with this hollow life! I won't!" The last thing she saw before the world went dark was Alistair's disappointed face.

Casey blinked as her vision cleared. A cold wind blew over her. The girl looked around. She was…home? Yes…she was standing outside her own home. How had she gotten here? Was it all a dream? She looked down. She had her bag, she had her clothes, and they were dry. The ground was wet where it had just rained, but she was completely dry. How…?

Suddenly she heard her mother's voice inside. She took a step forward, clenching her fist in determination. Something in her hand made her look down again. In her palm lay a key and a little bell. A shiver ran up Casey Ferguson's spine. As she put the items in her pocket, to head inside, she glanced at the time. It was 1:22am.

Tekima "Miss Kima" Wiland is a mid-twenties Western Australian, who lives on the coast with her long term boyfriend and pets. She has been writing stories privately ever since she was 8 years old, but began in earnest when she was 14 and met a friend who matched her passion for telling stories. She has moved to several different houses and schools and would like to one day travel so as to diversify her knowledge base. Currently she writes with friends, including some from Canada and England, in private stories to improve her skills.

She has always had a passion for anything creative

and has said she wants "...to leave behind something beautiful to be remembered by." She also enjoys painting and crafting artwork to sell, and hopes to be a professional artist.

Find Miss Kima and her artwork on Facebook:
https://www.facebook.com/MissKimasCreations
Follow Miss Kima on Twitter:
https://twitter.com/MissKimaKima

CAKE
by Typhanei Celeste

ONE

Have you ever had a dream so real you had no idea you were asleep; one so warm you never wanted to leave, and yet the second you woke, you could not remember a damn thing? Tilly did. He dreamt like that all of the time. So, he wanted to stay there; wherever "there" was, it was a hundred times better than his waking life.

Today was like always; a deep gasp brought him back to horrible gray reality, leaving a feeling like drowning still heaving in his chest. Next, he heard Lug coughing his head off in the other room, and as usual, the baby began crying at the sound.

He was then instantly awake. He had to help take care of Little Fry because Misty was usually so out of it from all of the *Aryan* she used. Tilly didn't judge her for it; she shot it up because it helped her pain, and it enabled her to do what she *had* to do to make money—she sold her body.

Creepy old guys in big cars who wanted to do all kinds of nasty things would drive up, and they would always have some medicine to give her. After they fucked her every kind of way, (beat her, strangled her, and sometimes even made her dress like one of their own kids in their plaid skirt-and-blouse-uniforms typical of prep school), they'd pay her with the card she needed to buy diapers and milk. Then, they'd push her out of the car like a pile of garbage and peel off—back to their big houses and warm food; back to their pill-head wives with plastic faces, their spoiled 'poor little rich kid' brats, and back to their job of making his and Misty's lives Hell on earth.

Tilly loved her very much; for all intents and purposes, she was his sister, and if he could, he would change their lives permanently. If he could bring himself to be like those Blue-blooded bastards, he would kill one and move them all into a sprawling estate, giving them the ending they so richly deserved, in poetic justice. Unfortunately, they were all stuck in this hellish existence together.

He was supposed to *wait* on those asshole rulers—the Masters, the Elites, the Rich, or Nobles. Different names for the same ruthless bastards. Tilly had been taught about them all his life while living under their bullshit rules, classist labeling, and mistreatment.

Because of all that money, they were tainted. They were corrupt in the marrow, quite literally; their inbreeding was infamously frightening. The older generations seemed to produce crazy offspring whom they didn't just tolerate, but held in pride. The worst of the worst rotten Rich were willing to do *anything* for their own satisfaction whatever the cost; both opportunistic and sadistic. One could never tell what they wanted, either. You could only presume it would not feel good. It never seemed to matter if it was bloodlust or asset greed, as long as they beat the gluttony of their mighty parents. He'd be lying if he said he didn't live in fear of them. He did. They basically ruled his life, but he'd be damned if he would beg and serve them, acting like nothing was wrong.

Being a Rebel was risky as hell. He'd figured out the only way to survive without licking their boots was to hustle and sell himself like Misty, only at least he was stronger than her physically. He did not get beaten or raped nearly as much as she had. This made him feel responsible for her, even though he watched after her as much as he possibly could, and she was quite stubborn.

The same was true of all of his bunkmates, in one way or another; they sold whatever they could get their hands on—drugs, sex, stolen goods—and they all protected one another. Together, they eked out a miserable, bare existence in an abandoned warehouse building condemned long ago by some previous generation; people who probably hadn't realized how lucky they were.

They were the poor, and worse, as Rebels. Independent of the meager crumbs handed out by the Elite, they also flew in the face of every law to make it on their own as hustlers and street kids. After the last war, the epidemic, and 'The Fall,' the Rich Rulers had revealed themselves—as if the assholes had just been biding their time, waiting and watching. That, or they'd actively contributed, which was another idea often theorized. It didn't matter, the end game was the same; they had risen with all their power, money, and influence—like some octopus—thrust deep into everything that had built America. They had already been buying government officials long before Tilly was even born, now it was just blatant control. There were no votes anymore, no illusion of democracy for anyone but the rich, and so the cancer of the vicious circle of this oligarchy kept metastasizing and spinning on track.

The same families were always in power because they had always had money, and there was no real middle class. Tilly had been taught financial and political history, despite there being no real institutions of learning anymore; there were plenty of stories from the old-timers.

'*They*' had risen, and only the poor remained to take care of all of their little wants and needs from minute to minute, be it a pleasurable orifice, a punching bag, or in the case of the traitorous Workers, a willing maid. The Poor—the ones who'd survived the damn plague—had further divided themselves into the Rebels and the Workers. They were like bees—only with a whole group of queens. There were more Workers because most people shut their mouths and followed like sheep, blinding themselves to the overwhelming truth. Tilly understood this meant his kind were quite outnumbered.

Even more dangerous, just to make a card, they *had* to break the law. They basically took their lives in their hands getting out of bed. Tilly knew, too, the way things had been all his life (and still were) simply could *not* be right... He really wanted to do something about it, but he could barely keep up, could barely keep down his fright, and honestly, sometimes, he barely wanted to live. The Elites had made it like this on purpose, of course, because in truth, Tilly and his crew were the traitors, but he'd heard that every great thing that had happened in history—including the creation of this supposedly once-great country—had begun with some kind of treason against someone. Rick said you didn't make it anywhere without stepping on someone's toes, and Tilly thought he was probably right.

Little Fry was this tiny, funny-looking, wrinkled thing; his face was always wrenched up like he knew what lay ahead for him. Tilly held him carefully as he gave him some milk in an old glass bottle from the cooler they kept for food; its ice has melted a while ago, leaving tepid water. Fry was literally a miracle baby—in more ways than one. Tilly knew he certainly deserved more than what they could give him in this world, which was why Misty had tried so hard to terminate, which she could have been locked up or executed for. It was a pregnancy that was rare in the first place, since most of their class weren't fertile. They either had trouble getting pregnant—ever since the epidemic, birth rates had gone down, everyone said. When a poor kid did get knocked up, they usually couldn't carry it...or worse, it came out wrong. In rare cases like hers, many would take matters into their own hands, like she had.

There were no doctors for them; they couldn't afford care, even if it was offered. Luckily, there were a few people this side of the tracks who knew of things they could never comprehend. They'd gone to Dr. Rick—an acquaintance and friend to all of their kind—and he'd given them some herbs like parsley, cinnamon, pennyroyal tea, and old OTC drugs like aspirin, and she *had* bled...yet she'd continued to grow. When she got bigger and even more desperate, he'd told her about the coat hanger. He described a time more than a century ago that he called The Jazz Age, when women apparently did that kind of thing a lot because they drank 'bathtub booze' and got pregnant. You were supposed to be able to give yourself a miscarriage if you drank a shitload, but Doc said not to do that and they'd listened; after all, he knew a lot more than either of them.

Misty had sobbed the whole time she tried to rid herself of the growing baby in her, even though she'd known it was a mercy killing, but eventually it was obvious she was going to give birth regardless. Misty was so torn between her natural feelings of love for the little thing and terrible guilt about the world she was bringing him into—not to mention her very real and justified fear of something being horribly wrong, especially after everything she had done—it had been a horrible time. But he'd turned out fat and healthy, as Doc said.

It had been so hard, having enough food, not to mention getting the right things together for the baby that was determined to come. Dr. Rick had helped them tremendously, but there was only so much he could do. Misty ended up having to go out on the streets again, even though it was so dangerous. The Rich did not want traitor street kids like her having babies because they were against the Elites' so-called natural order. At any time, one of those rich asshole johns could have taken Misty, and Tilly would never have seen her again. It wouldn't have been the first time, either; plenty of their friends had simply disappeared after trying to do something about their situation. Shit, all Greg had done was graffiti some places around the city, and he'd been gone within the week. In reality, it hadn't just been the plague that had affected their fertility, Tilly was smart enough to figure that out, too. The Workers seemed to have babies like rabbits. Tilly and Misty had both come from 'subversive stock,' both their parents had been activists, back when you could still do things like fight. Tilly's parents would have be so disappointed in their son, but he did what he could…for the time being.

Luckily, Misty knew some of her johns, and she only went with them, saving every little card she could get so that she had enough food. Rick had helped score some vitamins for pregnant girls, and they'd gone into The Hills and broken into a house to get some baby stuff from a Rich bastard's nursery. That had been a pretty good score, but they'd almost gotten caught by one of the damned Workers. Now more than ever before, Misty had to be careful not to be caught or killed by *them*, or the traitorous Worker bees, or else Little Fry would grow up without a mom in addition to everything else.

Dr. Rick always pointed out the irony of their class to him; no one got away from serving Them in some way, and he was right. Misty and Tilly *did* wait on them…in the worst ways; they just didn't do it with their heads bowed. They made it impossible to live if you didn't serve their rigid purposes, fit specific molds, and in that way, Tilly supposed they were subversive. Rick had taught him that word, along with many others; he had so many books, which were now banned—well, at least to poor street kids. Rick was definitely at risk, which was why he went about his business very quietly; he even had a day job working for The Elites so they wouldn't suspect him of any kind of treason.

Tilly was always asking him for his books, but it took forever to read them since he'd mostly taught himself after his parents died—Rick was now continuing the lessons. There were schools, but what they learned was how to serve the rich, and above all, obey. Tilly had not gone because his parents had refused to send him—not that he'd had any interest anyway. There weren't any real lessons. Rick told him school used to be all about books, but now there weren't any at all; they were absolute contraband. You were better off having a shitload of drugs—the Rich didn't mind that at all; drugs were legal, too, and expensive as hell if you wanted their *real* drugs. Lug made drugs from the weirdest shit; whatever he could find to mix together, really. Lug was smart like Rick; he knew chemistry, and he called himself his own 'guinea pig.'

Tilly had heard of a time in history—not that long ago—when there were places filled with books for free, and when even poor people had things like televisions and phones you could carry around. He'd even heard about those magic machines Rick called computers, but it had not been like that for a long time; not since the war and the plague that had followed. Tilly's parents hadn't even seen a computer, nor had he or Misty. Dr. Rick was quite a bit older; he'd become like a parental figure and teacher, and Tilly was grateful. Maybe if he kept up his studies with Rick, he could do something; that was what Rick said, that Tilly was meant to help the revolution. He could only hope as he looked into Little Fry's face, suckling away on his bottle. He was truly a miracle. "Meant to be," as Rick said. He was only 6 months old, now, and Misty was out hooking again, shooting up Lug's Aryan or Heroin, whenever she could get her hands on the real shit. She stumbled into their makeshift kitchen area, her hair a mess, to look for something to pep her up for the day.

"Aw, thanks, babe," she said. Tilly shrugged.

"S'okay, I like it; he's pretty cute for somethin'

so funny-lookin'." He grinned at her and she smiled back, but her eyes were forever haunted, deep circles lining them from sickness and lack of sleep. Or too much, Tilly didn't know.

"Is he wet? I'll change him, just lemme get some Kick in me, okay?"

Tilly wanted so badly to tell her to stop, but he couldn't; he understood all too well.

"Okay. I gotta go meet up with Rick in a little while."

She rolled her eyes. He hated when she did that.

"He's getting your hopes up, Till; there ain't gonna be no *revolution*, you know that. We're stuck like this until we either give up and serve them, or give up and die. And if ya ask me, death is better." He hated when she talked like this. "Here, give me him; you go learn to read, as if that's gonna help."

He handed Fry over and told her she was being a bitch but he loved her anyway, then he left, thinking she was probably right.

Two

Mary awoke to the sound of a baby crying in the other room. Shuffling feet and low murmurs told her she was not the only one awake this early; even with her eyes still closed she perceived the shadows passing before the bright sunlight streaming through the cracks in the boarded windows. In a rundown, four-bedroom house, she lived with ten other people and their kids. Like her, they were all from the wrong blood, wrong side of the tracks, wrong everything. Sometimes the really nice Masters would call them 'commoners,' but that was simply a euphemism for servant. Mary was a maid for the Watson family who apparently were distant relatives of the famous Rockefellers; they certainly seemed rich enough. Mary didn't know for sure, didn't *want* to know; she kept her head down, took her pay and was grateful she didn't have to live like a rat like the poor fuckers in tents under the bridge or squatters in condemned buildings.

Mary rolled out of her little air mattress on the floor and turned on the one lamp she owned.

"Aw, man! Mary, Goddamn, girl, we can't *all* work at the fucking Watsons...goddamn crack of fuckin' dawn..." Liz groaned and put her pillow over her head, turning her back to Mary.

"I'm sorry, hon."

"Yeah, yeah." She seemed to mumble and slip right back into snoring almost simultaneously.

Liz was a call-girl, usually working only at night. Liz had been smart; she'd gone to work at an escort service with a madam, their clientele were rich, so she didn't really get hassled. The poor schmuck street kids and Rebels were hustlers on corners in the worst parts of the city, so there was a difference, despite it being illegal. At the moment, though, she was a 'kept' mistress, which always confused Mary; if a man wanted a woman all to himself, why would he chuck his wife for a prostitute in the first place? She didn't ask questions, though; she found it best to keep all her thoughts to herself. A skill she'd learned in school that had earned her high marks, and given her certain privileges others didn't have.

While she got benefits, she also had the burden of more responsibility. She'd been with the Watsons since she was old enough to first do laundry, then the rest of her chores, and while she had of course been taken advantage of, there were so many times she'd avoided that awful fate by simply being invisible. She'd also walked in on her employer and his various family members doing appalling things; had she been anyone else, she was sure she'd have been killed by now for all she knew, but she kept plugging along, quietly, and discreetly.

It wasn't like she didn't make mental notes. She did. She simply kept them to herself and her journal; even her friends and roommates knew little about her work. Then again, they were all Workers, they knew the cost of gambling with their employers' personal affairs—even speaking about them was risky; if one person said something amiss... She had friends who weren't as adept as she was at keeping secrets and *they* liked to gossip; a couple had paid dearly, too. She didn't understand why they couldn't keep their mouths shut. She'd gotten herself a diary with money she'd saved, and she kept it in a niche in the wall, behind the wallpaper.

Most of the Workers in her house couldn't read, anyway; they didn't need to for their jobs, and that's how it worked. True education was partly necessity and mostly privilege—unless you had money to attend decent schools, you'd best show some talent for secretarial skills if you wanted to read and write, otherwise it was labor all the way. Her aptitude had been tested quite young, and she was also fortunate that her parents had served in the same capacity, and had the same ability to shut the fuck up about the Elites' idiosyncrasies.

THREE

The estate was palatial; Mary didn't even have all the words to describe it, but every time she showed up for work, it took her breath by the sheer size. She had to climb her way past all the perfect landscaping, up the long curved driveway to simply get to the front—with its beautiful columns and archways—another walk led around the main house and other outer buildings to the service entrance where she made her way inside.

She hung her jacket on the hook and said hello to

the other maids on duty; one was Mary's predecessor, exhausted and leaving for the day. They hugged warmly, Sophia's old frame bending with time, it seemed.

"He's in a mood today, hon." Sophia winked at her.

"Parker?"

"Who else?" Mary helped her shove her jacket on to leave. Parker was the youngest son of the Watsons, still at home, and quite a handful. At only fourteen, he had cornered Mary several times, his eyes gleaming, and when she'd tried to demurely refuse his advances, he would get brutal. No one had to teach Mary about sexual sadism, she knew all too well the more she screamed or fought, the worse it would be, so she'd kept quiet as always, and eventually, unable to keep himself hard, he'd lost interest and she'd thanked a God she wasn't even sure existed.

His father was the owner of several corporations—she didn't understand how it all worked, only that everything she or anyone bought basically paid him. Parker's mother, too, was from a very wealthy family and she worked from home on her 'PC'—a machine she barely understood—mostly wrestling with stocks that manipulated the rest of the world; what little there was left, anyway. They didn't seem to work nearly as hard as Mary, and yet they had more money and power than they or their following generations could even spend, but that was also because they'd been born into their money.

Mary looked lovingly after Sophia, her only living parental figure. Her parents had both had bad hearts, and Sophia had taken her in, training her for her position, helping her to read, everything. The only reason Mary didn't live with her still was because she'd had her own family to tend to and Mary had no right to intrude, despite Sophia's protestations to the contrary. She had an open invitation to Sophia's full house with her husband, three daughters, two sons, and now their children, and while that was awful tempting it was also important for her to be independent.

"Hey, Mare," Toby conspiratorially whispered and nodded her over. She smiled; he was a mischievous sort, always with a sharp wit, a glint in his eye, and smart ass answers that got him into trouble.

"What's the haps, Tobe?"

"I got a little somethin', sweet stuff," he chuckled, holding out a palm with two pills. She gratefully took them, giving him a little kiss. "Oh, that's all I have to do, huh? Wow, cheap date. Remind me next time I'm feeling a bit frisky." She laughed.

"I think you're forgetting I have a vagina, babe," was her retort. He mocked confusion, screwing up his face.

"Oh, is *that* why we ain't together? I knew there must be a reason." He winked at her and tapped her butt with his own hip. Mary loved his attitude, and thought he was brave for many reasons, not the least of which was his sarcasm, humor, and obvious preferences—the Rich liked their staff to breed, the only reasoning behind anyone's sexuality being looked down upon that she could understand. After all, she knew for a fact that certain Watsons had their own predilections; their family members could be—and were—absolute predators, in fact; a trait they seemed to foster and nurture. He reminded her to be careful—*after* she'd already popped the pills—and then told her (again) to call him if she somehow found herself alone with Parker. Toby was like a brother, and if it weren't for the mitigating circumstances, she would have seriously thought of him in a completely different light; it was getting time for her to find a mate, or else she might find herself paired up with someone the Law chose for her instead, and she did not want that to happen.

Toby twirled through the gigantic kitchen, humming while he got breakfast ready, and along with two other staff members, began prepping each culinary delight that each family member had requested for the day. She got the tiny bit of certified, official mail together and set trays for them, and soon enough, she was buzzing. She wasn't absolutely positive of what she'd taken, but Toby usually had the good stuff, not some street garbage. The day was in full swing.

FOUR

Tilly and Rick had decided to take a break from their lessons and now they were flying high on hallucinogens. Rick explained that ages ago, throughout time, humans had taken different kinds of psychoactive drugs in a kind of journey through their mind, into the larger universe; it was called a vision quest by the Native Americans who used to live here.

A person could always do drugs for fun, but to do it for deeper reasoning and higher consciousness, one had to prepare; there had to be a certain ritual to help the mind concentrate on the real objective. Rick had taught Tilly how to meditate, how to take all of his noisy energy and focus on one goal: to become a tool for change and start a revolution.

Tilly didn't know how much—if any—of the world was left, and it certainly seemed too crazy to say 'change the world,' but he couldn't let himself think of the rest, he had to take it one step at a time. If it weren't for Doc, he would never have the courage to even think he could do anything except maybe scrape by, maybe do one nice, big score, but Rick, he'd turned him around. Tilly no longer thought only moment to moment, especially now that Little Fry had come along. No, now Tilly could see a big picture, and he did not like it, could not tolerate the idea that he and Misty—and Rick, too—would die like their parents as just more victims for the bloody-handed rich monsters and leave Fry all alone in this big horrible world. Change had to come, and it had to start somewhere, why not with them?

"Oh, man, that taste! Gets me every time!" Tilly threw his guts up into a bucket as Rick assured and cajoled him, wiping the heavy sweat from his brow.

"Get past it. Concentrate on the light in your third eye; watch the pinhole open like the shutter on my camera... Let the light come streaming into your mind, flood those neurons..." Doc's voice was smooth and even and pot smoke hung thick and heavy in the air, a pungent perfume spiced with the sour-bitter green taste in his sinus cavities.

With his eyes closed, he could see amazing colors, and a tiny pinhead-sized hole, light in the distance, and as he breathed, the colors breathed and throbbed, ebbing away from the light as it pierced through. Rick's voice was far away, now, an echo of an echo somewhere back in time, and as light poured forth, suddenly, Tilly was traveling on his quest.

He did not know exactly what signs or advice he was supposed to see or get on this trip, but he certainly hadn't expected to see and feel what he did. There was a girl his age waiting for him, and he felt her energy all the way deep into his bones, like he knew her, but he had never before seen her in his life. She was beautiful, graceful, and serene with an unassuming wisdom of quietude, as if meditation came to her as naturally as Tilly's angst came to him. She was mysterious and familiar and all at once he knew their destinies were tied together. He didn't know the why, when, or even how, he just knew it was true.

When he was back in Doc's house, recounting everything, he tried to recall if they'd had any conversation, and he could not; there wasn't much more to his journey than that, either, which in a way was kind of disappointing.

"Don't be so hard on yourself, kiddo, you're just starting." Rick said, smiling. Tilly was having none of it; he was almost pouting, his brow furrowed, he tried to understand.

"I'm supposed to be…becoming better. For the cause. Not havin' a wet dream, dammit!"

"I doubt it was that. Look, neither you nor I know who she is in the grand scheme of things, but in your big picture, it appears as if you've got someone to meet. You won't know where or when, but either it will happen, or maybe she's a guide and you'll recall some important info she gave you. Patience, my boy." Doc was so mellow and faithful, Tilly could not understand it, but he was still learning; Rick was probably right, as usual, but still, he was disappointed in himself.

"I just wish I could change things now. I...I feel worse now that I think I actually can do something."

"Of course you do; that's why ignorance is bliss, kid." Rick looked at him soberly and said, "'It's always darkest before the dawn,' ever hear that before?" Tilly shook his head, thinking about it, knowing Rick would explain. "It means things always seem worse before they get better. That's what you're going through: growth, and growing, changing, it's hard, ok? Just try to go with it." He patted Tilly on the back and ruffled his hair like he'd always done. Tilly felt like a kid, but it was not unpleasant.

He tried to cheer up, tried to concentrate on his other lessons, but he couldn't shake the girl or the feeling from her his visions had given him.

FIVE

Mary had a very strange and busy day. As she left in the evening, for the first time she could remember, she'd seen and heard shit she couldn't put out of her mind. She wished for once she could talk about it, but there was no use in that, so after work, she and Toby left together to get something to soothe their nerves. He was frazzled; one of the kitchen staff was still fairly new, which meant young, and she was driving him nuts. He didn't have the patience Mary had to have.

They walked back towards his car, around all of the gorgeously ornate architecture that still managed to awe them. The estate was in the Hills, away from all the riff-raff of the city where people like Toby and Mary lived. They hardly spoke, there was hardly a point since they couldn't talk about work; they knew the rules.

By the time they hit the drug shop, where the druggist knew them both by name, it was late. Finally, Toby began to get his sarcastic humor back as they started talking about other things. She forced him to let her pay with her card at the pharmacy then they took off toward her house to get some clothes to spend the night with Toby. She was sure Liz would be appreciative, and she needed a break, too. They would pop some more pills, watch a movie, and talk; she'd get far better sleep in his nice bed—something she was still saving to acquire.

That night, amidst some tossing and turning, Mary had the clearest dream. In it she met a guy she'd never seen before, yet knew she was supposed to know in the weirdest feeling of intuition and déjà vu she'd ever had. She told Toby the next day as they got dressed for work.

"Oooh, maybe he'll be your Mate; sorry to disappoint, hon, but you don't have the right equipment for me." They chuckled together.

"That's fine," she replied, acting sad, "I spent ages crying over you."

They bantered like that the whole time, managing to get to work early. Almost immediately, she knew it was going to be another day for her journal.

Parker was becoming obsessed with some other horrible subject, now, by the look of the old booklets he had laying around. Women and men strapped and chained, their faces contorted in looks of utter terror with leather-clad men built like colossus torturing them. She couldn't help but notice he'd lost any interest in sex—or in his case, *rape*, though she'd known it wasn't really just sex when he had come after her, it had seemed like attraction at first, before he got nasty and brutal. Now, he'd become severely withdrawn, locking himself into some room off of his own—a door she'd never noticed because it had been behind his bookshelf—doing God knew what. Mary wasn't worried about him, she was worried for the rest of the world, really. A flash of the new, very young girl serving as sous chef in Toby's kitchen kept popping up in her head. The girl could only be about ten to twelve in Mary's estimation.

After trying to wait on Parker, she made her way to Watson's office, and overhead more information that she didn't want. Of course, *his* twisted business deals were one thing, Mrs. Watson's *plans* were another. In spite of herself, Mary listened, hearing two voices with that impeccably educated English associated with the Rich Elites. They were talking about certain delicacies and some party for very important people; Mrs. Watson was a Socialite, and prided herself on her affairs to impress.

She just *felt* this kind of suspicious dread, though she could not pin down anything in particular as the cause. She felt it deep within, and that depth of premonitory feeling brought back a glimmer of her dream, just for an instant; those sparks of intuition and déjà vu shivered through her again. Holding her breath, she continued eavesdropping, a part of her wondering—with more than a speck of guilt—why, but the rest of her mind sure she must bear witness to…*something*.

"Yes. We'll have those nice sweetbreads. There are a few statesmen I expect to have, too, mother." Peyton Watson was speaking with her mother, as it turned out, apparently going over the menu.

"Darling, you must try the brains, you *do* still have the recipe I gave you, yes?" Her mother's face never seemed to change.

Peyton nodded, and her mother added, "You need the very purest! Now, for preparation, you have whom?" Her mother was abrupt and sounded like an expert.

"Oh, mother, I have my ways." Peyton and her mother shared a conspiratorial grin. Her mother patted her, saying, "I certainly hope you have it all figured out, my dear. And just what is wrong with employing the Service?" Mother Watson gave her daughter a withering stare. "Since when are they not enough, hmmm?" Peyton sighed.

"It will be fine, mother. Relax. Here." She actually got up and got her mother the expensive liquor from the carafe herself. Mary almost gasped then; she'd never seen any of them help themselves—except to what wasn't theirs (she was thinking of the men who had taken what she had not wanted to give).

"Now, then. When do they arrive?"

"Oh, the day after tomorrow, right after our 'scholarship program' goes into effect."

She tried to shake that same feeling she'd been having, something like a vague perception of some plot not totally understood in her mind—perhaps she didn't really want to figure it out; she just didn't *know*…anything, for sure.

Mary knew she needed more information, that she'd have to essentially snoop, something she had never done before. She drifted silently down the long hallway from Mrs. Watson's office, reeling from a precognition she'd never had; she knew things had to change.

Six

"Mary, you've got me worried, what's eating you?"
Mary shook off her thoughts, not daring to tell her
mentor that their bosses' dirty laundry was now so
unsettling she was thinking of rebellion. Sophia
would be crushed; all her training and dutiful
raising of Mary…she couldn't disappoint her this
way over a few strange days bouncing around in her
head.

"Oh, I might have a little bug, don't worry,
please." Mary hugged Sophia, still rattled; she clung
a little too long and Sophia noticed, feeling her head
and fussing over her like the mother hen she was.
Mary reassured her, "Oh, Soph, it's okay, I
promise…just that time of the month." Sophia held
her shoulders and looked at her for a few moments,
and then she was gone.

It was the early morning hours of a busy day,
everyone humming around, and Mary knew today
was the day of 'the statesmen' party that Mrs.
Watson had been so feverishly planning. That
suspicion and dread had not faded, but increased; it
was like someone had switched on a light in her
mind that just got brighter, illuminating possibilities
that used to be nothing—just blank, negative space.

Mary made her way to Parker's room only to find him missing; she knew he was in that mystery room beyond his own, and she did not look forward to her task. His huge, flat screen television, mounted on his wall above other entertainment machines, played a crazy movie full of violence and classical music. The characters were all dressed in the same all white costume and spoke heavily accented English, yet she didn't understand what they were talking about. The narrator spoke of 'oh, me brothers' and 'droogs' and sat in some kind of restaurant or club full of white mannequins drinking what could only be milk but which they called 'moloko.' Mary shook her head; Parker was always watching the strangest films. This one was old but looked futuristic, and she wondered what the hell it was, but she hadn't time to figure it out; not today. She made her way to the northernmost corner of Parker's bedroom—where his bed was opposite his living area furnished with the large screen and an overstuffed couch large and comfortable enough to sleep in itself. The movie with British accents and Beethoven's music faded into the background as she rounded his bed.

As she approached the closed door of what she had presumed to be Parker's side of the attic, she heard it: a slight mewling sound, weak and miserable. Mary did not want to, but knew she must investigate for a couple of reasons. For one, she couldn't assist Parker in starving himself and expect to keep her job, and for another, she'd never find anything out unless she got up her nerve.

She got Toby, and he motioned her forward as she turned the knob carefully and quietly, easing the door inward. She grabbed her mouth, in spite of the fact that she was not really shocked; it was still surprising. She was confused and disoriented by the space. There was a gigantic, finished room where she had thought only storage space existed. Somehow, he'd made it into a kind of dungeon; with dim lighting and various tools everywhere, it looked like some shed from those old horror movies she watched with Toby. Hammers, drills, saws, and other frightening-looking tools she couldn't name were everywhere—hanging, tossed aside, and littering the floor. She heard noises up ahead and around the corner.

"Aw, man!" Parker's voice, then a crash from deeper within the cavernous space. As she rounded the corner, she saw the bare construction of wood inside the huge mansion's walls. Shadows leapt here and there from Parker's candlelight lanterns. The eldritch flicker lent itself most appropriately to the creepy place. She looked back at Toby, who'd followed her halfway; she could just see him in Parker's bedroom, but it seemed like another world.

She tiptoed, being as sneaky as possible. Metal clanging sounds and the occasional curse from

Parker were the only indications that the place was inhabited. The space had several tables and workbenches and when she finally saw him, he was sitting at one of them. Thankfully, his back and side were toward her and he was too busy to turn around because if he had, she was fairly sure she would have fainted.

Blood covered what she could see of him—splattered all over his apron, smudging his face, and streaking his hair; his hands and arms were virtually covered up to his elbows with the various colors of fresh and old, drying rust-colored claret. She tried to tell herself it wasn't blood, but only a glance revealed a cat hanging from the rafters by a noose, its guts spilled open, dripping viscous fluids.

She did not stay long enough to see what he was working on so diligently, all hunched over like the madman he so obviously was. She almost shit herself as she turned on her heel and ran back as quietly as she was able, trying to trace the same way she had taken. Toby got closer in her view and she was finally able to shut the door, gliding it gently back into its track, the click even more comforting than Toby's hug. He pulled away from his squeeze and looked expectantly at her, questioning with his eyes; he cocked his head, and she debated with herself on what, exactly, she should say.

"You're white as a sheet!" He giggled as he realized his joke about her complexion—she may have looked sick, but she was not white by any stretch, and never could look pale. She was one of the darkest people she knew. She couldn't help but smile and smack him on his shoulder. She almost burst into a hysterical laughing fit, some lunatic nervous tick, but she knew she better not do that or she might not come back. She sniffled as she realized her eyes were running, too. Toby was serious; he handed her a tissue from his pocket and tried to comfort her.

"Do you wanna talk about it?" He said this with a shift in his eyes and posture, his discomfort clear to her. She shook her head and took a few breaths.

"No. That kid just…worries me sometimes," She did not like the shakiness in her voice, but she had to fake it; they both knew better than to talk about the poor little rich kid.

"I just… I don't think I should bother him about food…" As Mary spoke, she could have sworn she heard him sigh in relief, it certainly reflected in his face.

"Okay, sugar, look, why don't you write a little note and leave it? Or, we could knock and do it the right way…" As if on cue, another blood-curdling sound of pain echoed through the space beyond the door and into the main bedroom. They exchanged an uncomfortable glance and tried to cover the awkward position they found themselves in.

"Look, sweetie, I've got to get back to the—" He

started as another sound pierced through the walls; Mary could swear it sounded human, but then again, most death cries sounded alike.

She remembered when Parker was only ten, he'd had an imported snake—some exotic animal that did not belong in America, let alone their part of the country. He loved to feed it live rats and as it grew, he worked its appetite up for larger rodents like squirrels and then rabbits. Inevitably, he would just have to feed the damned snake when she was around, watching and helping tutor him—not at all worried about the kid she thought just had a simple crush. She'd seen almost every single little cute, fuzzy creature you could name get its life snuffed out by that fucking serpent as it coiled and squeezed the cute little furry mammals and rodents to death, their shrill cries so upsetting to her that she'd cried a couple of times, but she had to put up with it. Next, the reptile would unhinge its jaws to swallow the prey whole. Rabbits' screams were very similar to what she heard now, behind the walls of the Watsons' mini-castle. Apparently, she was right; most mammals sounded similar when they were in pain or dying. A chill ran down her back, goosebumps popping out on her arm, hair standing on end. He'd always been a violent little prick; his parents must have been proud, they obviously financed his little project to give him extra room.

Toby held her shoulders, giving another short but

sweet hug and kissing her on the cheek. She gave him a weary smile and dismissed him.

"Go on, Tobes, I can deal...I mean... it's not *really* a big deal, you know? He's just a kid, learning about himself and all that," As she said this, she almost laughed—not just because it was utter bullshit, but also because she was only a few years older than Parker. Still, it was a decent cover, and Toby silently gave her a short nod and wink. He couldn't tell that she choked back another loony laugh; that some shrill howl that marked some borderline in her sanity and morale was trying to bubble up from inside her being. She fought it off, trying to clear her mind of the dead cat in the weird 'serial killer compartment' off of Parker's main room.

"Okay, honey. Sorry; just tell the Watsons he isn't eating if you have another problem, okay?" Mary nodded, thinking this situation was fucked; she was damned either way, really. At least if she told—and it would have to be worded precisely right so as not to seem like some petty tattle—she would still be reprimanded, but maybe not fired.

"I'll be down to help in a bit, okay?" She kissed him again and he took off, leaving her in Parker's obsessively tidy room, or studio apartment was more accurate. She'd never had to clean up after him, save for his food tray and dishes; the rest of his room was immaculate, which used to impress her.

Now, she stood here, looking around at what she could do and wondering how in the hell she hadn't gotten into trouble for not cleaning; honestly, she didn't know—even with all of her impeccable training and impressive skills—if she could ever clean it to his standards.

"Oh, well…" she mumbled to herself, grabbing the laundry hamper from his walk-in—a closet bigger than the dining area in her house.

Mary went about gathering all the laundry, and she noted how excited and almost frantic the Watson family was about the day. It seemed disproportionate to any important lunch, dinner or even all-day event only the Super-Rich would host (and boast).

When she got back to the kitchen, she noticed the hors d'oeuvres were starting to get plated. Toby ruled the kitchen almost like a sergeant, making everyone move like well-oiled machinery. She was sneaking a smoke in the coat pantry, looking into the huge kitchen beyond, feeling guilty that she wasn't helping. But before she could even ask if her assistance was needed, Toby marched over to her, a strained look on his face.

"Mary, honey, I really hope you have other domestic affairs to tend to; I mean, you *should*, today of all days." He was brusquer with her than he'd ever been and she found that it did sting, even though she understood. She was also disappointed;

she thought this might be an excellent opportunity for her to look around.

"Well, I thought you could use th—" He cut her off with a quick wave of his hand.

"Honey," he breathed deeply, and a horribly cold look crossed his face for just an instant, which again caught her off-guard; this was not the Toby she knew and loved. He seemed like one of them, in fact. His prickly cold demeanor was gone as quick as it had appeared and he smiled warmly at her, his little reserve of patience softening his voice into explanatory rather than callously demanding.

"You know what's going on, right? We're not breaking the rules by talking. You understand that this is a crazy-important dinner party for Congress, right? Honey, you're just not experienced; I need experience today, okay, my sweets?" His voice and face were completely normal and Mary thought she must be even more on edge than she'd thought. Toby was anything but cold; he was one of warmest people she knew, and one of only two people she cared so deeply for she'd die for them. She really needed to reign her craziness in, especially since she now had to find another way around the 'Watson Castle' to find answers.

"No, I know. I'm sorry, Tobes… Hey, do you have anything? I left my shit at your house…" She trailed off as he smiled, digging in his pockets and handing her an entire bottle. The label said

'Relaxation Combo Kit' on it, consisting of a few different types of downers, pain killers, a couple of sleepers, and maybe one peppy pill, give or take.

"Aw, thank you!" She almost squealed and stood on her toes to kiss his well-shaven cheek that always smelled great from his cologne and just a vague hint of food from being in the kitchen constantly.

A deafening metallic crash made her jump, and he yelled behind him at the staff. Then he looked at her, grabbed the hand with the meds in it, and said, "For God's sake, Mary, open those now!" There was that snappy tone again, but it wasn't nearly as cold as she'd thought.

"Give me one, babe. Goddammit, these fucking *morons*!"

Pushing in the door to the gigantic kitchen, she heard him yell at his underlings.

"What are you idiots *doing* in there? I can't leave for less than *five* minutes?" He was incredulous. "Are you *kidding* me?!" Now he was angry, which was his personality; he'd always had a fiery temper, was passionate and great in the kitchen, which was exactly why the bosses never reprimanded him. He took the two pills she gave him and chewed them dry. She hugged him and almost ran to the laundry room, leaving him to storm through his kitchen, yelling at the staff.

She could still hear him even as she got into the

laundry room, which was technically another building. The size of two large kitchens, it was always warm and always smelled wonderful. Like the kitchen, it had a huge island for a folding table along the length of the rectangular-shaped out-building. An ironing board was set up in the far corner with hanging racks along the wall. Various detergents, softeners, deodorizers, perfumes, and starch all topped the shelf above the hanging clothes.

She was next to the line of industrial machines against the wall; a load was already going in the washers and dryers, 'with all kinds of digital bells and whistles,' according to Sophia. She leaned against it, heat seeping into her bones as she popped a nice mix of downers and pain pills, grateful he'd given her the whole damn bottle. She didn't know how she'd make it without *something*.

The amount of laundry was staggering; she knew there would be more, but this was absurd. She began to relax as she sorted the laundry; her plan would be almost effortless now, it was just a matter of thinking it through.

Yet once she got into a familiar rhythm, pangs of indecision stabbed at her; she wanted so badly to go back to her ignorance. She argued with herself that she didn't need to know anything, simply take her check and be grateful she was a Worker in lieu of a street kid; she told herself it was a compliment she'd heard what she had, which was really nothing at all, now that she thought about it, right? So what if her rich bosses liked to eat weird shit? That was no crime. So what if they *did* commit crime everyday on the stock trade marketplace, right? She almost burst out laughing; she was being ludicrous. They were her employers and more importantly, they were the all-powerful, all-knowing Rich who made all the rules! She most definitely did *not* want to get in their way, and that was that.

SEVEN

Having made her decision, she hummed along as she did laundry. How simple, to load or fold, and wait for the bells and whistles to tell her what to do next. She was lulled by such a familiar habit; soon enough, the previous days and all those weird feelings of dread dissipated like the steam from the iron.

She was so relieved, in fact, that when she got to the second floor to make up the long table in the formal dining room (used only for receiving proper guests), she didn't even think much about running into Sophia, despite the strangeness of her being there at all, let alone her attitude. She was *never* there late in the afternoon and should have been long gone. They passed each other with not a second thought…at first. Somehow, she missed the difference in the China cabinet, as well. Between being chemically slowed down, the comfort of an old, repetitive routine as well as the relief from any responsibility for the dread and suspicion that had been her constant companion had induced a kind of mesmerism. She was so mellow, in fact, that she missed these things that would have caught her eye just a day before. She thought she might be missing things 'accidentally on purpose,' really; she didn't want to know. She'd decided to turn that flood light off in her head.

"Oh, hi, Sophie." Her voice was low but not slurred, slow but not noticeably intoxicated. "Wh— are you getting extra hours?" Mid-afternoon and she was sweating and trying hard not to show it, but the humidity of the laundry room and running around left her hair damp. Sophia seemed busy, but not frazzled; she *seemed* as cool and collected as ever.

"Well, there you are, dear. Look at you. You know how important today is, don't you?" Mary nodded. Even if she hadn't eavesdropped, anyone could tell they were getting ready for some large supper.

"Now, see how important it is to keep your head down? After helping with this banquet dinner, your service will be invaluable! They'll know that you're irreplaceable." Sophia stroked her chin, beaming with a pride that Mary could feel, and she was grateful. More proof she was doing the right thing.

"Thank you, Sophia. I sure hope so. I mean, I learned from the best, you know." She smiled like a child, basking in Sophia's pride and maternal glow.

Suddenly, Sophia's eyes shifted around to see if they were alone, then they turned hard. Her grip tightened on Mary's shoulder. Those bony hands Mary had thought were weakening from age and a lifetime of service were now more like talons, digging into her flesh. She again had that 'Twilight Zone' feeling; *nothing* was right, nothing was as it had been just a second ago or how it *should* be— how it always had been. How could that be? Sophia's teeth clenched, her jaw muscles working… Mary just froze. She had never seen her this way before, not even when Sophia had been completely aggravated with her.

"Now, you listen. I know you've been snooping. I *know* you've seen and heard things that you don't *like*." She wrinkled her nose in disdain, mocking Mary when she said 'like,' as if it was a reference to something like pickiness—some mundane creature comfort you'd belittle a child about in order to make them grow up. The tone was hard enough to wrap her head around; Sophia's instant change from sweetest grandmother ever, to cold, hard boss was mind boggling, but it took a few minutes for her words to actually sink in. She continued unabated, Mary's stunned look doing nothing to affect her.

"…I'll be goddamned if yet *another* of my trainees are going to fuck up *my* family's good name. Freemans have served Watsons for generations, since *long* before The Fall. I have Watson bastards in my family! I'm on the inside, and my future generations should be taken care of for life, do you understand? Don't even think that there's any way around this; we *serve*, that's what we do—it's what we were *born* to do. Today is your final test; you either shut up, keep your head down, *or* you end up like your dimwitted parents, snooping and tattling…as if anyone would care! They are the powerful, no matter what they like…here I thought you were a natural. What in the hell has gotten into you? It's a damn good thing you've kept your trap shut, given me time to talk to you."

She wagged her finger and Mary wondered if she'd actually downed a hallucinogen by accident and this was all just a bad trip. This was *not* Sophia…could not be! Mary had known her since she was eight years old—this sweet, motherly, even *grand*motherly type who led by example and positive reinforcement had *always* been her bedrock. She depended on Sophia's good nature and patience—she just hadn't realized how much, until now, when she needed her. She was glad she hadn't said anything; she tried now.

"Bu—wh—I d—don't kn—know wh—" Mary

could not speak. No matter. Apparently Sophia had enough to say for both of them.

"You just do your job, and you do it right, you understand?" Again, she changed, from that calloused tone back to a more plaintive plea. "You want to make me proud, right?"

Mary nodded, not trusting herself to speak. Sophia patted her hip and gave her one more penetrating look—as if she could tell what Mary was thinking—and then she walked away, leaving Mary wide-eyed. It was then that she noticed the other things she'd never known about before today, as if someone had stripped a veil from before her eyes—one she hadn't even known existed.

The wall-lining China cabinet—supposed to hold a variety of the Watsons' best wines, gold-plated China, collectible Lalique crystal heirlooms and the like—revealed an entry to what she'd previously assumed was the interior of a wall. Somehow this extravagantly giant, dark-wooded piece of furniture that had been antique long before The War, had a portal, like in a book. She was reminded of that wardrobe story from ages ago that she'd heard as a kid, and that made her think of all the other stories and their hidden doors—the rabbit hole, the looking glass, and of course that great golden brick road— all leading to those other magical worlds that somehow peacefully coexist next to so-called reality. Mary was still young and full of wonder, despite living in such a dreary world, and she was thinking now that maybe those classic children's writers had known something. Perhaps they'd written more fact than anyone cared to believe. She was quite literally awestruck.

Her arms still holding new linen for the table, she felt like she was in a dream, and the feeling would not shake off. She went through the motions, removing the old white table dressings and fashioning new napkin holders and settings in the red that had been requested, all the while hearing all kinds of strange noises from the rooms beyond that secret door. Should she look? Should she spare herself anymore threatening surprises? She'd even thought of running, because one thing *did* stand out about what Sophia had said; they *had* known her every move, they *had* been aware of her the whole time—of course they had.

She thanked that Maker she still wasn't sure about for her natural demeanor and the stiff upper lip Sophia had engendered in her personality. She thanked whatever 'Powers that Be' for her intuition and ability to think without saying a damned word. Again she thought how good it was she hadn't said anything. A shiver ran down her spine as she felt that damned déjà vu again, this time it was not at all pleasant, but a feeling that she was nothing but a puppet or plaything and that she had never acted of her own free will. Instead, all of this had somehow been written and she was just part of some larger plot just playing her bit. The dominoes were all in order, falling just as they had been set, and there was absolutely nothing she could do to control them. She did not like this feeling at all; in a world of abject powerlessness, this was like the coup de grâce of all the hopelessly enslaved.

Why didn't they simply make robots, then? Why did they have to keep the lower class breeding as slaves, as Workers? She didn't understand how human labor was better for the Elites when the only difference was their very ability to think in a free-willed fashion; humans could incite riot or cause anarchy—like the street kids. Thinking of them almost made her feel better; *until* she realized that they may just be part of the 'Big Picture,' as well. They too would simply be going about their parts in some predestined show, written by the Rich, unknown to everyone but the writer of this 'reality play.' But surely she was going too far; surely they weren't *engineered*, right? After all, they only caused trouble, rebelling against everything, breaking laws, and going against any order; they lived very hard, short, horrible lives just so they could do what they wanted, but was it just the illusion of freedom? Again, that shiver, as though perhaps they were all part of the same damned setup, and *no one* had any choice, save for the Masters themselves. She wasn't even sure who, exactly, that would be, either. She rubbed the goosebumps and chills from her arms, her teeth gritting against an inner chill that was yet one more thing she had no control over.

EIGHT

A cry snapped her from her reverie and she knew exactly where it came from; the hidden door behind the china cabinet. She jumped, almost spilling the centerpiece of flowers from the table. Sophia's voice played over in her head and this time she clued in on the fact that the woman had mentioned her parents—her parents had snooped, she'd said; parents Mary barely remembered. What in the hell had she meant? They had both worked for the Watson family, along with Sophia, and they'd worked themselves into the ground...or so she'd been told.

Whatever the reason, that suspicion and dread had resurfaced, and in force. Now there was something else, too—a worried curiosity she simply couldn't slake. She looked around the huge dining area to see if she was being watched though she knew very well there may just be hidden cameras that she wouldn't be able to find.

Two great, tall windows imposed on the space. Taking up most of the walls on each opposing end of the huge table in the center of the room, sunlight streamed through the thick, velvet curtains that were drawn to each side. The windows revealed the magnificent spreading space so expertly manicured outside; rolling greenery that led to flowering vines that entwined the walls of the estate and the bushes in front of the window were perfectly cut. She couldn't see the flowers, but she knew they were there, and at the edge of the property were gargantuan trees, beautiful and older than the hills.

The house had been built long before The War and following plague, which might go a long way toward explaining why, exactly, they even *had* secret passages. Now that she knew about the cabinet, she recalled a choice area in the library, as well, like in the movies. Actually, with all of the grand fireplaces, there was no telling how many hidden doors there were, not to mention *where*.

Everything was quiet now; the roar of silence was almost worse than the cries she'd heard in Parker's little abattoir. She made herself breathe and worked around the table until she found herself at that special, secret door. She looked in and found that—like Parker's room—there was far more than simply the framework of the house. Some strange padding was on the walls, covering the internal woodworking. A smell like the kitchen wafted through the small corridor that led to the left and deeper into the very house itself. What the fuck was going on here? Mary couldn't turn back; she *had* to know what in God's name was going on, what Sophia had been on about, and why. She had to satiate the dreadful knot of some kind of suspicious intuition that had been tightening in her gut for days.

Walking forward, she heard familiar voices; Toby and Sophia had somehow made their way into this area, which in itself was as big as a house. As she turned the corner, she was almost sure they'd heard her—their powers of sensing when she was around were sharp as hell and just a bit creepy. She listened.

"...I told her; now it's up to her," Sophia was saying.

"I know, but mom, come *on*, do you really think she's *ready*?" Mary drew a sharp breath, holding her hand over her mouth. Toby had never spoken of his parents; she'd assumed they were dead, like hers. A strange bang accompanied other noises she just couldn't put her finger on, but that sounded at once familiar and suspicious.

Rounding the corner, she was surprised to find another kitchen—much smaller than the main kitchen downstairs, it was nonetheless a kitchen, and the entire hidden room was dim, as though they simply couldn't provide enough light for this sinister space. That was the least of her worries; it was *not* what made her stop in her tracks.

Appalled, she covered her mouth as she gasped and almost screamed. She could not believe her eyes, did not *want* to believe, either. There was Toby, wearing an apron that was like Parker's; stained with what could only be blood. On the chopping block island was meat, and suddenly some of Toby's statements about purity of food and sweet meats totally made sense. She was sickened, and her stomach retched as she squeezed her face with her hand. Her heart beat was so loud she was sure they'd hear it; it jumped up into the back of her throat as her guts sank. She slid down the wall, in utter shock and hysteria. She knew if she let go of her mouth she would vomit and scream. If she'd stayed on her feet, she would have fallen.

There, right before her eyes, was a dead human *child*, its little body cut open, a meat cleaver sticking up from the cutting board. It looked like a horror movie, and her mind rebelled, whirling around the truth of what she was seeing; it had to be fake, it just had to be a doll, right? Surely this was a prank…

The small stove had a pot and skillet sizzling upon it; the steam drifted toward her, and she recognized it. That smell was a common one; every day in Toby's kitchen, for at least one meal that scent could be sniffed—it was distinguishable from every other meat. "Only the purest," he would say; in fact, she'd just served some to Parker. All of the suspicion and dread she tried to pass off as paranoia were now distilled into a feeling of pure disgust and shock so severe she didn't think she could stay lucid; she felt she was going to black out any second...or maybe she just wanted to, which was likely; anything to make this all go away.

This is not real, this could not be happening... this mantra went through her brain over and over, a denial that made her grit her teeth so hard her jaws felt like they were breaking. There wasn't just a child; there were several. Like animals in some slaughterhouse, they all had some horrid wound gaping in their little foreheads, their faces reflecting their youth and innocence. They were eating fucking children. She didn't look close enough to see which kids they were, she didn't have to; they were the kids of The Poor.

"Oh my God, oh my god..." Someone was repeating this sentiment constantly, and she noticed with dismay that it was her voice, far away, as if she were floating above her body. She realized she was making noises too late; they were already looking at her and it was terrifying.

"Mary, hon, what did I tell you? I need experience today." Toby was so cavalier, so off-hand, that it furthered that feeling of 'Twilight Zone' displacement.

This can't be real, right? They're just babies! Her mind was reeling, spinning out of control.

"I *told* you today's 'test' was vital, didn't I Mary?" Sophia admonished. "Now get up from there, dammit! Don't be a complete ninny."

"Bu—bu—but that's a—ba—" She stammered and sputtered all over herself. She again almost puked when she felt, as well as *heard* her own stomach growl.

She knew this smell, and she was further repulsed when she realized she had probably eaten it herself. They were fucking cannibals! They...*ate*...fucking *children*! She shook her head, which did not help her since the room was already revolving around her.

"Okay, Mary, settle down, now, okay? Now just think about it; you don't want Peyton to come in here, do you? You don't want to end up on this slab." Toby spoke in even tones, as though he was speaking to a child...

"*...a dead child?*"

He laid the knife down by the child, and began coming toward her. She saw a nice-sized refrigerator next to the oven, which was cooking something, too. There was another dead child in the sink; it had the top of its little scalp peeled back, the androgynous little face crumpled forward to reveal the white-ish colored skull beneath and that, too, had a cut through it. Again, words drifted through her mind: "Darling, you must try the brains," Old Mrs. Watson had said. She understood all of a sudden that *all* of the Watson family ate human meat; three generations of cannibalism. Shock, awe, terror, and revelation all mingled together to make a convoluted mess of her mind.

Pieces of the truth of the situation began to emerge; mysteries she'd never considered to be nefarious were now suddenly clear. Missing Workers' children, their signs up all over the city—signs that grew old and weathered and never had any solution or closure were now explained. Cases in which the parents had thought the cops had just been lazy, the assumption being that all kids ran away—to where, she'd always wondered, and now she knew. She was sure that Rebel kids must be used this way, too, and yet all this time she had believed them to either be in jail, in a camp for rehabilitation/re-education, or even executed.

Toby was before her now, his hand out for her to hold and hoist herself back up. Only then did she feel the tears streaming down her face; she'd been crying silently for a while, snot leaking from her nose, and hadn't been the wiser. Her mind was captivated by the dead and butchered children, her mind still rolling back over these terms she hadn't truly comprehended; this must be the 'purest meat' that with glittering eyes Toby had spoken of—an in-joke she hadn't been in on until now…and it was no joke.

Her eyes were fixated on the kitchen and dead

kids she wanted so badly to erase. Words like 'cannibal,' terms such as 'baby killer,' and questions flew through her head as she shivered uncontrollably, probably in shock. She wiped her face with her own apron, again feeling nauseous. She reached for his hand and he pulled her up, his strength surprising for how small and wiry he was.

"Bring her here, son. Let's have a nice sit-down and think, shall we?" Sophia held her hand out toward a little dinette set across from the kitchen area. There were cards dealt out on the table along with pennies, and the dining area was more like an employee lounge. There were even spaces—like little cubbyholes—for the Workers' things, along with a coat rack in a space much like the service entrance. She saw another door that was almost hidden from view, more from the camouflage caused by the same black padded material that covered all the internal walls, and which seemed to insulate the area.

"Okay, Mary, now quit crying, you'll be fine; once you learn to deal with our bosses' weird...appetites, you'll find out how being loyal to the Watsons has benefits." Toby was trying to speak in those smooth tones reserved for hysterics, neurotics, and children; children, for God's sake! Her mind screamed at her, but Toby's soothsaying continued. When she didn't respond, he spoke to Sophia.

"Mom, I think she's in shock, her skin is cold and she's not speaking!"

Sophia made her way over but Mary simply stood there, lost in thoughts in her own head, unable to move she was so freaked out.

"Come on, honey. Let's sit down…" Sophia led her to the dinette area and sat her in the sofa. "Toby, baby, make us some tea."

Mary mumbled a tamer question to keep her mind off of the horror-show elephant-in-the-room.

"Toby's your son?" Sophia smiled.

"Not just mine. He's half Watson. I told you, my family lines cross with theirs; it's why he has such a desired position so young, why he went to Cordon Bleu Academy, and why he's never in trouble. Yep, he's set for life. There are a lot of Mr. Watson's half breeds working for him; they also get private allowances so no one else gets jealous… But you needn't worry about that now; you've got to work on your objectivity. It's just meat, right? It's simply a delicacy for them, and besides, most of the kids have something wrong." Sophia stroked her hair, putting it behind her ear.

"I need you to straighten up now, honey; we have got to get this party ready!" Toby brought her some hot tea and asked if she had any pills left. She nodded and he told her to take a couple more.

"We're prepping for a couple of important samplers, so you drink your tea, and then you will go back out there and finish your job. I mean it, now; I know you can do this…" Sophia patted her hand and the pair went back to the kitchen.

The sound of the knife slicing through flesh was so disconcerting. Her brain would not stop its exhaustive chatter, and she almost spilled hot tea all over herself.

Thunk!

The sound made her jump; the meat cleaver. She didn't even look up, she simply put down her tea, gathered her courage, and ran.

NINE

Tilly and Rick were working on weapons. Every day was a different lesson with different challenges, most of them intellectual, but if they were going to have a revolution, they would have to fight and they'd need weapons. They were working on bow hunting, crafting their own bows and sheaths of arrows and personalizing them. Doc made up a paste of crushed oleander leaves and some other choice herbs from the garden to make poison-tipped arrows surely to be lethal as hell.

Tilly went out hunting down materials in various rundown and condemned buildings all over the city. They used their bows to hunt some food rather than shooting the meat. Whether it was rabbit, birds, raccoon, they ate it all; you couldn't be picky when you were a street kid. The grocery stores were closer to the Hills, on the border of the urban jungle and the 'burbs; they charged exorbitant amounts for basic food products, especially meat. Tilly, Misty, Lug, and Rick only had so many cards; even on a good, busy day or after a large score, they could only afford so much. They almost never bought meat or refrigerator stuff for Tilly's place since they only had the cooler. Rick had a fridge and he would keep things for them, but it was rare they could afford that stuff—or even wanted it because it was so much—and it wasn't easy to steal.

Tilly liked hunting, but he didn't like hurting animals. Doc had taught him to thank the Great Spirit for the nutrition, and thank the animal's spirit for its sacrifice, and that made him feel better. He also learned to use every bit of it; he'd put skins out in the sun to dry just like his hand-washed clothes.

Misty promised to cook for them if Tilly rounded up enough to eat, so he made his way toward the grocery, toward the 'burbs where there was more land, greenery, trees, parks, and therefore more little mammals. Sometimes, if he went into the Hills and west at the right time, he could go to the few houses of 'survivalists'—people who had been 'prepared' and grew all their food, kept animals for milk, eggs, and meat, and had plenty—and he'd snatch a little something. Their wild berries were delicious. He'd stolen a pig once, but there was so much meat; they'd all gorged themselves and had to stuff Rick's fridge, and still there was some left, which luckily Lug ate; he could out-eat anyone.

On his trek toward one of the farms, he saw her; she was running like there was someone after her, but he didn't see anybody but her. He was caught off-guard, utterly by surprise, and instead of ducking into a hiding spot, he just stood there like a stupid deer in the headlights. Luckily she was just a Worker and he didn't see any Masters, or else he would have kissed his ass goodbye.

As she drew closer, a strange feeling grew within his chest and stomach; he knew her...but how? He knew he'd seen her, knew she was very important, and yet she was a total stranger—a stranger that was obviously a traitorous Worker loyal to the damn Elites; he should have been sprinting away from her, but he found he couldn't.

When she was in earshot, he could hear her crying and repeating something to herself. She was a mess and it was obvious that she was in some sort of trouble. This made him feel a bit better.

"Well, if you skipped out on a shift, I guess you won't be worrying about me, then..." Tilly mumbled to himself when he decided his curiosity and the situation called for some investigation.

"Hey! Hey, you. Stop, girl!" He yelled at her, waving her over to him. She stopped dead in her tracks, sobs wracking her lithe frame. She was a beautiful girl, about his age, with dark skin supple and shining in the sun. Tears shone on her face, and dried tracks showed she'd been crying for a while. She was obviously embarrassed; she took her apron and smeared her face, trying to wipe all signs of her grief away.

"Hey there, are you okay? I mean, I know that's kind of a dumb question, but you know, I mean…well, I mean are you hurt?"

She stared at him like she couldn't believe her eyes; she rubbed them and looked up again. She was halfway over the bridge from the Hills and he had just gotten on it from the urban side. She shook her head and he took that as her answer. He walked slowly toward her, trying to understand where he'd seen her before. He finally got it as she walked toward him. He was absolutely stunned; his vision quest had come true! She was the girl of his dreams, or visions, as it were.

TEN

Mary's nails dug into the flesh of her palm as she looked at the boy coming toward her. She couldn't believe that he'd just walked right out of her dream. She had that strange sense of déjà vu as well as the excitement you feel with a brand new gift; she also had a hard time swallowing the situation all at once on top of the horror and repugnance she still felt acutely.

He was speaking to her, the guy from her strange dream…this whole day had been an exercise in the bizarre and horrible, what more was left? She was afraid to ask. But, somehow, she was not afraid of him. As she approached, they looked at one another with absolute recognition and something about his presence made her feel as though she could talk to him. Despite his bow slung over his shoulder with a sheath of arrows, she did not feel threatened. At least he wasn't eating little kids! They drew closer together and somehow knew the next part of their journey had not even started yet; another domino fell into place…

Typhanei Celeste and Rayven McCoy were born December 17th, 1979 in Virginia, but have lived in Florida most of their lives. Although twins with similar interests, they are quite different and have forged very diverse paths in life. While Typhanei has moved back home to be with their mother, Rayven retains her independence. They can only be seen together when Hell has a cold.

Typhanei Celeste's first love was reading, which came in handy as she was bitten by the entertainment bug as a young child and had a flair for the dramatic arts, resulting in a theater award by age fourteen. At that time, she was also playing guitar, and wrote poetry and songs until she had to stop due to injury and illness in her twenties, when she began focusing on research and prose. She finished her first manuscript in 2013, and has written several short stories as well as a novella. She has a genuine love for learning and her favorite subjects span the arts, sciences, and history. She recognized a love for the art of taking pictures in 2008 and is following in her mother's footsteps as an amateur photographer. On a full moon, you can see her skulking about, trying to attain the perfect picture of night and the stars as seen from earth. She lives in Tampa, Florida with her beloved mother and believes reality is nothing short of a psychological construct in a vastly misunderstood universe.

Stay up to date on her latest stories at:
typhaneiceleste.wixsite.com/typhanei
Follow Typhanei on Twitter:
https://twitter.com/typhanei
Find Typhanei on Facebook:
https://www.facebook.com/typhanei

GRIM HOPE

by T. R. Wiland

Amala sat in her hospital bed, her short brown hair caught in the light of the sun peeking out from behind the rain clouds beyond the window. She did not pay attention to the drip attached to her little body, nor the uncomfortable gown she had to wear. She was used to it by now—she had been there a long time. She was not sure how long, but she was sure she had missed a lot of homework. She missed her friends, and playing outside. She wasn't really sure what was making her sick, but she felt fine at the moment. She spent most of her time colouring, drawing, or playing with her doll or stuffed rabbit.

Most of the time she was tired, sore, and lonely. She didn't like the multitude of tests she had to go through, the scans and needles; needles were always the worst. She cried every time and the nurses tried to calm her, but more often they just made it worse. Today she was particularly exhausted; there was a lot of walking, and she was already weak and malnourished. The day had just taken a lot out of her. She was nearly ready to sleep, but heard a sound that made her smile. She looked up from brushing her doll's hair as the door opened.

"Hello," said a little voice. Amala looked up. She knew the one who had spoken. It was another boy from the ward. He never said his name, but he was friendly and played with her. He had wonderful stories that Amala loved to hear.

"Hello again." She grinned, glad to see him again. He had been visiting when the nurses weren't around, particularly at night time. He didn't like the nurses, he told her, and so he hid when he got the chance.

"I had more tests today," Amala told the boy sadly. He was wearing his blue pyjamas, as he always did when she saw him. "I hate tests."

"So do I." The boy nodded as he came over to sit on the edge of her bed. "What sort of tests?"

"A scan and a needle." She screwed up her little face as she remembered it. "There was a scan machine... It looked like a big one-eyed monster with its tongue sticking out... The nurses told me off because I was afraid it would eat me. The grown-ups don't get it, how scary everything is!" She drew her knees up to her chest and sighed. She didn't like how scared she was of everything. The nurses, the doctors, tests, even just being in the hospital itself frightened her. Everything was so white and bare and the lights hurt her eyes. It was never this bright at home. There it was dark, with plenty of places to hide.

Her house had lots of nooks and crannies she could seek refuge in. Her mother collected a lot of things—books, magazines, clothes…boxes and boxes of random, fun stuff. They were stacked all through the house, piling nearly to the roof. When her Daddy was cross with her, she often found a place to hide from him. He liked to collect metal and car parts in the back yard, and books, lots of books. Her Auntie called her Mummy a 'hordor' but Amala didn't know what that meant. She just liked to hide and play with the cats. Her favourite was Mittens, a light grey fluffy cat that Amala had looked after since he was a kitten, and their older cat, Soup, had babies. Many of the others were given away, but she was allowed to keep him. Mittens went missing one day and Amala had been so sad when it happened. Her brother had been getting rid of smelly rubbish in the kitchen when he claimed to have found Mittens, but Amala wasn't allowed to see him. She remembered her brother saying Mittens wouldn't come back. Amala was even more sad and confused; she loved that cat. Was he mad at her for not finding him? She missed him very much.

She'd told her friend and he had looked sad too. He had been just as sad as she was. He understood her. She had come to trust him and tell him more than she told anyone else.

"Sometimes I like to pretend I don't have to be here anymore," the girl confessed.

"You can leave, you know," the boy told her cryptically.

"I wish I could!" She sighed, then shot him a little smile. "I would eat cheese on the moon and go to a princesses' ball every day!" She laughed softly; the boy laughed, too.

"You could sail there on a pirate ship!" He grinned. "And you would never have to return!" Amala thought about that for a moment.

"That would be nice," she muttered to herself, then looked at him. "But it would be good if you came with me." The boy stared at her in surprise.

"You would wish me to join you?"

"Yes. We're friends!" she insisted.

"Very well; then it is settled. We shall escape this place together! Leave it to me!" He petted her hand gently, then passed her her stuffed rabbit. "Do you want to hear some more stories?" Amala had previously told him she had trouble sleeping, but when he told her his exciting adventures, she dropped right off. The girl bounced a little in her bed excitedly, but stopped when she was hit with a coughing fit. But she did manage to nod her head.

"Yes please," she managed, taking the glass of water he passed to her. "Thank you."

"You are most welcome." The boy smiled, but Amala always thought he looked sad. She wondered if it was because his Daddy hurt him too. He put the glass back and took her hand as she settled in to listen. He told her about a magical ship that sailed not just the sea, but in the clouds, where she would be free to see the sun as much as she liked. Slowly her eyes lowered and closed, and his words became a vision.

Amala giggled as the fresh, salty air whipped her hair around. She held her little hands up in the air and let out a whoop of joy.

"This is so amazing!" She held her hands out like a plane and zoomed around the deck of the wooden pirate ship. She felt so alive, so free.

"Ahoy matey!" called a familiar voice. Amala's little face lit up like it was Christmas.

"Nanna!" she cried and rushed over to her. The woman scooped her up and hugged her.

"Come on, little bee, you are the Captain! Where are we going?" Her grandmother smiled. Amala looked around to see there were people with her— her big sister, Stephanie, Mr. Hammond, her teacher at school, and Grandy, too, a few friends from school, and... the boy from the hospital! He

looked at her with a mysterious little smile through the crowd. Amala raised a hand and pointed to the sky.

"We are going to have a picnic...on the Moon!" the girl cried decisively. A cheer went up and her friends wandered around to do their work. Amala headed up to the ship's wheel, the tapped the centre of it twice with her finger, and with a heave and a creak, it rose from the blue water, and began to float upwards into the pink sky.

ഗ ⁊

Over the coming weeks, she noticed her friend would visit her every day. Sometimes he sang her songs in a funny language, and he began to teach them to her.

During the days, she noticed that everyone seemed even busier than before, so much so that some of the nurses had forgotten to bring her her lunch on more than one occasion.

There were many tests, more scans, more needles. Her friend always came by at the end of every day. He always seemed to know what would cheer her up. On the days she felt hungry he would bring her a big chocolate chip muffin. She would always split it with him.

Amala always looked forward to Thursdays—

visiting hours were from 11 until 2, and her mummy would visit her on those days. She used to bring Amala some cookies, ones she made herself. Then she made cake; Mummy said she made it, but only used the containers of the cakes at the shop to carry it. Mummy was very clever to make it look and taste the same as shop cake. Then her visits came later into the day, and they got shorter, too. Amala wished Mummy would come on other days as well, but Mummy said she was always tired and sometimes had other things to do. The last few visits Mummy only brought her a sandwich like the ones in the machine downstairs. Last time she forgot to bring anything.

But still, Amala waited to see her Mummy today. It was not cake or sandwiches she liked, but to see her mother and give her a big hug. 11 o'clock came round—Amala knew the time as she learned it in school. She waited a little longer; maybe Mummy was just a bit late again. Eleven thirty came and went, then twelve passed without interruption. Then one o'clock. The little girl just sat, waiting, hoping that the door would open. Finally it did, but her face fell when she noticed it was just the nurse.

"Everything alright, dear?" she asked.

"Uhm…is my Mummy out there? She was supposed to visit today," Amala managed in a small voice.

"Oh…I'm not sure, dear, I'll go and check." The

nurse hurried off. It finally got to two o'clock. The nurse must have gotten busy, because she never returned. Neither did her mother. The girl held out hope right up until the time read five minutes past two. A feeling of cold settled over her, and she lowered her head into her arms. Her little body shook as she began to cry.

She barely ate that night. The nurses seemed worried and tried to get her to have dinner but she didn't want any. She felt heavy, like she was weighted down and squashed into her bed under a lead blanket. She curled up for ages and eventually cried herself to sleep.

She awoke to feel someone sitting beside her. She looked up, her expression hopeful, but it was only her friend. She felt a little disappointed. Clearly it showed on her face.

"Am I not who you were expecting?" He asked with a little smile, he did not seem bothered by her reaction.

"My...my mummy didn't visit me today." The girl mumbled in a shaky voice, her earlier sadness returned; tears stained her cheeks and she was curled up against herself. The boy's smile dropped. For a moment he looked angry, but the expression was quickly replaced with one of sympathy.

"I am sorry," he told her. He didn't say anything

else, just placed a hand upon her shoulder and let her take the deep breaths to calm herself. After a little while she let out a big sigh and sat up, then leant over and hugged her friend. He petted her head and began to tell her some more stories.

"Once upon a time, there was a child, a little boy, much like you, and he was always outside. He wandered the forests and trails, always climbing trees and rocks near his home, always exploring. He had an older brother who was always having to fetch him. The brother was never one to go outside much, and was often reading or inside and didn't seem to bask much in the sunshine. They were very different, but cared about each other very much." A sad look crossed the boy's face and Amala was filled with curiosity. "One day, the boy had gone out to play, and the boy's father told the brother to go and fetch him for dinner. The boy had been out all day, which was strange—usually he was not out so long. The brother searched and searched. Finally, after a long time, when the sun was beginning to set, the older brother found the boy…at the bottom of a small cliff." There was a pause and Amala petted the boy's hand. He continued after a moment. "The child was hurt, very badly, and the brother felt panic and guilt. How long had he been there? The brother rushed to his side and tried to help him, but the boy could not walk. He smiled, saying that he was glad to see his brother before he passed." The boy shook his head. "It was then the brother heard a voice. 'You cannot save him.' The brother turned to see the God of Nothing behind him."

"The God of Nothing?" Amala asked.

"Yes. In those times, the people believed that when you stopped living, the God of Nothing took your soul away to the Underworld. He spoke, and told the brother that the boy must go with him now. The older brother begged the God to spare him, and offered to go in the boy's place. The God thought carefully, and said, 'If you wish to save him, you must agree to become my servant.' The brother agreed." The boy shifted in his seat. "The brother took the boy back to their family. After that, the God took the brother away, and he was imbued with special powers and given grand, otherworldly tools. From that day, the people came to know the brother only by his new name. And when their time had come, Death would be the one to take them away."

Amala sat in silence for a few minutes. Then she turned to the boy with a smile. "I like that story. The brother was nice. If he came for me, I would not mind." The boy looked at her in surprise, but then smiled. He sat back and began to tell her some more stories, until she fell asleep.

The next morning, Amala did not feel very well. She curled up in her bed and stayed under the covers; she felt cold and did not want to get up. She heard the door open, but pretended to be asleep. She did not want to talk to the nurses right now.

"Amala?" called a female voice. One of the nurses. "Ah, she must be asleep."

"Probably for the best, she needs her rest." That was a male voice, it must have been one of the doctors. "When she first came in...I'd never seen such severe malnutrition in my whole career. God, what kind of life must she have had?"

"You wouldn't think she was dying from the look of her." The nurse said sadly. Amala lay still. *Dying?* She was dying? Her friend must have heard the nurses talking about it, that's why he told her that story! "Is there anything that can be done, doctor?"

"We have run multiple scans, so many tests, there is nothing we can pinpoint, nothing definitive. I called her parents, but her mother hung up on me."

"She didn't visit the girl yesterday either."

"It seems she is unable to face her daughter. Perhaps she blames herself. Or maybe she has given up."

"That's absolutely disgusting...." After that, Amala stopped listening. Mummy had given up, because she was going to die. She'd heard adults talk about death, about how scary it was. But Amala wasn't afraid. She knew the brother from the story, he was Death, and he was nice. If she had to go, well...she would miss her mummy and everyone…but she was sure it would be alright.

It was a long while later that she eventually sat up and ate some of her breakfast, left on the tray by her bed. The nurse bustled in again and smiled at her, the kind of smile people use when they are sad or worried, but pretend everything is fine. Amala had seen her mother use it a lot.

"Hello there, Amala! Good to see you're awake."

"I feel a little funny today, but that's okay. When I leave here I am going to see my Nanna." Amala smiled. She felt a little better. The nurse gave her another one of those smiles.

"Ah, yes. You know I spoke to the Doctor and he said you're doing very well. That you might be able to go home soon—ah, excuse me, dear." With that, the nurse hurried out of the room.

Amala spent the day drawing and writing. She wrote a letter to her mummy and her friends, and she drew some pictures of some of the people she knew, including one of her friend that visited her. It was a quiet day, one that made her remember everything before it. Today felt like the start of something new.

Amala awoke to the sound of her door opening; it didn't sound like a nurse. Slowly she sat up and looked over toward the sound. There in the moonlight was the pale face of her friend. The girl grinned happily, but it faded when she saw his sombre look.

"What's wrong?" she asked worriedly.

The boy let out a gentle sigh. He looked down at the ground for a moment, then back at her. His expression was regretful.

"It is time." A strange feeling filled the girl, there was a tingling sensation on her neck and a weird cold wash ran down her back. She saw shadows grow darker, and the boy before her began to change. He became taller, his limbs extended, his skin grew paler, and his little dark dressing gown seemed to be alive as it curled around his form, becoming darker and more fluid, as though it were smoke. He towered over her now, looking down upon her as a large shape loomed behind him: wings, two massive dark wings extending from his back. Amala stared, wide-eyed in wonder. She looked up to his face. He was paler, and a man, not a boy, but she knew this was her friend. His eyes were the same.

"You're an Angel!" she gasped.

"Yes. I am sorry for the deception Amala, but it's time to come with me now."

"You're the older brother from the story, aren't you?" she asked, gazing up at him in awe. Something in her had resonated upon meeting him. She had known he was special but she found herself unafraid, and not all that surprised. His wings were beautiful. Black as night, but in the dim light of the room, they shimmered with many colours: pink, blue, purple, and green. Death was said to be frightening, but Amala did not see that at all.

He nodded, but with a slight frown.

"You...are not afraid." It was not a question. Amala shook her head.

"The place you have to take me, what's it like?" In response to her question, he gestured to a light glowing from behind him, stepping aside so she could see the source. There was a doorway, bright from what seemed to be daylight beyond it. She could see little but the streaming brightness, her gaze shifted from the 'man' before her to the door, and back again. Suddenly she seemed hesitant.

"Do we...have to?" she asked, her nose crinkled up. The Angel standing before her, bowed his head.

"I am afraid so." He looked her over. "You want to stay? You told me you didn't like this place."

"Well..." Her face showed a look of concentration. "I will miss my mummy. I...didn't get to say goodbye."

"I know. I am sorry, I did not think she wouldn't come." Amala didn't seem wholly convinced, and pulled out another crayon and began to draw.

"I better leave her a note," she said thoughtfully, making careful lines on the paper. "What is it like through there?" she asked the Angel as he waited for her. She still seemed unsure. He offered her a warm smile.

"It is warm, and you can have parties like in your dreams, sail ships, and explore castles..." He paused, and his smile widened. "Your grandparents are waiting for you too,"

Amala looked up with a gasp. "Nanna and Grandy are there?!" Her face split into the biggest smile. The Angel nodded. The girl quickly finished her drawing, and laid it neatly on the bed. She took a deep breath, her stuffed rabbit in her arms, and bobbed her head.

"I'm ready." She walked to his side and was about to take his hand when she stopped to look up at him. "If I go, will you still visit me?" The Angel was stunned.

"You wish still to be friends...?" Never had a human asked him this before, but she nodded enthusiastically.

"You are my friend; you made this less scary." She reached out and her little hand took his. The Angel stared at her for a few moments, before giving her a wide smile. The girl just grinned back at him, and with that, he led her through the door of light.

SHOPPING CART UTOPIA
by Helen Andronaco

Dawn came along quietly that fateful Spring morning; the weather remained too cold for bugs, and most birds were still on vacation down South. There wasn't much traffic as the sun rose. Trees were starting to bud and the winter's snow had finally melted into the ground, which made morale high in the parking lot outside of the local Easy-mart—at least, higher than it had been all winter.

Outside, several shopping carts gathered at a designated space and discussed their passions. Shopping carts are typically very actively interested in human beings and enjoy eavesdropping on all conversations within listening range. They are very quiet and even if they risk moving on their own, nobody catches on. That fateful Spring morning, several carts had gathered at the farthest designated space from the Easy-mart building, right next to the street and the Bonus-mart lot, where, for the record, there was no designated cart space and therefore rarely any Bonus-mart carts around.

However, that particular morning there were. It was a human's doing of course, carts were very bashful around carts from other lots, even the neighboring ones. It didn't matter that most of them were made in the same factory, they just weren't on the same team and that made conversation awkward, though polite. Shopping carts as a general rule were never rude unless thoroughly provoked.

At the designated Easy-mart shopping cart space next to the Bonus-mart parking lot, a group of eight or nine carts had assembled to chat. It was turning out to be a lovely sunny day and they had assembled quite peacefully, shared gossip and questions about their favorite humans, and offered support to one particular cart who was upset by a human who'd backed into it in the darker hours of the morning.

It was at the moment when one shopping cart said, "Quiet, there's a human coming to her car at the Bonus-mart lot!" when the carts immediately quit discussion and watched and waited, and listened.

The human woman was pushing a Bonus-mart shopping cart towards her silver hatchback and talking on her cell phone. She was noticeably happy with her life, as the smile on her face was bright and warm and even contagious for the carts to feel uplifted by her presence; her laughter carried loud and clear across the yard of grass that separated the lots from each other and as she drove away, leaving the Bonus-mart cart half up on the curb, everyone missed her.

Shopping carts are typically shy and so none of them wanted to be the first to start chatting once the coast was clear. It was actually the Bonus-mart cart that broke the spell.

"She wasn't all that great, you know." the cart said. "She was very rude to the cashier, at any rate."

If shopping carts could nod, several of the Easy-mart carts would have nodded knowingly. One of them replied, "Human women can be quite difficult to understand."

"Especially the ones who drive those large vehicles." Another chimed in.

"The human who backed into me this morning was a woman, and I had thought she was very nice."

Instead of turning back to a Bonus-mart cart rack, the Bonus-mart cart hopped the rest of the way onto the grass and moved slowly towards the Easy-mart carts. "The thing about humans is, they're always in a hurry. Male or female, young or old. They may pretend to be nice or mean, but all they're really thinking about is rushing to the next thing. It's very tiring, if you ask me."

Some of the Easy-mart carts were taken aback by the Bonus-mart cart's forwardness and backed away from it uneasily, but the others stood their ground—they were manufactured more recently and consequently more trusting towards foreigners than the older carts.

"I like it, though." said one of the newest Easy-mart carts. "I like the very busy people. They are quite efficient and make me feel highly useful."

All shopping carts agreed that feeling useful was grand, and typically such a statement would have been met without any argument.

But the Bonus-mart cart did not agree. "But we're taken for granted by them, you know."

An older shopping cart spoke up, "Taken for granted? They make us."

"That may be so, but they use us." the Bonus-mart cart retorted. "They make us so that they can use us and then forget about us, and then throw us away when they can't use us anymore!"

Some of the carts gasped while others contemplated the Bonus-mart cart's statement in silence. The removal of inefficient carts was not something they liked to discuss and therefore the issue was typically ignored, as carts preferred to be carefree. However the Bonus-mart cart continued, "They don't know we have feelings. They don't know we watch them, care about them, remember them, understand them—and I don't think they would care if they did! They would lock us all up!"

"They wouldn't lock us up." said one of the carts.

"Humans are very unpredictable," said another. "They might lock us up. Then again they might not. I don't think I could say which."

"Whether they would or wouldn't is irrelevant," said an older cart. "They will never know about us."

All the shopping carts fell silent to consider what the older cart had said. It was right. Humans never would know about the carts; they communicated in completely different ways and that was that.

One of the newer Easy-mart carts finally broke the silence. "What's the point, then? Why do we all waste our time doing what they want? If they don't appreciate it, why should we?"

The Bonus-mart cart said that it didn't know, and all the carts were stunned into silence.

At that exact moment, an old man pulled his truck next to the Easy-mart space and grabbed the Bonus-mart cart to use for his shopping experience. This caused several of the Easy-mart carts to silently gasp in horror and wonder, and when the old man was no longer in sight, they began chattering about it like old ladies at a tea party, unable to think about anything else.

At first, the Bonus-mart cart was nervous. Initially it debated breaking free of the man and rushing back to the Bonus-mart lot, but it knew it was too late. Visions of the Easy-mart managers tearing it apart piece by piece for trespassing ran through its head, and as the doors opened to let them inside, it was so nervous that it jammed its wheels and came to a complete stop right in the entryway.

But the old man was stronger than he looked and just pushed the cart again and they were inside. The Bonus-mart cart waited anxiously for an employee to notice and cause a commotion, but the old man just did his shopping and nothing happened. Nobody seemed to care. After passing five Easy-mart employees with no commotion occurring, the Bonus-mart cart began to relax and take in the view. Easy-mart, it noticed, was exactly like Bonus-mart.

There were rows and rows and rows of things humans liked and needed, organized by their purpose. The lights were bright, the ceiling was high, the floor had probably been waxed and washed a couple of days ago but it was already covered in scuff marks and dirt, and the occasional wrapper of some kind of food.

The old man pushed the cart to a checkout lane and placed his various groceries onto the conveyer belt. He had come to Easy-mart for a large bottle of detergent, a pair of tennis shoes, a box of tissues, and a small pot of magnolias. He patted the handle of the shopping cart like a father patting his young son's head and said, "Well done, laddy, we're almost outta here."

This surprised the Bonus-mart cart so much it almost jumped. But, shopping carts are creatures of great self-control and it was able to remain calm and stationary. The old man paid for his items and placed them back into the cart and pushed it back out towards his truck.

By the time they reached his truck, to no surprise of the Bonus-mart cart, the other Easy-mart carts had disappeared from the cart-rack.

The old man put his items into the back of his truck and then pushed the Bonus-mart cart towards the cart-rack and then said, "You're on your way to Shopping Cart Utopia, eh, buddy! You'll make it!"

And so, the pieces of the lifelong puzzle all began to fit together for the Bonus-mart cart. This old man must be its guardian angel, and now it knew that Heaven existed! Shopping Cart Utopia! Of course! The cart became extremely excited and nearly started crying out with joy that very moment, but waited until the old man had pulled away and double-checked to make sure that it was alone.

Shopping Cart Utopia! It decided it must leave at once. But where could it be? The Bonus-mart cart decided that it would just continue to travel away from Bonus-mart. It decided to leave at once.

The cart pushed itself through the lot, no longer caring if anyone noticed. All humans that did notice attributed the scene to the wind, even though it wasn't a particularly windy day. The cart was soon out of the Easy-mart lot and on the road, heading out of the city. By sundown, it had reached the very outskirts of the city limits. Exhausted and confused by its new surroundings—green stuff on the ground and small cozy looking buildings and relatively litter-less roads—the cart decided to rest.

It dreamt of freedom and Shopping Cart Utopia, where carts of all kinds were safe to roam as they pleased and talk as loud as they wanted—where they could make sweet cart music and dance the nights away; where they could explore their passions and discover the answers to secrets no slave cart could ever know. In its dreams, the Bonus-mart cart was at peace, and it woke up the next day with a fresh excitement for the rest of its journey.

But a big red suburban swerved to avoid hitting a squirrel and plowed right into the shopping cart, breaking it into several pieces. The driver of the car was in a black suit and frowned and swore as he backed off the curb, dragging parts of the Bonus-mart cart onto the road. The driver didn't get out to take them from his car, he just continued driving until they finally broke loose.

The Bonus-mart cart was dead. Its body parts are still lying in various sections of that road, waiting to find Shopping Cart Utopia.

Helen Andronaco was born in May 1987. She lives in Connecticut and spends a lot of time in her imagination. Unsuccessful at global domination, she focuses her attention on writing.

Read more on absoluteneptune.com

THE UNMAPPED
by Carly Janine

PART ONE

The girl was walking down a deserted street, placing one foot in front of another at a snail's pace, engrossed in her phone and music that streamed from the phone to her ears via tangled, dirty ear buds. She appeared to be looking for something, tracking it from her handheld device. Suddenly she stopped, jerked out of her reverie by a blinking light on her phone. She had found something!

Warily, the girl looked around before ducking into an abandoned warehouse. The light from her phone shone upon her face, making eerie shadows in the dusty entryway. The girl slipped a flashlight out from her pack and held it high, shining the light through the thick cobwebs and jagged shadows. She moved around some boxes before she spied it, lonely and forgotten in the corner. It was an artifact. This one looked like a toy doll, but her device could detect trace amounts of magic still clinging to the doll. Overjoyed, she tucked the doll in her satchel and slipped back out the front door.

Nearly running, the girl retraced her steps back down the street in the coming darkness. The streetlights in this part of town no longer clicked on at twilight as they used to. In fact, this whole area was now Unmapped, which meant the rest of society had given up on keeping the streets maintained, the lights on, or providing any services to the people-of-the-edges that lived, or ventured, there. In some parts of town, the buildings crumbled and gave way to little pockets of Nature, which folks referred to as the Regrown. Jeva had a special tie to the Regrown, but even so, at night the Unmapped was no place to be caught alone after dark. Strange beasts were rumored to walk the streets of the Unmapped once the sun went down, and rumor had it that this may even be why there was a sundown curfew for all citizens in the first place.

"Miss Opal! Boy, do I have something for you tonight! Miss Opal?" Jeva called into Opal's Antiques and Magickal Artifacts as she threw open the door and scooted herself and her pack over the counter. The shop was on a mostly deserted street, but the first street lamp burned dimly down the block. Back in civilization. Jeva turned on a cut-glass dragonfly lamp and opened up her pack, exposing the doll to the light. Up close, the doll didn't look like much. She was antique for certain, one eye staying open while the other closed and rolled a bit. A tattered blue dress and ribbon in her dark curls showed how she had once been loved and cared for. Jeva stroked the doll's hair absently while calling out again for Miss Opal.

"Yes, I am here! Whew, dusty back here." Miss Opal emerged from the back stockroom and eyed the doll in Jeva's hands. "Where'd you find this one? Wait, don't tell me."

Jeva just smiled at her. "How much?" she asked softly.

Miss Opal was a form of enchanter. She would take the doll and strip it of its magick. Once she had separated the two, which was a skill few people possessed, she could sell the magick itself to those who had no magickal powers of their own. The doll would become the empty vessel it had been before someone had imbued it with power.

Being a true antique, the doll would fetch something, but the real money came from the magick itself. Once split, the magick could be used as it was, or used to enchant another item with whatever properties were intended. It could even be combined with tech modules to help bring AI creatures to life, or power bots and droids; the possibilities were endless. 50 years ago that would have brought amazement, but these days even the most spectacular things seemed common, cheap. It took a lot of magic and a lot of power to impress anyone these days, and most were too tired from simply trying to make a living to even bother investing their time in learning the arcane knowledge required to use the magick.

Miss Opal squinted at the doll.

"There is magick here, that is for certain. I should think I can give you $325 for it. I still have to separate the magic from the item and see if I can even find a buyer. More naturals like you around and soon I will be out of business!"

Me, a natural? Jeva thought. She did have certain affinities; she could code and track, and when she journeyed she often saw glimpses of another realm—but it always faded away just before she could get there. Jeva thought if perhaps she could get through that barrier and into the realm itself, she could find someone to help. Things had gotten so bad lately. $325 would pay her food and rent for about another week, that was it. She sighed.

"Ok, $325. More than fair. Thanks, Miss Opal."

Miss Opal opened up the cash box and briskly counted out some bills for Jeva. She pursed her lips, then added an additional $20.

"$345. God knows where you went and found

this thing."

"Thanks, lady." Jeva gave Miss Opal a hug, surprising the old woman.

"Be careful out there; it's getting dark. You don't want to be caught out after curfew. Are you sure you don't want to stay the night?"

There was a cot in the back that Jeva had used more than once, but she currently had her own place she wanted to get back to. Sparse though it was, it was hers, for now anyway, as long as she could keep the rent paid.

Jeva shook her head and stepped back out into the encroaching darkness. Her pack settled on her shoulders, ear buds back in place, she set off on a brisk walk. Her place wasn't far from Miss Opal's, which was one of the reasons she chose it. Not that she had much choice. Real estate wasn't exactly a teeming industry right now. She made her living on freelance coding projects, tech modules and droid/bot parts, and obtaining magickal items for Miss Opal.

As she walked, she noticed the large number of other citizens hurrying home as well. Some held briefcases and suits while others were dressed more casually. They all shared a slightly anxious expression, glancing often at the droids circling overhead. Being caught out after curfew would garner an expensive ticket, and multiple offenses could land you in jail.

Jeva scanned her phone screen as identification and the apartment complex gate clicked open. She paused, glancing over her shoulder before entering, closing the gate quickly behind her. In contrast to the fancy outer gate, a simple old-fashioned metal key opened the front door of her studio. It had one window, facing an alley, and across the alley, another window stared back at her. She never opened the blinds.

Tossing her backpack onto the floor, Jeva crossed the room and grabbed a cold drink from the fridge. Her mind was occupied with thoughts of what Miss Opal had said about her being a natural. If she was a natural she didn't need to collect magick or artifacts, though they could amplify her powers. Powers? What powers? She sighed.

"What's wrong, Jeva?" piped a wee automated-sounding voice. Across the floor rolled a small round robotic device—a bot. A series of lights flashed as the words came out, indicating a speaking voice. It was like a conscious Roomba, with personality.

"Oh hey, Robot. Nothing, just have a lot on my mind tonight. I was thinking about magick and Miss Opal and, oh, I don't know. But I feel like I need to do a journey. I feel like I am so close to a breakthrough with this strange realm."

"What kind of breakthrough?" The bot vibrated and hummed, her only family now. Jeva was only

17, but she had been emancipated from her abusive family at 15. Robot she had assembled herself, and he was really part of her little family now.

"I don't know. I keep seeing glimpses of the realm but it's not enough. I wonder if I could GO there? Or somehow get a message to the people there? What would I say? I don't even know! But it feels important, and I know better than to ignore my intuition for too long."

She had learned these tricks from Miss Opal over the years—how to center herself and quiet her mind; how to open up her inner eye and see.

Pulling a small stick of wood, *palo santo*, from her bag, along with a lighter, Jeva lit the end and blew the fragrant smoke around the room. Not only would it clear the room of any negative energy or dead spots, the smell always cheered Jeva up. It smelled clean and pure, and made her think of earth magick and shamanism. She was tired, but she wanted to attempt a journey before bed. From a bookshelf she grabbed a rattle made from bones and feathers, and turned to face each of the cardinal directions, calling in spirits to watch over and guide her as she journeyed.

Once the spirits had been called in, Jeva set her phone to play a droning drum beat, repetitive like a heartbeat, and sat back and closed her eyes.

Almost immediately she was transported.

She could see a woman sitting at a vanity,

watching herself in the mirror. The woman was beautiful, with long red curls and big brown eyes. She looked like...a fairy. She was a fairy. But she had no wings—just a smallish stature and a regal air about her. She could pass for human. The fairy looked up, and in the mirror her eyes met Jeva's. The woman gasped and spun around, but she was alone.

Back in her apartment, Jeva opened her eyes and inhaled sharply. It had seemed as though the woman had known she was there, had seen her perhaps. But it was impossible. Journeying was for fantastical visions, clarity, awakening.. but was it really real? If the woman had seen her, could she get there herself and stay?

"What happened?" piped Robot.

"I saw a girl, no I saw a *fairy* and she saw me, too. I scared her, I think."

Robot beeped comfortingly.

Her mind reeled. How could she ever sleep now? Jeva wanted to go back into the journey immediately, but something stopped her. The woman had seemed shocked to see her, but not necessarily happy. What if she showed back up and scared her again? Or worse yet, got attacked? Jeva felt like she needed a plan. She asked her spirit guides for help and inspiration, closed sacred space, laid down, and fell into a fitful sleep—colorful dreams and messages winding their way into her consciousness as she lay.

Meanwhile, in the fairy realm, the woman with the red hair narrowed her eyes. Someone had been spying on her, and she was determined to find out just who the young lady was who had popped up in her vanity mirror.

The next morning, Jeva awoke feeling heavy and lethargic, as though she had traveled thousands of miles in her sleep, which perhaps she had. She turned on some good house music and tucked her ear buds in as she danced around the little studio making breakfast. She nearly stepped on Robot as she got herself ready for the day.

"Hey watch it, little lady." Robot couldn't do a southern accent, but he did have a sense of humor.

"Sorry! I was just rustlin' up some grub. Want some?"

All she got back were some clicks and beeps, which meant her question wasn't worthy of a response.

"Well, I did have one idea…"

"What's that?" asked Robot.

"I thought maybe if I went into the Unmapped again today, I could look for some upgrades for you and maybe see about doing a journey from one of the Regrown areas. Besides, there's always a chance that I can find another antique, and if the journey works, maybe I will have better luck from somewhere in Nature."

"What if you scare the fairy woman again?"

"Well, if she's seen me once maybe she will be expecting me. Besides, I don't seem to have much control over where I land. Maybe I won't even see her."

"It makes me nervous but you are the boss. Boss!" Robot approximated laughter.

"Why does it make you nervous, Robot?"

"Because if you don't come home I will live an uninteresting existence in this square of a room, until someone comes in and takes all of your stuff and puts me in a box somewhere for all eternity. Terrifying, isn't it?"

Jeva laughed merrily. "I'm coming home—don't worry, Robot. Besides, I'm only going to my special tree. I feel so safe there, I don't think anyone could hurt me there."

Robot clucked worriedly but did not continue the conversation. Instead, he whirred and rolled out of sight behind the bed.

"Ok, be that way! I'm outta here Mr. Pouty-Face."

While they had been talking, Jeva had finished up breakfast and cleaned up, finally pulling on some long pants and a long-sleeved shirt. She grabbed her pack and made sure to bring her rattle and *palo santo*, along with some water and snacks. She was good to go.

Jeva slipped the long key into the lock and

locked Robot in the apartment, as she did every time she left. Her phone and Robot were the most valuable things she owned, and it wasn't really safe for her to bring Robot out with her on too many adventures, especially into the Unmapped. He was small and portable, but he also drew a lot of attention with his personality and noises. Miss Opal had never even met him, although she had heard stories.

If she needed him to analyze anything, she would bring samples back home with her. He could scan plants and modules and all sorts of things, giving her information that she often couldn't get from her phone. He was one smart cookie, thanks to her. Jeva had learned coding at a young age, and was near-genius level with it now. She created applications for her phone and used them to keep track of the areas of the Unmapped that were Regrown—like her favorite tree. Since huge areas of the Unmapped had no roads, or blocked roads from fallen buildings, it was very difficult to map. Hence, nobody had tried.

Jeva slipped her ear buds back in place and zoned out into her phone as she walked, deftly avoiding fallen branches and rocks that dirtied the sidewalks…where there were sidewalks. She opened her Regrown app and selected her favorite tree. It was a beautiful tree, tall and gnarled, with branches that spread and drooped, making it perfect for climbing or nestling beneath for a nap. It had a serene feeling to it. The first time she had found the tree Jeva marked it, making it the first thing she mapped in the Unmapped.

She resettled her pack on her back as she walked, turning down this street, crossing through that abandoned building. Her walk took her deep into the Unmapped. It was a bright, clear day and she spotted no drones overhead as she ventured out away from the city.

Eventually Jeva found her way to the tree, sprawling out of the planter where it had once been a sapling. Now it commanded a quarter of a city block, bursting from the concrete that had once contained it, ripping out the sidewalks that tried to stifle its roots. The tree was winning the war against the building it had once stood in front of.

Moss covered brick, and water dripped from an old rusted pipe nearby. It was practically an enchanted clearing. Moving close to the tree, Jeva once again called to the four corners to open sacred space before loading up her drum file on her phone. She settled in among the branches and leaned back against the trunk of the tree, crossing her booted feet at the ankle. Once again, she opened her eyes to the fairy realm.

The red-haired fairy was waiting for her. As soon as Jeva opened her eyes in the fairy realm, she saw her. The fae woman stood up and crossed the room she was in, stopping right in front of Jeva. "You're the girl from my mirror," she stated calmly.

"Yes, and you're the woman from my journey..." gasped Jeva, surprised to have once again found herself facing the same person and place, as though no time had passed between journeys.

"What do you want?" the fairy seemed to glow, and seemed perhaps a bit cold, but her question was sincere.

"My name is Jeva. I have come to you from one of the Regrown areas of the city. I was hoping you could help. Things have been so bad lately, our people are broke and ill, our society has killed all the Nature. I want to help heal us, but I think we need to work together somehow. Can you come to the tree?"

"I don't know. Yes. Maybe. I will try," the fairy said, speaking softly. "My family is associated with trees. They act as a focal point for our power. You may be surprised to find that my people have already been to your city and walk among you at times, though most prefer to stay near the Regrown areas of your Unmapped."

There were fairies here? In her world? Jeva's mind reeled.

The Fairy continued, "You must have some natural ability to be able to journey and speak to me in this manner. Do you have any magickal items on *you?"*

"I have my rattle, it is magickal for opening sacred space, and some palo santo.*"*

"Sacred wood? Someone has been teaching you the Old Ways."

"Yes, Miss Opal is my teacher," said Jeva.

"Wonderful. She must be aware of your natural talent." This could be very useful for us, thought the red-haired woman. "Stand back!"

Jeva sat up and opened her eyes, yanking the droning drumbeat from her ears as she moved. The woman stood before her.

"My name is Lelianne," said the fairy. Jeva peered closely at the woman, taking in her slight frame and tawny skin, brown eyes and long, flowing red hair. Lelianne was dressed in faded greens and browns that blended in well with the moss and the tree, yet muted enough not to stand out so much against the relentless gray of everything else. In fact, Lelianne and Jeva were dressed similarly, although the cut of Lelianne's clothing was definitely finer and somehow foreign.

"Nice to meet you, Lelianne," Jeva said with a smile. Her spirit guides surrounded her, filling the sacred space with light that twinkled and crackled in the morning sun.

"I see you have some protectors. Not to worry." Lelianne addressed the spirit guides and other beings that had been called to the magickal workings.

"I wonder why my last two journeys led me to you, Lelianne."

Lelianne's eyebrows knitted together briefly. "I'm not sure, but I do know one thing; you must have some tie to our land or our people. I wouldn't be surprised if you had other powers. Do you find you have a kinship with animals? Can you track?"

A tie to the fairy realm? Jeva was startled. It wasn't something that had never even occurred to her before. She had certainly never been there, although since she had begun hanging out with Miss Opal she had seen different aspects of the realm over time. How could she be tied to the land? She knew her family; she wasn't some changeling orphan. Or was she?

"I don't have a whole lot of experience with animals, but I can track, people and probably animals, too. I also prefer to be in Nature, and especially near this tree." Jeva lovingly placed her hand upon the warm bark of the tree, feeling stronger once the connection was made. What a day.

Lelianne looked quizzically at Jeva's phone.

"Oh, I've been mapping the Regrown areas within the Unmapped. I made a cartography program for my phone," Jeva explained.

Lelianne gasped. "You have a map?"

"Well, sort of. I have pieces of map. It has taken

me a lot longer than I expected due to the advanced decay of the infrastructure. I mean, buildings falling down don't make for easy travel, and I have to always be back in the city before curfew…"

Lelianne nodded. "The darkness here is thick, and there are things within it better left unseen."

As they were talking, the sun moved higher in the sky overhead.

"Now, what is to be done?"

It turned out that Lelianne had the ability to travel between the areas that were Regrown and the Fairy realm. With her help, Jeva's map could be completed much faster.

"Why are you helping me?"

"Well, we could be sisters, couldn't we? Besides it isn't every day a human being just appears in your mirror. There must be some reason we have been brought together."

Jeva smiled. Perhaps her map was not an impossible task, after all. It gave her hope, which was no small thing in an uncertain world. Hope could carry you through the storm and right out into smooth waters.

PART TWO

The next few weeks were a blur of hard work. Each morning Jeva said goodbye to Robot and ventured deep into the Unmapped, which was ever-so-slowly becoming mapped again. Jeva never saw anyone else on her walks. At least, no other humans. Occasionally she picked up a small artifact for Miss Opal or module for Robot, but for the most part everything was picked clean. Empty.

One day, while moving through some homes that had been blasted, she found some useful modules for Robot. They would upgrade his memory and allow her to write some new programs. She rushed home with excitement and soon had coded a working program to upload the schematics from the map she was creating on the phone into Robot's memory, and cross-reference any plant matter found with both the internet and a database of current scientific knowledge. Both were really necessary, as most of the plants and animals that had lived during the century before were gone. Instead, new flora and fauna had begun appearing within the Unmapped.

Most people didn't want to spend the time to dig through the archeological mess that the internet had become, or lacked the devices and knowledge to access it. People mostly relied on bots and upgrades from the city to keep them informed and answer their questions. Jeva preferred to scavenge information directly.

"There you go, buddy." Jeva adjusted some final settings before gently setting Robot back on the floor.

"I feel absolutely fabulous!" Robot rolled around in circles.

"I was thinking about inviting Lelianne to visit, what do you think?"

"I want to meet the fairy," Robot said, and beeped happily.

"Ha ha ha, okay, okay. I will ask her. I was thinking we could all have tea with Miss Opal at the shop. You can come too, I'll smuggle you in my pack. She has been ever so curious about you."

The next morning when Jeva met Lelianne, it was by a babbling brook surrounded by reeds and strange cat-tail like plants. It had once been a water pipe, now broken and hollow and rusted, mostly obscured by plants. Jeva even spied a water-creature as it flitted past down the stream.

"Lelianne, we have worked so hard the last few weeks. I have really been enjoying our time together. I was wondering if you would like to come with me into the city, meet my chosen family, Miss Opal and Robot. We could have tea, you could stay over, go back to work in the morning."

Lelianne chuckled, "You've put some thought into this."

Jeva found herself blushing slightly. "Well, yeah, maybe," she admitted.

"Of course, I would love to come."

"Wonderful! Want to go today?" Jeva bounced

with excitement, pleading with her eyes at Lelianne.

"Ok, sounds good. Now let's get to work."

Jeva set out pinpointing coordinates around the edges of the brook, saving them in strings and creating a 3-D schematic with her phone as she went. When she was finished she would have an accurate representation of the water source, complete with samples of the plants to take back to Robot. She also mapped out the warehouses and factory remains that surrounded the brook. It was tedious, but Jeva was detail-oriented and so engrossed in her work that she barely noticed the hours slipping by.

"Jeva, I do believe the time for tea is nigh!"

Jeva jumped, then grinned. "Already? Let's go."

The two girls chattered for awhile, then walked in silence. Parts of the street were missing and sinkholes had opened up, swallowing other parts. It took concentration and care to get through the Unmapped.

Soon they reached the edge of the city and Jeva's apartment. Drones buzzed overhead, endlessly circling, a seemingly bored facade. Always watching, yet there were never enough eyes on the footage from the drones, especially now, so for the most part, it was mock safety. Real surveillance. Though short-staffed, the drones were always recording and could be played back, so it really was safe. Or was not safe, depending on your outlook on being recorded at all times.

Lelianne eyed the automatic gate and jumped like a cat when it slid open. Not slick, she thought.

Jeva just smiled and pushed through to open the door.

"We're heeere!" Jeva called out to Robot.

'Hi! Friend! Lelianne, it is nice to meet you. Salutations and felicitations! And hello, Miss Jeva."

Lelianne bowed.

"Come on, into the backpack, it's time for tea." Robot gave his best robot sigh before scooting into the backpack whirring and clicking and then becoming silent.

Gingerly, Jeva swung the backpack onto her back, and they were off.

A little bell rang as the door to Miss Opal's swung open. Miss Opal was standing behind the counter with her back to the door as they entered.

"Hello—oh, hello, girls!" She turned around and her face lit up. She practically fell over herself as she hurried over to give Jeva a big hug.

"You must be Lelianne. Jeva has told me much about you."

"Same," said a laughing Lelianne. "She loves you! Also, Miss Opal, if you don't mind, I was hoping you might be able to help me with something."

"Anything for a friend of Jeva's, my dear. If I can, that is."

"Well, I'm not sure if Jeva has told you, but within the fairy realm there are many different skills and affinities one can have. My family is connected to trees in particular. All animals and plants, of course, but trees are really where our hearts lie. Jeva's favorite tree within the Unmapped has special meaning for us, as well. I have certain skills with trees, like hearing their thoughts and inclinations, and to an extent I can heal them, but I was hoping you might have some tree magicks of your own. Is there anything you can conjure up that would help to promote the growth of trees and plants? It would help the Regrown immensely."

Miss Opal looked thoughtful for a moment. "Let's get to tea then I will see what I can do."

Miss Opal walked to the front of the store and hung out a CLOSED sign. She looked carefully down the street before locking the door. She then led Lelianne and Jeva to the back of the store, where she had a whole little apartment. Not only was there the cot where Jeva had slept from time to time, there was a kitchen and a squat table with four fat chairs and, along one wall, racks stacked high with jars and packets and seeds, and all sorts of things.

Jeva opened up her backpack and set it on the floor. Robot came scurrying out. Miss Opal clapped with delight.

"Ta-da!" said Robot.

Everyone laughed, and the girls sat down at the table. Miss Opal had already laid out some biscuits and cakes and cookies. The tea kettle began to whistle. Miss Opal poured them some piping hot tea and the friends talked and talked. Lelianne told them more about the Fairy realm and Miss Opal shared her knowledge of plant healing magicks, promising to send them home with some enchanted items to help encourage new growth. Miss Opal had lots of questions for Lelianne about her family and their tree affinity. Robot was silly, as usual, and Miss Opal seemed to love him immediately.

A few hours later Jeva, Lelianne, and Robot made their way back to Jeva's studio apartment to sleep.

The next day, the girls said goodbye to Robot and set off to continue their work. As they were walking down the street, Jeva stopped suddenly. "Wait, Lelianne, why don't we stop back by Miss Opal's on the way back out? See if she needs anything?" It was a random request, and it surprised Jeva as much as Lelianne. "Surely. Maybe she would like some breakfast or coffee after our nerd session yesterday. It's early still."

As they took the corner to Miss Opal's block, Jeva's stomach churned. Not only was the street deserted, which wasn't unusual, but there were no birds chirping or cars moving or, well, anything. Even worse, she spied broken glass littering the cracked sidewalk in front of Miss Opal's shop. Jeva started to run, Lelianne close behind.

The girls burst into the shop and found it in disarray. The bookshelf was knocked over, books spilling onto the floor, some flung open carelessly as though they had been rifled through. The front glass case was smashed, though pieces of antique and enchanted jewelry glimmered among the shards, untouched.

Jeva ducked under the counter and ran to the back. The cot was upended and bedding all over the floor. The cupboards hung open, one hanging by a single old hinge, swinging softly. Miss Opal was nowhere to be found.

"Someone must have seen us last night, seen Robot. I wonder, I was so careful, how did this happen?" Jeva wailed.

Lelianne frowned. "Most disturbing. We must return to the Regrown at once. I may be able to work some magick back in fairyland to uncover the culprit. I can't do much from this side, though."

Jeva's thoughts were racing. Who had done this? Had she messed up? Was it *her* fault that Miss Opal was gone? She was starting to panic, so Jeva sat down in one of the fat chairs and took a deep breath. She had to focus. Miss Opal was really the only other human she cared about, she had to be okay.

"Let's get Robot and go now. I don't want to leave him at home."

Whoever had been watching them must have been waiting for them to leave, because when they got back to Jeva's gate, they found the scanning device busted and marks all over the gate. Jeva stared at the jagged marks for a minute before comprehending that they were grouped together in fives, like fingernails or claws. She shuddered. Whatever it was had given up on the gate, at least temporarily.

Jeva touched the scanning mechanism with one finger, then tentatively lifted the cracked face. The wires underneath were intact, and after a minute of fiddling she got the lights to turn back on. Her phone scanned successfully, and the gate slid open.

"C'mon," Jeva called over her shoulder to Lelianne as she rushed in, pulling the long silver key from her pocket as she bounded up to her front door.

Inside, everything was intact.

"*Robot!*" called Jeva.

"I'm here, mistress," squeaked Robot, sliding out from under the bed. "I heard the most dreadful noises, I am so glad you are back and seem to be uninjured. Do you know what was outside?"

Jeva shook her head. Robot had heard the intruder at the gate. She wondered if any of her neighbors had seen it, but dismissed the idea of going door-to-door and knocking to find out. They had to get back to the Regrown.

"You're coming with us," Jeva said firmly to Robot. Meanwhile, Lelianne had returned to inspecting the claw marks on the gate.

"This isn't good," Lelianne called.

"What isn't good?"

"If I didn't know better, I'd say these claw marks came from a hand not much larger than either of ours. What do you know that is our size that can claw metal?"

Jeva was stumped. She unceremoniously dumped Robot into the backpack, ignoring his offended huff.

"Let's go to our tree," Jeva said.

The two girls cautiously emerged from the apartment complex, before turning and taking off down the street at a brisk pace. Soon they reached the last streetlight and passed it, continuing on into the Unmapped. Jeva pulled up a screen on her phone, inspecting the different routes to her favorite tree. She decided to lead them in a way she didn't usually go, just in case. It was longer but most likely safer, and it would be difficult to follow them through the twisting streets and pathways of the thickening wild.

"It occurs to me, if it is easier for me to cross over at the Regrown points, perhaps it is easy for others as well. Our foe could be someone from the realm of fairy."

"Do you have any enemies?"

"Not enemies, per se, but all the families of fairyland do not always agree. As my family is tied to trees, we are mostly close with the other Nature families. There are families aligned with things that are perhaps not as benign as ours."

"Like what?"

"Well, there are elements like Chaos, Decay, Darkness. These things are ruled by families within fairyland as well. There are a lot of politics involved, but for the most part the families live in peace. Every once in a while there will be a disruption, but it is nearly always settled by the High Fairy Council," Lelianne finished.

"Not only are the Regrown areas portals, they also seem to be a natural source of magick. If they had an enchanter like Miss Opal, I wonder what they could do," Jeva responded.

Lelianne looked alarmed. "We have to hurry, I need to get back and warn my family."

At last the girls reached the clearing where the great tree grew.

Miss Opal was lying underneath the tree, seemingly in a trance. A dark figure loomed over her.

"No!" shouted Jeva and Lelianne simultaneously. While Jeva hesitated, thinking she had no weapon or plan of attack, Lelianne rushed the figure immediately.

"What is going on!?" beeped Robot.

"Not now, Robot." Jeva approached Lelianne, the figure, and Miss Opal slowly.

Lelianne reached out for the figure, leaning forward, but it suddenly disappeared. Her hands passed right through the spot their body had been, so she lost her balance a bit before she recovered and turned the fall into a crouch. She leaned over Miss Opal.

"She's breathing," said Lelianne.

"Who, or *what*, was that? Is she okay? *Will* she be okay?"

"*That* was a Decay fairy. I think maybe they were trying to transport Miss Opal back into fairyland through the portal."

"Can you wake her up? What did they want?"

"I don't know what they wanted. I think I can wake her up, but we have to get her back to my family or get my family to come here. Will you wait here with her and Robot, I will go fetch someone to help."

"Yes, of course."

While Lelianne teleported back into the fairy realm, Jeva reached into her backpack and freed Robot, and groped around trying to find her palo santo.

"I'm going to open sacred space, Robot. It will make me feel better to have my guides around."

Robot just beeped worriedly around Miss Opal. He circled her a few times before curling up under her arm to snuggle.

Jeva used her compass app to find the cardinal directions, then pulled out her magick rattle and shook it in each direction, using ancient invocations as she worked. Soon energy snapped and crackled all around her, golden-white light drifting through the clearing like fog. Once the circle was created, she returned to Miss Opal's side and sat down next to Robot.

A good amount of time had passed. Jeva and Robot tinkered with the map, and Jeva added a new flower that was growing near Miss Opal. Finally, a portal opened up and through it stepped Lelianne and another red-headed woman. She wasn't as athletic as Lelianne, and she was far more decorated. Jewelry graced her ears, neck, wrists. She looked regal, but also somehow earthy, in the same way that an earthiness clung to Lelianne. She looked as though leaves would either scamper out of her way, or rush in to cushion her fall. Powerful.

The new woman turned her gray eyes to Jeva, "No change?" she asked briskly.

"Nothing. She hasn't moved," Jeva answered.

"Lelianne, take her feet."

While Lelianne moved to sit at Miss Opal's feet, she said to Jeva, "This is my sister, Olivia. She is a healer. She will help us!"

Olivia had moved to sit at Miss Opal's head. She gently lifted her head and placed it in her lap. The magick in the air hummed. Each leaf on the magnificent tree seemed lined in light.

Olivia began to sing softly, a low song in a strange language that rolled and lilted. Magick swirled out from her heart, enveloping Miss Opal in the golden-white light. Suddenly, Miss Opal gasped. Her eyelids fluttered open.

"Miss Opal!" Jeva was filled with joy. Robot simulated a clapping noise.

Slowly, Miss Opal sat up. She leaned against Olivia for support.

"Who did this to you? Why?" Jeva asked.

Miss Opal answered, "It was a Decay fairy. I think they are planning some sort of attack. The Regrown areas would die if they were overrun with Decay fairies. If there were enough of them, they could attack the city! They must want your map, or Robot, or both."

"That would explain why they attacked my gate, I suppose," Jeva murmured. "Gosh, what should we do? Can we seal the portals?"

Lelianne said, "The portals are natural, and I don't think any enchantment would hold them closed for long. Besides, more and more of the Unmapped is becoming Regrown. Soon all of the Unmapped will be wild and free."

Olivia added, "We can probably close them if we absolutely must, but not for long, so if we are to use that we must be strategic."

"If the Regrown have fairies that have been tending to them, I wonder...do you think they would fight if need be? To protect the Regrown?" asked Jeva.

"We prefer not to fight, but to protect the magick of this new Nature, I am sure they would. Nobody wants the darker fairies to control an abundance of natural magick. I do hope it doesn't come to that," said Lelianne.

"I might have a better idea," Jeva said.

"What's that?" inquired Lelianne.

"Well, while you were getting Olivia, we were working on the map. I even found a new flower to add to the registry. Take a look."

Jeva hit a button on Robot and he switched to projector mode. Light streamed out of him to form a holographic image in front of the women. It was the map, and it was nearly complete. Like a labyrinth lit by ancient torches, pieces of the map were lit up. The places that were still dark were few and far between, mostly in the southeast corner of the Unmapped. Where streets were missing, alternate routes had been carefully mapped. Their labor was nearly over.

"Anyway, as you can see, the map is almost done. We have a map, of the Unmapped! And I think we should share it. The pieces that are missing will be filled in by everyone else. If we wait, we may miss this opportunity to make the knowledge both less valuable to the darker fairies by sharing it, and more valuable to everyone else that could have an interest in studying the Regrown."

Lelianne and Olivia both looked doubtful. "Share it with who?" asked Olivia.

"Everyone," said Jeva firmly. "I can send a copy of the map with Lelianne back into the fairy realm. And I can give Miss Opal a few copies to sell in her shop. Once the humans and fairies all know about the Regrown and the extent of it, and how beautiful it is, they will come here. It will become a safe place, a healing place."

"Won't the humans ruin it? asked Olivia bluntly.

"*Olivia!*" gasped Lelianne.

"Maybe. But maybe they will send in scientists to study these amazing new varieties of plant and animal life. You never know with us. The Regrown cannot stay secret forever," answered Jeva simply.

"Wouldn't giving the information out be like handing the key to our enemy?" asked Lelianne doubtfully.

"I really think that people will care for the spaces. Besides, worst case scenario we have the fairies that have been tending the portals to watch over each Regrown site, prepared to fight. What do you think, Robot?"

Robot chirped "Mistress, I have seen humans be both kind and cruel. I do think caution is needed with this Decay fairy as we know not her intentions precisely. But if you think it will help to share the map, then perhaps we should."

Miss Opal nodded. "Their side has chosen aggressiveness. I believe the most loving response would be to share the map. Just think of the karma if we had an opportunity to stop an attack like this and did not take it, or worse, responded with violence and many lives were lost that need not be. The magick should lend itself to the protectors, making them strong. I wonder what happened to the protector of this glade, though."

Jeva started. It hadn't occurred to her that there could be more fairies there, watching, yet choosing not to intervene. Lelianne had mentioned there being creatures in the darkness in the Unmapped as well. It wasn't totally safe yet. But her mind was made up. She wanted to get back to her apartment and get to work making copies of the map.

"I think we should get Miss Opal back to the city before it gets dark, and help her get her shop put to rights. After that, I want to go make copies of the map. Each of us should have a hard copy just in case, and I will make some for Miss Opal to sell as well," Jeva said.

Lelianne nodded. "Okay, let's do it. Olivia, why don't you go back to Fairy and spread the word. I will bring you a copy of the map in the morning. I want to go help Miss Opal and Jeva."

Olivia gave a curt nod, obviously not yet

completely on board, before disappearing into the portal.

Jeva and Lelianne helped Miss Opal to her feet and the three women slowly made their way out of the Unmapped, with Robot once again riding along in the backpack.

It took a few hours to clean up the mess that the Decay fairy had made of Miss Opal's shop. The girls set Miss Opal to rest on the cot in the back while they went to work righting everything. Robot kept Miss Opal company, showing her funny videos and telling her stories.

It was fully dark by the time they said goodnight and stepped back outside. The streetlight flickered, but held, sending feeble light their way. The darkness cut thickly between each light. They walked quickly, and Jeva used the flashlight application on her phone to cut through the darkness between the lights. Still, by the time they turned onto her block they were practically running.

Jeva scanned her phone at the gate, shuddering at the sight of all the claw marks, before slipping inside. Lelianne followed close behind her. Once inside the apartment, Lelianne collapsed on the bed. Jeva chuckled at her friend's display of exhaustion. They luckily hadn't run into any officers and seemingly escaped the drones under the cover of night.

Jeva set to work making copies of the map.

Robot rolled out of the backpack to help. Soon they had a dozen copies of the map on discs, flash drives, and nicely printed.

"We can drop some of this stuff off with Miss Opal in the morning." Jeva finally succumbed to a giant yawn. Soon both girls were asleep, with Robot standing guard.

Jeva's phone alarm went off early the next morning. After a quick breakfast of yogurt and granola, the girls were off to Miss Opal's shop. The bell rang as they opened the door to the store, darker inside than usual due to the front window having been blocked out for repair. Miss Opal breezed in from the back. She seemed to be in a really good mood.

"I have something to show you!" Jeva and Miss Opal said together simultaneously. They both looked momentarily startled, then started to laugh.

"You first," said Miss Opal. Jeva pulled out the printed copies of the map and the flash drives.

"I was thinking we could sell the flash drives, but the printed copies we could put up on lamp posts around the city. You know, give everyone an equal chance to find them," Jeva explained.

"Wonderful. Maybe I can work on putting up printed copies on the posts while you go back to the Regrown," said Miss Opal.

"Back to the Regrown?"

"Yes. I have made you an enchanted amulet. It

327

glows, so it is a source of light, but more importantly it will cloak you when you go into your journey space. You should be able to see into the realm of Fairy without being seen. I think we should find out exactly what the Decay fairy is up to."

Jeva gasped. "Amazing! But I could never afford to pay you for such a thing, at least nothing near its worth…"

Miss Opal said, "Well, the way I see it, if I didn't do this I would feel like you guys rescued me for nothing. I have to contribute to this, if for no other reason than to make sure nobody else gets taken. We must find a way to end this."

Lelianne added, "I agree, it is a wonderful gift, *and* as much as I hate to rush you, we should go try it out immediately. Who knows what the Decay fairy is planning, or how releasing the map will affect their plans."

Jeva nodded. "You're right, Lelianne; we should go. I really hope, by sharing what we have learned, that others will come into the Regrown again and make it something beautiful. Thank you, Miss Opal!"

Jeva gave Miss Opal a big hug, her arms softening into the goodness of being hugged for just a moment, before she stepped back. Miss Opal secured the amulet around Jeva's neck, and the girls were off. Their chatter floated down the sidewalk as they walked toward the Unmapped.

Jeva chose a Regrown point that she hadn't used for a journey before. She felt too exposed and predictable going to her favorite tree, so instead she picked another set of trees. Lelianne's power would be at its maximum. Small white mushrooms littered the ground around the trees, and a thick green moss grew up the trunks. Not nearly as old as the great tree, this little grove of trees stood close together in a ring, the branches twisting up in strange directions reaching for the light.

Lelianne set herself up to watch over Jeva as she journeyed, while Jeva quickly opened sacred space and called upon her spirit guides. She asked to find the Decay fairy and see what was going on, if it was in the highest and best good for all. Curling up at the base of one of the trees, Jeva set her phone to the drum track. Before long she was deep in a trance.

The Decay fairy was standing at the bedside of another Decay fairy, who looked very ill. The room was silent. Another fairy entered. The fairy who had taken Miss Opal, and presumably clawed Jeva's gate, spoke:

"Our queen is ill and we have lost the enchanter. How will we gather the magick to heal her?"

The new fairy said, "I have news. They have finished the map. Not only that, but they have released it. A scout found this copy taped to a streetlight within the city. Now everyone knows where all of the Regrown points are."

"Clever. Now we will have people and fairies crawling all over. The only answer is war. We must take back the enchanter or find another, and now that we know all of the Regrown areas, we must use this knowledge to save our queen!"

Jeva listened with growing concern. If the Decay fairies launched a full-on attack, would they win? She didn't think that controlling the magick was worth anyone losing their life. How could she stop them? She was grateful for the enchanted amulet that hung about her neck. Miss Opal was good to her, like a mother. She wondered if the Decay fairy felt the same way about her queen. Suddenly, an idea began to form in the back of her mind.

The fairy who had entered merely nodded before turning around and leaving. She left the first fairy pacing intently at the foot of the queen's bed. Plotting, planning.

Jeva's eyelids fluttered open. "Lelianne!"

Lelianne had been watching Jeva as she journeyed, but she still jumped when she heard her name called. "Yes?"

"Do the Decay fairies have the power to heal?"

"Well, no, healing is a very specific gift. I can use my magick to heal trees, and some trees have healing properties so in that way I can *aid* in healing, but it is not usually enough for illnesses far advanced. Their talents lie more in decay and destruction."

"I have an idea," said Jeva excitedly.

⋇ ⋇

Miss Opal—who, at their request, had joined them in the small grove of trees within the Unmapped—set the final jar aside, trapping within it a pulsating golden-white light. All around them, jars were stacked—dozens of them. Now ensnared within the glass, the magick could be used in any number of ways.

"Are you sure about this?" she asked.

Jeva had been thinking all day. She didn't want to fight. She didn't want to be responsible for the lives of fairies and humans that would be lost. Wise beyond her years, she saw the usefulness of the darker fairies, and how their power and magick helped make room for new growth. Without Decay, there would be no Regrown.

"It is the only way," she answered. "We must help them heal their queen. Come on, let's go; it's getting dark."

They didn't run into any new adventurers on their way out of the Unmapped, but as they walked Jeva could feel eyes following her from the shadows. Her skin crawled and the hair on her arms stood on end. She heard strange snuffling sounds in the darkness. She walked faster, but the sounds did not diminish. Lelianne and Miss Opal matched her pace and the three of them found themselves half-running down the street as the light faded.

Soon they reached Miss Opal's shop, where they all decided to stay for the evening.

In the morning, Lelianne and Jeva returned to the grove to find all the jars of magick gone. In their place was a silver-handled mirror and a note that simply said, "Look at me."

Lelianne looked at the mirror suspiciously, but Jeva approached it without fear, hoisting the heavy mirror up into the air before peering into its surface. Instead of her reflection, she saw the queen's chambers once again, although this time the queen was sitting up. The Decay fairy was still by her side, looking worried but no longer pacing. Jeva felt awkward, but she finally said, "Hello?" to the mirror. At once the Dark Fairy at the queen's side stood up, looking straight at Jeva through the mirror.

"Greetings. My name is Jolene. Allow me to introduce our queen...Queen Elsinae."

The Decay fairy finally had a name, as did their queen. Why didn't Lelianne's family have a queen? She would have to ask; maybe they did for all Jeva knew.

Jeva bowed stiffly at the mirror, causing the queen to smile and Jolene to laugh outright.

"Forgive me," said Queen Elsinae, "I would have

come to you but I am still too weak. I felt it necessary to thank you, however. You've saved my life and prevented a war. This is something I never would have dreamed possible. The rift between our clans in Fairy had become so great, I feared nothing would bring us together…and yet you have. You have given freely to us, and shared your knowledge—with your people and fairies alike. You are unique and must be rewarded."

Jeva marveled at the queen's voice. It was like honey, smooth and flowing, with a cadence that was comforting. She forced her attention back to the words the queen was actually saying.

"Furthermore, I am not sure if you are aware of this fact, but you are kin to us as well."

"Kin? What do you mean? I know who my family is." Jeva had left her family long ago, but she remembered vividly her childhood of deprivation and harsh words.

"That may be, but someone in your family was a full-blooded fairy, or you would not be able to see into our realm as you do. So I have thought of a gift for you, should you accept it."

Jeva couldn't believe what she was hearing. She could be related to Lelianne, or the Decay fairies, or some other form of fairy entirely. She didn't know, and wasn't sure how she could ever find out.

"Please accept this gift with my purest intentions, Jeva of Humankind. I bestow upon you the power to walk within our world. As Lelianne and Jolene do, you will be able to step between the human and fairy lands. I hope this enables you to learn more of your story, and perhaps we shall soon meet in person."

Beside her, Lelianne squealed with delight. The queen smiled at her.

"And thank you, Lelianne, for all that you have done to help see our sister through these last few months. You are a true friend," Queen Elsinae continued. Lelianne bowed, much more gracefully than Jeva had.

"I need to rest. Thank you, ladies, for all that you have done for all of Fairy. I assure you the magick will be put to good use."

The mirror went dark in Jeva's hand, and she set it back on the ground before turning to face Lelianne, grabbing her by the hand, and spinning her like a top.

"I can't believe you pulled that off!"

"*We* pulled that off, you mean," Lelianne corrected, laughing. "Gosh, I can't wait to tell Miss Opal and Robot. Let's go back to the city."

Jeva closed the sacred space, thanking her guides for keeping her safe, and for leading her to this place of serenity from which she was able to act and think clearly.

"Do you need to go home?" Jeva asked Lelianne.

"Nah. Olivia can hold down the fort without me

for a little while longer. Besides, I wouldn't want to miss this story. And guess what—this means when I go back you can come with me if you like!"

"Now *that* sounds like fun."

The two girls walked carefully through the shattered remains of the city. More and more, signs of life were peeking out between the cracks in the cement, and upon the windowsills. Snails crawled up pipes, and strange, spider-like creatures spun nets in the darkest corners. Jeva snapped pictures of some of the creatures with her phone as they walked—little tidbits for Robot to mull over at home.

They heard voices ahead and instinctively the girls froze. Lelianne snapped out of it first, reminding Jeva that there was no war—that it was all over. Jeva stepped out of the shadows and into the light, only to see a girl even younger than herself, walking with her father through the Unmapped. She had an ancient phone and a sketch-pad, and she was speaking animatedly to her dad. Jeva smiled. She felt happy and whole for the first time in as long as she could remember. Jeva took Lelianne by the hand, and the two of them continued the long walk home.

Carly Janine is a writer and massage therapist living in San Diego, CA. She enjoys spending time with her daughter and doing yoga.

You can follow her blog at
nautiluscarly.wordpress.com
And her Twitter: @NautilusCarly
Subscribe to Carly's mailing list here:
ctowle@gmail.com

VIABILITY

by Danicka Winters

More than its grotesque appearance, the fact that it was *alive* was what horrified her. Ordinarily one would have thought even a breath of life would be impossible in a creature such as this, though Kara knew that it was in fact pretty normal. The misshapen head brought to mind a monster from a horror movie, and the hairless, pink flesh in its transparency made her recent breakfast threaten ascension.

Normally she spoke her mind easily, expressing her opinions on the morality of such things the moment she saw wrongdoing. Under the circumstances, however, she felt she was entitled to a momentary lapse into speechlessness. After all, the moment she'd laid eyes on the poor being, her breath had sucked into her lungs in a completely involuntary manner, and she'd been unable to fully release it since.

As appalled as she was, she was not frightened by it. There was nothing to fear in any living thing that couldn't have weighed more than half a pound. No, what frightened her were the people who were responsible for the abomination. A human embryo, alive and breathing, in a mechanical womb. Of course, fear was part of the draw.

"I knew you were the right person for the job, Kara. You've always had the ability to see beyond simple ethics and into the realm of possibility. As well as the real morality behind the science." The congratulatory tone in her former professor's voice made her squirm with pride inside, though a battering of guilt accompanied the egotistical and childlike pleasure at his approval.

"I take it there have been no special permissions given for this research, then?" She knew the answer before it came, but she had to ask.

"Well, not as such," Brian Reynolds, Ph.D., hedged with a cagey grin.

"Right. In other words you have funding from important sources that will be able to run interference for you. Now that you've had your fun shocking me, are you willing to tell me what the plan is here?" Kara knew the answer to that question, too, and she was only too well aware of what her likely response would be.

"Is your soul too high of a price to ask, if it's for immortality, fame, and glory?" Brian's grin only widened as he asked the question, though it caused her a stab of pain to hear it.

"You know full well I sold that to you five years ago, and I've yet to see it brought back to me," Kara retorted.

"We also both know it wasn't your soul I took. Or, at least, not only," he whispered in her ear. "And now I intend to claim that ownership."

The unholy shiver his words induced made it hard to resist his lure, but Kara needed answers. The scientist in her was itching to begin.

"No," she croaked. "The work first." It was all she could manage at the moment, and it was nowhere near enough to convince him that she was serious, despite her intense curiosity. Not even bothering to pay lip-service to her refusal, Brian pinned her against an unoccupied table, stripped her of her jeans, and then turned her around to bend her over the table. She moaned.

Instead of the feel of him entering her from behind, however, Kara was jolted by the feel of a needle piercing her gluteus muscle. She struggled at first, but Brian was stronger. Within a couple of minutes, she felt the drug kick in. As she began to float away from her body she recognized the sensation. He'd given her Ketamine, a particular favourite of hers, though the dose was small enough that she was still aware of her circumstances. She just didn't care.

He wasn't raping her. That wouldn't have been his purpose, because he knew she relished their twisted relationship. No, for some reason he wanted her out of commission enough that she wouldn't protest, and she couldn't think of a single thing she'd ever refused him. Or would ever.

"You know, I took something from you when we worked on that last project. Now I want you to see the fruits of that labour. Well, not quite labour, specifically, since you haven't gone through that just yet, but you will," he said with a small chuckle. Kara had no idea what he was talking about. Labour?

Brian stretched her out on the table, pulling stirrups up from underneath. Then he strapped her legs into them. He needn't have bothered, since she had no interest in refusing him, and even if she had she didn't think she'd be able to.

Instead of the expected heat of his penis, Kara felt the cold plastic of a speculum.

"I'll be right back," he announced, increasing her confusion. Kara couldn't even bring herself to turn her head to see where he went. A rattling and rubbery whooshing sound announced his return. A rolling cart. With instruments.

"Wha-" Kara tried to ask, but her voice was a near-useless instrument at that point. Brian answered her question anyway.

"I'm not going to hurt you, Kara. In fact, I'm giving you a huge gift. Just relax and let it happen," he said softly, with a slight chuckle at the rape comparison. Her brain tried to raise an alarm. It tried desperately to make the connection between what was happening, the grotesque objects surrounding them in the room, and the words Brian had spoken. But Kara was too far gone. It didn't matter how brilliant she was, because the Ketamine had done its job now.

Brian placed a block borrowed from an autopsy table beneath her neck. He reached toward the trolley and grabbed a thin rod. Kara's eyes fluttered closed. She knew what it was, and what it was used for, but she couldn't connect it with herself. She didn't even feel it as he probed her cervix. At first. For the moment she let the Ketamine float her away.

CB ⁊O

Brian laughed softly again. She'd be down the K-hole for a while, he knew, and he was finally going to get what he wanted from her. For some men that might have been sex, but for him it was immortality. Not merely the immortality that came from having one's own offspring, but the kind that came from fame and glory, too.

His offspring wouldn't just be brilliant. They would be perfect. They would be the children to which all parents would aspire to having as their own.

Kara didn't know it yet, but she was about to become the mother of a Goddess. And there was nothing she could do about it, even if she wanted to. She'd signed the paperwork so long ago, she wouldn't likely remember doing so. It had been part of her grant application when she first entered university. His research team had been looking for someone like Kara. Brian, himself, had been a prodigy, graduating high school at twelve and completing his Ph.D. at eighteen.

His university had been fighting to keep him on as a professor, though they tried hard to make it appear they were doing no such thing, offering him an assistant professorship position. Brian had been okay with that. He knew the game they were playing, and he didn't care about titles. He cared about the project their research team was in the middle of. It had been cutting edge, and it would give him an advantage when he moved on to his own projects.

Part of the project had involved finding other prodigies. Prodigies who might be looking for some assistance in paying for their schooling, because they needed to be willing to undergo some pretty iffy experimentation. Some of that experimentation involved drugs, and had resulted in a number of promising students becoming addicted and dropping out. There were, however, students taking a specific type of drug who began to learn at an alarming rate. Kara had been one of them.

Though she had certainly become addicted to the Ketamine, Kara was so intelligent she caught on to what was happening with the other students that were being given the experimental drug, and so she started stealing some of it for herself even though her group wasn't supposed to be on it. It was Brian who had caught her, and the only thing that had saved her from expulsion was his silence. In return he fucked her every night in the lab once everyone had gone home.

Brian knew Kara didn't have a clue how he felt about her. She'd never believe him because he'd been nothing but an asshole to her. He'd blown it when he'd blackmailed her into sleeping with him. He might have been able to make the sex pleasurable for her, but it had never been right between them because it was coerced. Not that it mattered at this point. He'd come this far being an asshole, and he wasn't going to change his stripes now.

Once again he was getting what he wanted by forcing Kara into it. He would deserve it when she turned on him in hatred, but his work had taken on a life of its own—in all senses of the word.

Brian withdrew the rod he had use to open Kara's cervix, and placed it beside the specially prepared catheter. It contained thirty microlitres of EmbryoGlue, and a very special embryo close to the tip. The one-cc syringe was completely airtight.

"It's time, Richard," he called out. The ultrasound technician pulled the cart forward with him as he strode up to the table. Brian didn't like using him, because he was a slimy little shit, but that was what he needed for the moment. Kara may have signed the paperwork allowing the procedure, but another technician might have felt the need to inform her before it was completed.

Kara was already going to fight this, tooth and claw, the moment she figured out what had been done to her. He just felt it would more likely be successful if the transfer occurred while she was in a peaceful frame of mind. If the embryo implanted successfully, it would take an abortion or a miscarriage for the pregnancy to fail.

There were sparks of lust glinting in Richard's eyes when Brian looked up to nod at him to start scanning. Brian wanted to kill him where he stood, but they both had a job to do for the time being. Instead he picked up the catheter and began inserting it, making Kara whimper. He glanced again at Richard's face. His jaw was slack as he stared down at Brian's hands moving between Kara's thighs.

"Richard, if you ever look at her like that again, I'll have you removed from the project." Brian watched in satisfaction as Richard jerked his gaze back to the ultrasound's monitor. Now Brian could concentrate on positioning the catheter tip optimally for implantation. Once it was in place he slowly depressed the plunger. He withdrew the catheter once he'd emptied the syringe, placed it on the cart, and covered Kara's lower half with a blanket that had been waiting on a lower shelf of the same cart. There was no point letting Richard get another look at her as he wheeled his equipment away.

Brian stared at Kara regretfully. At the moment he wanted nothing more than to slip inside her, but there was no way he would risk dislodging the embryo—either through the act itself, or her resulting orgasmic contractions. Besides, intercourse while the cervix was still somewhat open might lead to unwanted bacteria in her womb during a delicate phase of the process. More than anything, he wanted this pregnancy to be successful. He pictured Kara, heavy with child, *his child*, and he became so intensely hard he had to bite back a moan. He quickly locked the door of the lab so Richard couldn't return, stripped off the blanket covering Kara's nakedness, and undid his pants. He stared at her, as she lay helpless before him with her legs spread, and began to stroke himself.

 C？ ？

Well, first I'm going to have to clean up all the poisons that are running through your body right now, the small voice said in her head.

"What? Who said that?" Kara asked, and shook her head. "What poisons?"

I'm not sure. I only know they don't belong inside your body.

Kara turned her head to try to find the voice, but there was no one in the room with her. The only thing she could think of was that the ketamine was causing auditory hallucinations. Considering her level of coherent thought at the moment, however, it didn't seem likely. She no longer felt any of the effects of the shot Brian had given her earlier. Kara frowned. That didn't seem likely either, unless she'd fallen asleep for a while. She began to wonder how long she'd been at the lab.

You've been unconscious for a couple of days now, said the voice, answering Kara's unspoken question. *And yes, I hear your thoughts. There's no need for you to speak for me to understand you. You're not hallucinating or going crazy, by the way. I'm far more genetically advanced than you are, that's all.*

"Uh, who the hell are you?" Kara asked aloud, though she was pretty sure she already knew the answer.

I'm the child growing inside you. Are you my mother?

"I don't know. I'm sorry. I think it's likely you are, though. Brian said he took something from me a long time ago, and it seems pretty obvious now that it must have been one of my eggs. It stands to reason you were created from that egg."

Is Brian my father?

"Possibly. Well, probably. He's egotistical enough that he would attempt this kind of thing with his own offspring, rather than another donor. And somehow I don't see him wanting me to carry another man's child. Until now it would never have occurred to me that he wanted me to have his baby, however, so maybe not."

I'm not just a regular baby, though, am I?

"No, I would say you're certainly not." Before Kara could continue the strange conversation, the door opened. A vaguely familiar man walked in, smirking at her and practically panting with apparent lust. Kara tried to sit up, only to discover she had been strapped to the table. Panic flooded her system with adrenaline.

Don't worry. We can take care of him.

Kara had no idea what she could do to take care of anything when she was tied down, but the adrenaline continued to surge and spike in her as he came closer.

When he gets close to you, use your knees to crush him.

I'm not Superwoman, Kara thought. *How the hell am I supposed to do that?*

You will be.

☙ ❧

Brian walked into the exam room to find Richard's body on the floor, with Kara still strapped down, her eyes blazing. Not only were they blazing, but they were a different colour. Instead of the blue he was accustomed to, they were a bright amber, almost as if her gaze were truly afire.

"What happened, Kara?"

"Why don't you come a little closer and find out?"

"Uh, no, I don't think I will. What the hell is happening to you, and why are your eyes a different colour now?" At his question, Kara gave him a filthy look.

"How the hell should I know what's happening to me, Brian? Aren't you the one who did this to me? Besides, you're obviously full of shit, because eyes don't change colour." Suddenly her body relaxed, and the fiery anger left her eyes. She gave a gasp, and then a whimper he recognized all too well.

"What was that, Kara?" he asked, as he moved

closer and trailed his finger up the inside of her thigh. She shivered.

"No. You can't do that to me. Stop it," she gasped.

"Okay," Brian responded, and took his fingers away.

"I wasn't talking to you! I was talking to *her*," Kara replied, her frustration obvious.

"There's no one else here, Kara. Does that mean you don't want me to stop touching you?" Even as he uttered the question, his finger returned to her inner thigh. Her hips came off the padded table and she whimpered. She shifted and strained toward his hand, and her hospital-type gown rode up, exposing her fully to his gaze. When he pressed the heel of his hand against her clitoris, she convulsed in an unmistakable orgasm.

"Please," she begged. Brian knew what she was asking for, and he was more than a little inclined to give her what she wanted—if there hadn't been a dead body lying on the floor. Not that anyone was going to walk in on them, but it was just a little too gruesome even for him.

"Just a second. I need to get him out of here." He turned and grabbed one of Richard's wrists, and proceeded to drag him out into the hall. He'd have to figure out what to do with him later, but it shouldn't be that hard to get rid of the body. No one knew where he worked, and it was very doubtful anyone would even care that he'd gone missing. A momentary panic set in when he tried to think about how Richard might have died, but then a sort of fog came over his brain the moment he stepped back in the room.

Kara was biting her lip as she hungrily watched him strip off his clothing. By the time he was standing between her thighs, not a single thought remained of the dead man outside the room.

 CB 80

When it was over, Kara lay back on the padded table, panting. Brian remained between her legs, but had draped his upper body over hers. Not only had she had no control over her own desire, she realized, but she hadn't retained control of her body, either. Something had taken her over completely, and she had a good idea what that was.

Why would you do that to me? she asked the child inside her.

I need the genetic material, came the response.

Ewww. What the hell would you need that for?

I wanted to know if he was my father, so he had to get close enough for me to detect his DNA. Once I knew he was my father, I had to make sure he provided the material so I could continue growing. You won't be able to eat fast enough to allow me to grow at the desired rate. I want out of here as soon as possible. I have things to do.

Kara shuddered and Brian stirred against her. If the child grew too fast, there was every likelihood she wouldn't survive the pregnancy.

I won't kill you. Unless you give me a reason to. I'll need you for a little while yet, and I don't see the point of it.

Why not? You were pretty heartless with that other man who came in here, and it doesn't sound as though you have any real affection for me as your mother anyway.

You're wrong. I have a great deal of love, for you and humanity in general. That man was going to rape you. Not to mention the fact that I didn't want his genetic material to pollute me. I can't take all my material from you, or it will kill you, and right now I can't survive without you, so I need material from my father. I will be careful with you for your gestation period, and make sure that your body adapts in time to keep you safe. In fact, I can even make the whole thing completely painless for you. For now, though, it would be best if you ate something to keep up your strength. You're going to need it. Just make sure whatever they give you isn't polluted with chemicals. If I have to keep detoxifying you, I won't have the strength to grow.

Kara was quite happy to start demanding some food. She was starving. She had a baby to feed. Her baby needed genetic material, and Kara wanted to

351

make sure she could get as much as possible from her mother, rather than get it all from Brian.

"Get up, Brian! I want food. Lots of it. Now," she snapped at him, jolting him out of his slumberous haze.

"Sure. Okay. What do you want?"

"Organic. No hormones or antibiotics in the meat, and I want plenty of it. I need the protein. Fresh fruit, vegetables, and whatever else a pregnant woman needs to properly sustain the life of her unborn child. The difference is, I'm going to need a lot more food than most women."

Brian looked at her in astonishment.

"You know you're pregnant?"

"Did you think I was an idiot? Besides, she's been talking to me for the last hour and a half. If I weren't carrying a child, I highly doubt I'd be able to hear her talking."

"Jesus Christ! You know it's female, too?"

"Yes, Brian. I keep telling you she's talking to me. Now go get me some food before I do to you what I did to that asshole who wanted to rape me." She clamped her legs around him just tight enough to scare him, and released him just as suddenly. He stumbled away from her and put his clothing to rights. Kara smirked as he trotted off to do her bidding.

Her smirk disappeared when she noticed the telltale bulge of her belly. There was an unfamiliar tightness to the skin, and it was starting to feel as though it was going to tear.

Oh, sorry. I'll fix that. The relief was sudden.

What did you just do?

I just sent repair cells to increase the elasticity of your skin.

Elastin, you mean?

I suppose so, but it hardly matters what it's called. It all starts out as the same material. It becomes whatever it needs to become when it's sent there.

Embryonic stem cells, then, Kara responded mentally, which apparently didn't deserve an answer. She began to wonder if there was a way to find out how the cells were given their instructions. With current science they could tamper with the location or address information each cell received, but they still didn't know where the initial instructions came from. In the eyes of some scientists, those instructions might actually be construed as evidence of something more divine than science. Kara was skeptical, but open to the possibility.

Of course it's something more than mere science, mother. There's a reason you think of childbirth as a miracle.

Kara thought about it, but it was too big of an idea for her to deal with at the moment. First she needed to get out of these damn straps.

353

Just pull on them, her child stated somewhat impatiently.

I'm hardly strong enough to break these, kid.

You're strong enough. Trust me.

Kara shrugged and decided to give it a whirl. To her shock, the leather snapped easily when she tugged with her right arm. She could feel the new tensile strength in her bicep and pectoral muscles. She yanked her left arm with the same result. She did both legs at once just by straightening them. Then she undid the clasps and let the lined cuffs drop to the floor. Kara plucked at the ties of the gown she wore, and let that drop to the floor, too. Her hands went immediately to the mound growing beneath her belly button.

She had always wanted children, and she had secretly wanted them with Brian at one time. Even now, after everything he had done to her, a part of her loved knowing she carried his baby inside her. Shame flooded through her at the thought. He had used her in the most obscene way possible, and had finished up by implanting a genetically modified child inside her. It was the only explanation. This was not a normal pregnancy. The logical side of her nature was more than a little curious about the results of this particular experiment, but the soft, hidden, romantic side was heartbroken that it had *come about this way.*

I know you're sad, but there's more to this

situation than you know, mother. You were chosen for a reason.

Yeah. Because he thinks I'm brilliant and a good genetic match for him.

That is part of it, though not the whole. He emits other chemicals around you that indicate he has deeper feelings than he is willing to admit. However, it is clear that they aren't his priority at the moment.

Kara felt even more shame at the traitorous hope she began to feel at the thought that Brian might actually care for her. After all, he had completely violated her by forcing a pregnancy on her without her knowledge or permission. Never mind the fact that it was experimental and being kept off the books, or that he had been so unprincipled as to blackmail her into having sex with him to avoid expulsion from university.

Of course, Kara had been nearly as bad, since she had intentionally allowed him to catch her stealing the drug. It could have meant the end of her whole career as a scientist, but she knew the risk was minimal. She figured he would only make a move on her if he felt he could ensure her silence, so she set up a situation that would reassure him.

Her stomach growled, and then, low in her belly, she felt her baby move for the first time. Like a fluttering, or maybe even bubbles of some kind.

Is that you moving around in there?

Of course. I have things to do.

Kara shuddered again, but more from the surreal feeling of having a creature inside her that was doing things, rather than from any sort of fear. Of course, that was what pregnancy was like for all women, in a sense.

It might help if you gave me a name, Kara's child suggested. *Maybe you'll feel more comfortable if you can think of me in familiar terms, rather than just your offspring.*

What would you like to be called? Kara smiled at the realization that it was probably the first time in the history of humanity that a mother had had the opportunity to ask her own child what she would like to be named...and could expect an answer of some sort, that was.

I'm not sure what names are considered good ones, and my own tastes might be very different from the tastes of unmodified people. People name their children after beautiful things, do they not?

Yes, sometimes. Things like flowers or celestial bodies. Often children are named for things that came from other languages or cultures, too. Some names can mean loved by God, and some will have more to do with places or professions. Then there are the names that incorporate the mother's or father's name.

I think I would like something pretty, rather than those other sorts of names. I do not know what I will look like compared to others, though. Maybe I will be considered ugly. Would that be bad?

It might be considered ironic, and it's something you could be teased for, depending on the situation. If you are growing this fast now, you may not have to worry about going to school as a young child, which is where you encounter the most cruelty. You seem very knowledgeable already, so school might be unnecessary. How have you obtained this knowledge?

From you, and from certain genetic memories from my father. I know all that you know, in addition to those genetic memories. I cannot absorb anything else while in this state, so I will have to learn other things once I am done gestating. Presumably you have already gone through the necessary schooling for children, so I will not need to do so. We have yet to discuss any options for names, however. Do you have any suggestions?

How about Mira, which would be short for Miracle? You are definitely a miracle of modern science, and people wouldn't have to know your full name unless you choose to use it.

That is acceptable to me. And yes, I think shortening it would be for the best.

Okay, Mira. Do you want it formally shortened? We'll have to get you some identification somehow, so we'll need a legal name for you. We can keep it short, or use the whole name on the I.D.

Just keep it short. You and I will know what it means. We'll decide later if my father should be given that information. I do not know his character as fully as I do yours. I know what he was born to be, and what he was feeling toward you, but I do not know what he became by way of living his life.

Can you tell me what he was born to be? Kara was really curious about that, now that Mira had brought up the topic.

Only to the extent that his genetic memory provides the information, and it's not very reliable if you consider the changes a person's environment can make on their personality.

So nurture tops nature, is that it?

Mostly, yes, or I assume I'm right about that since I have a limited knowledge of these things based on your knowledge. Still, many people overcome what their nature would dictate, and many overcome what their nurturing would dictate, so it's not a simple issue. I would hate to provide you with information that might sway you one way or the other, and have it turn out to be harmful to you.

What do you mean?

Well, say I told you he was genetically predisposed to being highly affectionate and loving, but he had become someone cold and distant. You might begin to hope for love and affection, despite your knowledge of his current personality traits.

You might convince yourself that he was something other than what he's turned into. You could be hurt by that. Or maybe there's a trait in him that's dangerous, and yet he's overcome that. You would still be afraid of him for it, no matter how unlikely it was that he would hurt you. That would hurt him for no reason. You see my problem?

Kara gave up on that line of inquiry. It could be worse than useless. She fully understood what Mira was getting at. Sometimes it was better not to know these things. Besides, she was always better off judging a person by their actions, rather than their potential. Brian's actions thus far had rendered him completely untrustworthy, and she was more than a little pissed off about the whole situation she was in right now.

☾ ☽

"Here you go, Kara," Brian began, as he handed her the bag of fruit. Then he noticed she'd managed to get out of her straps, and he began to get really nervous.

"How did you do that?" He pointed at the leather pieces on the floor. Kara sneered at him before deigning to answer.

"Let's just say that whatever you did to our child has now made a few changes to me as well. Did you have any idea what you were doing when you made those modifications, Brian? What exactly did you alter in her DNA? Will she even look like a human being?"

"Yes. Everything about her is still human. I used germ-line engineering to enhance her in several ways. It's not as though I did anything that would be against nature. I perfected both your egg and my sperm, so that our child would be stronger, smarter, and more resistant to disease."

"It's pretty obvious you have no idea what you've actually done, Brian. If you did, you would know why I'm able to communicate with her, and you would have known that it would have a certain effect on me as well. You weren't expecting that, which tells me that for someone so smart, you can be pretty fucking stupid." Kara's contempt was obvious, and Brian couldn't even think of a suitable response.

One was unnecessary, however. Kara grabbed the bag of fruit from him and started eating. She had finished two apples, three nectarines, and a banana, by the time she opened her mouth to speak to him again, though it was only to ask him where the meat was.

"I've got it in the freezer. I can rig up a way to cook it using one of the Bunsen burners in the lab, but since you've obviously managed to tear free of the table I guess we can go somewhere else to cook it properly. It's not looking like I would be able to keep you here."

"No, you can't, but I'm not going anywhere. I want to take a look at what you've done so I can understand it better, and so Mira knows what's happening to her."

"Who the hell is Mira?"

"Our daughter. We picked out a name while you were gone. Get the Bunsen burner set up so I can get some protein into me. Mira needs as much of my genetic material as possible, which means I need to eat so she's not damaging me in the process."

Brian had never seen this side of Kara before. He didn't know what to make of it. But considering her new tensile strength he wasn't willing to test her. Besides, she was right. He hadn't expected any of these changes or abilities, and he wanted answers just as much as she did.

CB EO

They worked through the night, and on a hunch Kara decided to take a look at some of her own cells. She did this through the simple expediency of poking herself with a syringe and putting a drop of her blood on a slide. If there were any abnormalities, she could draw a few tubes to do some DNA sequencing.

When she looked through her microscope,

however, the abnormalities were readily apparent. Her thrombocytes, erythrocytes, and leukocytes were completely altered. At the moment, however, she had no idea what that meant for her. Her erythrocytes, or red blood cells, looked to be about ten percent larger. The leukocytes, which were responsible for protecting her from viruses and diseases, didn't even look like white blood cells anymore. As for the thrombocytes, Kara took a look at her fingertip where she had punctured the skin and sucked in her breath. Her platelets had not only stopped the bleeding, but there was no visible puncture mark. Apparently she had developed a rather advanced ability to heal. Would this continue once Mira was born?

The alterations will likely be permanent, mother, but they will not harm you. On the contrary, they should help you heal almost instantly and protect you from most diseases.

Kara had many questions that needed answering, but the truth was that science could only take her so far. In many cases only time would tell.

"Brian, what genes did you alter, exactly?" At her question, Brian looked up from his computer. He'd been looking at the DNA modeling of the embryo he had implanted in her—the one that had developed into Mira.

"Well, I made sure none of the known mental illnesses were retained, or any genetic abnormalities. I mostly just made sure she would be healthy, intelligent, and physically strong."

"So, you removed a gene that might be responsible for empathy or creativity because you didn't like the idea of her being manic-depressive, you've boosted her immune system to the point where autoimmune disorders are a distinct possibility, and you've made her far stronger than the rest of the human population. Has it occurred to you that this could easily kill her, or turn her into a monster of some sort?"

Sorry, Mira, she added mentally. *My concerns are reasonable, considering what he's done without even thinking of the consequences. You are my child, however, so whatever he's done I'll still be your mother.*

"I've removed all possibility of diseases, I would think, by boosting her immune system," Brian replied arrogantly, though she could see the doubt in his eyes.

"Allergies? Rheumatoid arthritis? Myocarditis? Even psoriasis, for Christ's sake? Did even one of these issues caused by an overactive immune system cross your tiny mind? Our child could end up being born with all kinds of problems, and look like some sort of lizard at the same time."

"I don't know how you could think that when you've seen some of the embryos with your own eyes!"

Kara slumped in horror. She'd had no idea when she'd been gazing upon them that those embryos had been her own offspring. Her stomach lurched.

Calm down, mother. Here. This will help. Kara's stomach quieted almost instantly.

Thank you, Mira. I don't need to be sick on top of dealing with all this. I need to be able to think.

Mira didn't respond, but Kara knew she was still busily trying to grow inside her. The bulge from her womb had grown noticeably larger since she had eaten the two pounds of steak Brian had prepared for her while she'd been studying some of his notes.

Kara was suddenly distracted by a wave of lust. She couldn't stop the moan that escaped her lips. Brian was the only available male, so she walked over to him and drew her nails lightly up the inside of his thigh. He was obviously confused by her sudden change of attitude toward him, but he wasn't the type to look a gift horse in the mouth. His response was swift, and within seconds they were mating almost violently on the steel counter.

ଔ ଓ

"What the fuck was that?" Brian wanted to know. Kara shrugged.

"You'll have to ask Mira once she's born. She's the one who keeps manipulating my hormones. You have no cause for complaint, apparently, since you're just as into it as I am."

"Yes, but I don't understand why it's impossible to resist. I'm not usually so animalistic that I can't stop myself from just taking you."

"Suddenly you're moral about the possibility of forcing a woman to fuck you? I don't think so, Brian."

"I mean I completely lose control, Kara. I don't like it."

"Sucks, doesn't it, to have no choice in something? Nice to see the tables turned. However, I think we have our daughter to thank for your lack of control. She's probably got me emitting some sort of pheromone or maybe a chemical that's restricting your inhibitions."

The look on Kara's face could only be described as smug, and Brian didn't like that, either. He was used to being the one in control with her. At one time he had used her desire for him against her, and now it was being used against him somehow. He was starting to worry that his experiment had resulted in something far more dangerous than he had anticipated.

In the meantime he had a body to get rid of, before it decomposed too much. The lab was kept fairly cool, but even that wouldn't stop the process. Not unless Richard's body could be frozen or something, but that wouldn't really solve the problem.

"Try cutting him up and using the strongest acid you've got in the lab. If you get the pieces small enough, disposal should be easy."

Kara's apparent ability to read his mind was more than a little startling. Worry was turning into fear, as Brian thought about what other talents might manifest themselves. And what would their child be like once the gestation period was complete?

"Don't worry, Brian. I'm not psychic. You're just staring at the body with a troubled look on your face. And now, of course, you were giving me the same look, so it wasn't hard to figure out what you were thinking."

Brian was more than a little relieved. The last thing he needed right now was Kara probing into his thoughts.

03 &0

Within a week, Kara was the equivalent of thirty weeks' gestation. She hadn't bothered to leave the lab. If she ran into anyone she knew, there would be questions—and she couldn't answer them. Besides, there was too much work to be done. Brian had finally managed to remove the last pieces of Richard's body from the lab, so the odour of decay was dissipating. It didn't bother her, though. Mira made sure Kara was shielded from the assault on her olfactory senses. She couldn't really smell much of anything at the moment. She could only detect the strongest traces.

Food was a different story. Brian must have spent a couple thousand dollars on the organic items she demanded, and she devoured them ridiculously fast. The only time she stopped eating was during sex, and she was considering the addition of IV fluids to increase her caloric intake.

"You never considered the possibility of an abortion?"

Kara looked up in surprise at Brian's question. She thought about it for a moment before answering.

"It never even occurred to me. I want to have this baby. I would have had your baby anyway, if there had been a more conventional route offered. Even if it had crossed my mind, I get the feeling Mira would have done whatever was necessary to ensure her own survival."

There was an uncomfortable silence after that pronouncement, but Kara knew she was right. She didn't need Mira to confirm or deny, and it wouldn't have taken more than a few chemical alterations to render Kara unconscious to prevent her from doing anything harmful to Mira. Her initial lack of consciousness was evidence of that, seeing as there was no logical reason for her to have remained unconscious for so long after the implantation. Ketamine would not have done that. Granted, Kara didn't think there was anything sinister in that. It was simply the safest way to ensure the implantation took hold, and to ease her shock. She just didn't know how the mechanism worked seeing as there had been no physical connection between them.

Actually, there was. I was able to latch on immediately. Once I had physical contact with the uterine lining, I was able to use some of the genetic material to reach out to the wall of your uterus. The umbilical cord developed right away and allowed me to communicate effectively with your entire body. After a couple of days, however, I had to wake you up. I was using up your calories at a dangerous rate, and could not continue to grow. I would have languished inside you, much like the embryos in those mechanical wombs.

Kara looked up at the embryos in question, wondering what could be done about them. Or with them. Knowing that they were her own children was breaking her heart, and she was determined to either save them, or destroy them and end their pitiful existence.

I can absorb their genetic material, Mira said. *Kara was alarmed at the very notion.*

You mean cannibalize them, don't you?

Not at all. They are conscious beings. I can hear them and communicate with them. They aren't really suffering, but they're not really doing more than existing for the time being. They have been unable to learn anything more than what a normal human baby learns, because they are not connected with appropriate genetic material, and they cannot connect with another intelligence in the way they are meant to. I can absorb them, and they can live as part of me. They're willing.

Are you willing to let me be a part of that decision, or are you just going to go ahead and do it, with or without my blessing?

I will respect your wishes on this. They are your children, not mine. It is, however, their only chance at life. They cannot be implanted any longer, because they've already created their connective cord and it's too mature. The plasticity of the embryonic stem cells is already diminished.

Won't that mean you'll have multiple personalities then? I mean, it sounds as though they would continue to be conscious within you.

That can be fixed. I can absorb the tissues and separate the consciousness so that it can become a part of my own ovum. They will remain there until such time as I decide to ovulate and procreate with an acceptable male. The difficulty will lie in finding one. He will most likely have to be created, but that can be arranged as well.

So far this is sounding like the best possible option, but give me some time to think about it, okay?

You have three days to decide. I will be born then, and will only retain the ability to absorb them for a short time. After that my skin will age very rapidly.

Does this mean you will grow old and die more rapidly than humans?

Not at all. I will age to adulthood very fast, as it is the optimal path to survival. The faster a species can attain the ability to procreate, the more likely its species will continue. I will remain fertile for many decades. Old age will likely be a very brief period again before I die. At least I will not have to suffer many of the indignities that strike the elderly of this planet.

How do you know all this? Kara was awestruck at what she was hearing.

It's the only logical outcome. Humans were designed inherently to take over one planet and then move on to the next. We're a very invasive species. In order to make the jump to an interplanetary existence, we also need to make the next evolutionary jump. That's me. My father designed me in such a way that this leap is now inevitable. Since I've obtained more of his genetic material, I've also been able to connect with his mind at a somewhat basic level. I can't speak with him the way I do you, but I have gained much of his knowledge, and can guess at a great deal of his intent.

His intent?

Well, he certainly wasn't thinking of humans becoming an interplanetary species. He was thinking more of his own mortality. He wanted you back in his life, he wanted children with you, and he wanted to make a discovery that would ensure his name be remembered in scientific history. Understandable goals, if short-sighted.

Kara felt the breath leave her body. Brian had wanted her back, and he had wanted children with her. It might seem like an obvious thing—that he wanted children with her—since he had done nearly the impossible to ensure that she carried his child, but she could have brushed that off as part of his need to etch his name in scientific annals. She was simply what he considered the best choice for a donor egg. That's certainly what she would have thought if Mira hadn't clued her in to his other motives.

The question was, once Mira was no longer screwing around with her hormones so that they were fucking like rabbits several times a day, and once she had a few moments of clear-headedness, would she be able to get past everything he had done? She had loved him once. Deeply. Or so she had thought. It was entirely possible her Ketamine addiction had played a role there. She had walked— or maybe ran—away from him, for her own survival. She had felt such a desperate need for his love back then, and was so certain he had none to give her. And now he'd gone to crazy lengths to tie her to him in ways she had never imagined were possible.

Most women would look at the situation and feel completely violated by what had been done to her. But then, most women hadn't fantasized about what it would be like to be pregnant with his child. Potent fantasies that had her wanting him desperately, and had very nearly convinced her to simply stop using her birth control. She knew there was something sick about that, so she had kept it to herself. Her dark, shameful secret that she hid by overcompensating.

Whenever anyone talked about having children around them, she would make a great show of saying she just wasn't ready to make those kinds of sacrifices, and maybe never would be. If a friend of theirs got married, and the woman changed her name, Kara would make a snide remark about the lost independence and vow to remain single. Brian had said nothing, so she had assumed he felt the same. Apparently he'd been hiding things, too.

For now it didn't matter. Kara had more immediate concerns, which meant she had to put her girlish daydreams on the back burner. There was no way she could make any decisions right now anyway. Not with her hormones being so blatantly controlled by another person. When she was herself again, that would be the time to think things through.

Kara felt Brian's finger at the back of her neck, making her shiver.

Again?

It's not me this time. Though I'm certainly happy for the additional material.

Kara rolled her eyes at her daughter's greed.

"What are you thinking about, Kara?" Brian's whisper in her ear had her shivering again. "You had the softest expression on your face."

In response, Kara felt her face turn bright red. The last thing she wanted to talk about right now was her laughable and pathetic desire for marriage, or even for children with him for that matter. She shook her head to try to avoid answering his question.

"You look so beautiful right now, pregnant with my child."

Kara felt so relieved her back was turned to him at the moment. His words had her turning to putty. He rolled his stool up behind her until she was between his legs, and his hand came around her waist to rest on her belly. He pulled her back against his chest. Mira moved to let him know she was there, and the moment was a fulfillment of one of Kara's most secret dreams. The fact that it was happening under such strange circumstances was enough to give her the jolt of anger she needed to pull away.

"Stop it! Both of you! Maybe, if Brian had bothered to ask me to have children with him, or had attained my permission in this experiment instead of forcing it on me, just maybe I'd be feeling the romance of it all. But as it is I'm extremely angry. I'm justified and entitled to my anger, so please just allow me to feel it in peace without screwing with my emotions."

She'd spoken the words aloud so Brian would know exactly what she was feeling, even though the words were meant for Mira. Brian, however, chose that moment to stand up for his heinous actions.

"Do these words ring a bell, Kara? 'The last thing I want right now is a little parasite hanging around me when I'm trying to win a Nobel Prize.' Or, how about these? 'What the hell is wrong with these women, giving up their freedom and their names to hang off some guy's arm. For what? A gold band?' Do you remember saying those things?"

Kara was in no mood to put up with his attitude.

"So you're justified in what you've done here? Taking away my choice entirely? Instead of asking me an honest question about my feelings, privately. Why do you think I said the things I did? Because we were in public and I didn't want to be humiliated by your complete lack of feeling for me in front of people. You were perfectly happy to coerce me into a sexual relationship because you knew I wouldn't want to be ejected from university, but you sure as hell didn't do anything to make me think it was ever anything more than fucking for you. As far as I knew, I was nothing to you, and I couldn't bear the thought of hearing you brag about that to your friends in front of me."

"Brag how?"

"By saying you were only interested in your work. If I had to hear those words, I would know for sure you didn't give a damn about me! I figured I was just putting off the inevitable."

"Instead of asking me an honest question about my feelings, privately?" He mockingly threw her words back in her face, silencing her. To her surprise he stomped off to his office, only remaining inside for about five seconds before stomping back out to her and unceremoniously thrusting a velvet box into her hand. He also held a small piece of paper that he folded in half—backwards. A receipt.

"Look at the date on it, Kara."

She did. She could see the date, but not the amount he had spent, since the receipt was folded. The item in the box had been purchased just before Christmas two years earlier. She remembered how they had been at dinner with a couple of friends the day before Christmas Eve, and their friends had announced their engagement. It took her a minute to remember her response to the happy news. Her heart dropped like a stone.

"You remember what happened, Kara? Jason and Brienne?"

Kara's face burned.

"Yes, I remember," she said quietly. Her reaction to their news had been so negative that the couple had soon made their excuses and left them sitting in the restaurant.

"Let's recap anyway. I believe it was something along the lines of how stupid it was to tie your life to another human being, when it was impossible for humans to remain monogamous, and that marriage was for people who didn't have real lives."

Tears rolled down Kara's face as she squirmed in shame, and the pain that had prompted such a horrible reaction. She had to say something to Brian to make him understand.

"We had been together three years by then. You hadn't once mentioned marriage, or anything other than wanting to fuck me. I kept hoping you would fall in love with me, but the words never came. Our anniversary, or what I considered to be our anniversary, had passed once again without any acknowledgement from you. I risked my whole career by letting you catch me stealing that drug, hoping it would start something between us, and it did—but it wasn't anything like I hoped it would be. Instead of starting a real relationship with you, I started what felt like an unending fling. It was bad enough that I was sure you didn't love me, but to constantly have people talking about marriage and children was just too much for me."

She stared at the velvet box in her hand.

"Am I supposed to look at this? Because I don't think this is the right time."

"No. You're right. It's the worst possible time for you to see what's in there." He held out his hand, and she dropped the box into it as though it were a hot ember burning her flesh.

"So now you know," he said, by way of wrapping up the conversation. Kara just stood there, numb, as he returned the box to his office. She waited until he came back before speaking again.

"Why didn't you return it? Obviously you kept the receipt. I'm sure they would have taken it back."

"Because I didn't want to, for one thing. There was another reason, but I'm not willing to share it with you just now. For the time being, why don't we just get back to work?" He grabbed his stool and wheeled it toward the microscope where he'd been studying Kara's latest blood sample. He sat down and pressed his eyes against the lenses.

Kara went back to work, wisely keeping her thoughts to herself. Well, as much to herself as possible, since Mira was privy to them also, but Mira didn't share her thoughts on the subject.

Something Kara was grateful for. Brian had behaved despicably, and so had she. And now she was back to her earlier solution—setting aside any decision-making until such time as she was no longer pregnant and forcibly involved in this highly-charged situation.

CB   BO

It's time for me to come out, mother. Though Kara had been expecting it all day, it was still a jolt. She felt huge, and knew it would be a relief to be done with pregnancy, but the short time-span made it far too surreal for her.

You said you could make it painless. Will you do that for me?

Of course. I don't see any need for you to suffer under the circumstances. You've proven more than satisfactory as an incubator for me. Kara nodded to herself and looked up. Brian noticed the movement and turned toward her, a strange expression on his face. If forced to describe it, she would have said it was a combination of love and lust, but she couldn't be sure.

"It's time?"

Kara's nod was directed at Brian this time. He walked over to her, solicitously offering his hand to help her from her stool. He kept a hand beneath her elbow to guide her back to the room where she had initially woken, pregnant with Mira. She shuddered, remembering Richard and his ill-fated attempt to rape her.

Labour was intense, but as painless as Mira had promised. She felt the contractions, but they were much like what women described as Braxton-Hicks contractions. Her belly would become rock hard, and her left leg would temporarily go numb, but other than that it was perfectly fine. Within an hour, Mira was sliding from her body. There were no cries, and no need to clear her airways; Mira had taken care of that on her own. Kara made sure Brian did not cut the cord, either. Once she had birthed the placenta, it was placed on Mira's belly for prompt absorption. Kara and Brian watched as Mira matured by at least six months.

Kara breast-fed Mira, providing her with the nourishing colostrum she would need to advance further. Mira grew again. Kara estimated she was the equivalent of about a year old by then.

"Please set me on the floor, father," Mira requested, startling both her parents. Hearing such grown-up phrasing from the mouth of an infant was just weird. Brian acceded to her request, however, since there was no reason not to.

It took Mira a few minutes to master the art of walking, but once she had done so she stared up at her mother and began to speak again.

"What is your decision?"

"Better that than death," Kara replied. Brian was confused, but became compliant once it was explained to him what Mira was planning to do. There was no point in denying her, since she was completely right. The other embryos would not survive much longer, and there was now no way to implant any of them in Kara's womb.

"Bring me to the first mechanical womb so I can absorb the tissue. It should be enough that I will not need any further help with the rest of them."

Kara swallowed, more than a little horrified at what was being done, but it was far too late to turn back now. Feeling fully restored, despite having given birth within the last hour, Kara stood up and headed to the washroom to clean herself up. Dressed in the clothes she'd worn to the lab initially, that she had washed by hand a week previously in the bathroom sink, she left the washroom to see how much her daughter had grown in that short span of time.

Mira looked at her as soon as she walked into the main lab area. She was fully grown now, and it was like a kick to the gut. Kara could have been looking at her twin.

"Did you do that on purpose, Brian?"

"Yeah. I didn't think it would be fair to have my daughter look too much like me. I wouldn't have been doing her any favours."

Kara was amazed at the depth of his knowledge

of the genetic code. He had to have found a way to map out everything from eye colour to skeletal structure. She hadn't realized he had been able to progress so far, though she supposed she shouldn't have been so surprised after everything else he had managed to accomplish.

"Can you still speak to me the way you used to, Mira, or is that gone now that you're no longer physically connected to me?"

"It's gone, of course. It wasn't a psychic thing or anything; just a simple latch onto the central nervous system."

"Simple. Right," Kara said sardonically. "Why is it that you could communicate with the embryos then?"

"They were modified like me. You do not have the ability to receive information without a physical link, whereas I do, and so did they."

"Are the others with you now?" Brian's question had Mira nodding.

"Yes, and I will find them new bodies soon. We just have to create a suitable male for me to mate with. I assume you still have access to the donor files," Mira queried.

"You assume correctly. Files as well as samples. We will have no trouble incubating another child that is similar to you. Of course, we'll need to use a different mother so there will be no genetic contamination from your own mother."

Kara sat down, horror once again seeping into her consciousness. She had never signed on for this in the first place. Now that her hormones were no longer being controlled by Mira, she was starting to see things far too clearly for her own comfort. She tuned back in to the conversation to find Mira discussing her with Brian.

"I left her fertile, by the way. You will have approximately three days before the egg dies. It's up to you."

It was then that Kara realized Mira had not released her from the sway of her hormones. One look from Brian was all it took for the desire to mate with him to take over her body.

ß   &

It was six months before Brian showed her the ring, and in that time she had given him twelve more children. All of whom were working in the lab. Mira had made sure the first egg was modified even more than her own. Subsequent children had continued Mira's good work, building on the modifications. They all looked like regular humans, though Mira was the only one who was identical to her mother.

By the third child, however, some unusual traits had shown up. Tough skin made them nearly invulnerable to penetration from sharp objects, and gills were hidden beneath their hair. X-rays showed unusual skeletal structures. Their bones were bird-like; hollow, lightweight, and yet extremely durable. Compared to most humans, their offspring were pretty much immortal. Kara wasn't sure how to feel about that, though she couldn't really complain. After all, every one of her pregnancies had increased her own survivability. It was Brian who was the weak one now.

Kara stared at the ring and realized something. Brian had always been the weak one. She had loved him once, and as emotionally flawed as she had been, she had never resorted to the kinds of measures Brian had taken to chain her to him. The heart-shaped diamond was ridiculous in her opinion, and even at her most sappy she would never have liked it. The inscription was even worse.

'Kara' mia.

Her name meant *beloved*, and so the heart was appropriate in that way, whereas *cara* would have meant *darling* in Italian, but the truth of the matter was he had never fully understood her. He might think he loved her, but he hadn't even known her. Even after three years together, he hadn't learned the first thing about her. Now he disgusted her.

Not that that mattered in the slightest. She was now pregnant with their fourteenth child, and there was no escape for her. Her children would keep imprisoning her, until one of them considered their evolution complete.

Kara couldn't even fling the ring in Brian's face, or tell him how she really felt about him. Instead, the ring now flashed from her left hand, mocking her. The false desire she felt for him overcame anything she might choose for herself.

My own children are helping him rape me, over and over again, she thought, realizing at the same time that she wasn't even allowed to feel despair over her situation. A flood of feel-good hormones and chemicals came from her brain.

Kara began to float on those chemicals almost non-stop. Every time she started to realize how unhappy she was, and how much she wanted to break free, her latest child would put a stop to it. Every time she opened her mouth to speak, to tell Brian what she thought of him, she would either fall asleep or be drugged by her own body.

03 80

Kara was careful not to think about anything at all during the final days of her sixteenth pregnancy. She allowed herself to concentrate on her work, and the genetic manipulation of the embryo that would soon be implanted in a very unlucky woman's womb. Once her fifth son was born, Kara told Brian she was going to the washroom to clean up.

She made a brief detour to the lab, ostensibly to

announce the healthy birth, and palmed a scalpel. Once inside the bathroom, Kara swiped the sharp blade across her left wrist. It hadn't been easy to penetrate the tougher skin, but she managed. Then she locked the door to bar entry. She was rapidly hypnotized by the spurts of blood ejaculating from the artery. Welcoming the weakness when it came, Kara felt the tears of relief leak from beneath her closed lids, tickling her nose as they trailed slowly across the bridge from one side. It was finally over.

I don't think so, mother.

Kara wanted to wail in despair, as she realized they were overlapping the pregnancies now. Then the unwelcome happiness overtook her once again.

THANK YOU

We really appreciate the time you've taken to read this book. If you've enjoyed the anthology, it would be very helpful to these writers if you left a review on Amazon, or any place you talk about the books you have read. An honest review can also help other readers decide if they would like to spend their time reading an author's work, so you would be helping them, too. Independent authors thrive on reviews, so we thank you in advance for your support!

IN CASE YOU MISSED THEM...

TIPPING POINT

Book One of the Tipping Point Trilogy
by Rain Stickland

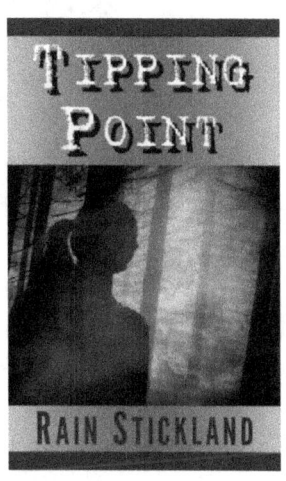

Mackenzie knew the power grid was going down. She was warned. So she spent years coming up with a way to survive and protect her daughter at the same time. When major cities start going dark, and supply lines to millions of people are cut, Mac is suddenly faced with an entire litany of situations she wasn't expecting, and isn't prepared for.

GROUND ZERO

Book Two of the Tipping Point Trilogy
by Rain Stickland

The world went dark, but Mackenzie was one of the
ones who had prepared for it. Not everyone is as
fortunate. Prescription drugs are no longer available, and
Mac's best friend is a type 1 diabetic. She manages to
find someone who can make insulin the old-fashioned
way, but she still has to get it to him before it's too late.
That means leaving the safety of her hidden farm and
travelling hundreds of miles to get there, without getting
killed along the way. Meanwhile, her daughter is forced
to contend with one disaster after another.

By Jill D'Aubery

In 1943 America is at war with Germany and Japan. Japanese submarines prowl the Pacific Ocean and high in the hills above Hollywood someone is sending radio signals to these subs.

Cold Canyon Drive is the story of two women who fought World War II at home: Valerie, a school-teacher, and her best friend, Betty, a war-wife. They have to deal with fear and loneliness, love and deceit, spies and smugglers, hermits, snakes, and a ferocious cat in a weird and sometimes frightening place called, Laurel Canyon.

BY TRACI SANDERS

Jewel has met the man of her dreams … the one person with whom she's meant to spend eternity. Harley is charming, charismatic, and although he can't carry a tune in a bucket, he's the most gorgeous man she has ever laid eyes upon—especially in his U.S. Air Force uniform.

Just days after the couple returns from their honeymoon, Harley is called to active duty in the Middle East. Jewel is heartbroken but determined to adapt to her new life as a military spouse and support her husband. Her plan is short-lived when Harley is killed in action just days after his deployment.

Unable to cope, Jewel withdraws from her family, friends, and the world around her, until Harley visits her with a message from the beyond.

Will Jewel surrender to the dark side to be with her true love, or will she discover that sometimes people are put in our paths for reasons beyond our understanding?

BY TRACI SANDERS

Local news anchor, Amber Woods, seemed to have it all – a thriving career, two beautiful children, and a doting husband named Drake. Life was perfect...until her world was turned upside down in one fateful night.

While the incident caused Amber to renew her priorities; Drake was unable to deal with what happened, and sank into a deep depression laced with infidelity and alcohol.

Hoping a change of scenery would salvage her quickly deteriorating marriage, Amber agreed to move to New York; but it didn't take long for her to discover that the past is not always left in the past.

Can Amber save her marriage without losing herself along the way? What will she do when darkness breaks her will to keep trying?

Coming Soon!

Perfections
Anthology

Imperfections explored the dystopian world in all its many colours. This time, however, editor Rain Stickland is taking the optimistic route. Of course, that doesn't guarantee people will be any happier. As the expression goes, be careful what you wish for.

Full submissions guidelines are available by sending a quick e-mail to: rain@rainstickland.com.
(Make sure you spell Stickland without an R.)

Salvage Rights
Tipping Point Book Three

For someone who wants to live a quiet and solitary life, Mackenzie is doing a terrible job of it. Somehow she and her daughter have managed to start rebuilding civilization on a small scale. But not everyone wants a return to law and order. There are those who look on the end of society as an opportunity, and they will stop at nothing to ensure Mac and Cameron do not succeed.